LIST OF TEN

LIST OF TEN

HALLI GOMEZ

STERLING TEEN
New York

STERLING TEEN
New York

An Imprint of Sterling Publishing Co., Inc.
122 Fifth Avenue
New York, NY 10011

STERLING TEEN and the distinctive Sterling Teen logo
are trademarks of Sterling Publishing Co., Inc.

ISBN 978-1-4549-4014-2

Distributed in Canada by Sterling Publishing Co., Inc.
c/o Canadian Manda Group, 664 Annette Street
Toronto, Ontario M6S 2C8, Canada
Distributed in the United Kingdom by GMC Distribution Services
Castle Place, 166 High Street, Lewes, East Sussex BN7 1XU, England
Distributed in Australia by NewSouth Books
University of New South Wales, Sydney, NSW 2052, Australia

For information about custom editions, special sales, and premium and
corporate purchases, please contact Sterling Special Sales at 800-805-5489 or
specialsales@sterlingpublishing.com.

Manufactured in the United States

Lot #:
2 4 6 8 10 9 7 5 3 1
01/21

sterlingpublishing.com

Cover design by Elizabeth Mihaltse Lindy
Interior design by Julie Robine

FOR JOHN CUNNINGHAM,
THE UNOFFICIAL MAYOR OF THORNHILL

TEN

Three letters. One puny syllable. The number didn't sound impressive, but I couldn't stop thinking about it. You could say I was obsessed with it.

It didn't help that the world shoved it in my face. In social studies we debated the Bill of Rights. And who picked the FBI Ten Most Wanted List? Please. I could come up with at least twenty psycho-quality people in New York City alone.

My theory was the world's fascination with the number started with Moses and the Ten Commandments. In biblical days, people knew better than to argue with a guy who parted seas. But I blamed my obsession on my psychiatrist.

Almost ten years ago, Dr. Hadley Quentin, or "Hardly Qualified," as I liked to call him, planted the idea to close my eyes, take a deep breath, and count to ten. It was supposed to relax me, but the last thing a six-year-old with Tourette syndrome and obsessive-compulsive disorder needed was a fixation on one particular number.

But I was young and desperate and let the number run my life. As if I had any say. It conspired with my brain and interfered with everything from walking to sleeping. Until I decided to take control.

To celebrate taking back my life, I created my List of Ten. And on April 6, the tenth anniversary of my diagnosis, it will be complete.

1. Get my first kiss
2. Meet someone else with Tourette syndrome
3. Be pain-free
4. Find a babysitter for my baby brother
5. See the space shuttle
6. Talk about Tourette in public
7. Give away my Tim Howard autographed picture
8. Drive a car
9. Talk to Mom
10. Commit suicide

FEBRUARY 1

One, two, three, four, five, six, seven, eight, nine.

I stepped into the room the same second I got to ten. Also the same second the bell rang. Yeah, it sounded cool, but required absolutely no talent or planning. I counted my steps every day, so it was bound to happen at some point.

Of course, I still had to make it to my desk before class started. In other classes I'd be considered late and heading to the teacher's desk to pick up a detention slip, but Mrs. Frances didn't care. Probably because it took her a few minutes to get her stuff together, and right now she was preoccupied with her computer.

My desk was in the front row, but on the far side of the room. I stood in the doorway and debated which path to take. The long way down the side, across the back, then up to my desk, or the shortest across the front. My neck twitched. My hands squeezed into fists.

Since class hadn't started yet, everyone sat in their best

conversation positions, facing away from the teacher. Abhy and Spencer argued about whether Luke Skywalker was Rey's father, and three girls puckered and posed in front of the phones they held at arm's length. Their fascination with Instagram selfies would make it possible for me to walk across the room without being noticed.

I took a deep breath and the first step. One. You'd think I was heading toward the electric chair. It was just science, which happened to be my favorite subject. Another step. Two. I stretched my legs to maximize the distance. Three. Four. Five. Six. Seven. Eight. Nine. Ten.

I was three desks from mine, but it didn't matter. I'd hit the magic number. I bent down, touched the floor, and just in case someone saw, fumbled with my shoelaces like that's the real reason my hands were near the nasty floor. From the corner of my eye I saw Jason's eyes on me. Busted. Heat rushed from my neck to my forehead, and not because they turned on the heat in this school. I stood up, took three giant steps to my desk, one, two, three, whispered the remaining seven to get to ten, and fell into my chair.

My neck twitched. My hands squeezed into fists. Repeat. I pulled *A Farewell to Arms* out of my backpack. If anything could take my mind away from here it was World War I. I read and annotated until Mrs. Frances stood up, barely visible above her computer monitor, and pushed her wide black-framed glasses farther up her nose.

"New term, new seats," she announced.

For one breathtaking minute, my body froze. Okay, it was liter-

4

ally scared stiff, but the neck twitches and hand squeezing stopped. I savored the stillness.

Then the minute passed.

My head bobbed to my left shoulder. My left shoulder lifted to my head. Repeat. Head bob, shoulder lift. Head bob, shoulder lift. Of course it came back. I'd done the neck twitch every day, every hour, every few minutes since I was six. But right now it was out of control.

I pleaded with Mrs. Frances. My mind to her mind. My eyes to her's. *Please don't do this. Don't change my comfortable hell.* She moved to the front of the room and studied the paper in her hand.

"Okay, everyone pack up your materials and move to the back."

Chairs scraped around me. Papers fluttered. The mumble of voices drifted behind me.

I took a deep breath. One, two, three, four, five, six, seven—

Mrs. Frances looked up from her paper. Her eyes landed on me.

"Troy, pack up your books."

My chest tightened. She interrupted me in the middle. And on an odd number.

Eight, nine, ten. I shoved the book in my backpack and started again. One, two, three, four, five, six, seven, eight, nine, ten.

I stood up, trudged to the back, and fitted myself into the corner. Mrs. Frances consulted her paper, called out a name, and pointed to my old desk. "Bradley."

One of the selfie girls giggled. Bradley moaned.

"Mrs. Frances, can I have another seat?"

"What's wrong with that one?" she asked.

Bradley glared at me like this desk-switching event was my idea. Mrs. Frances could have said half the class had Ebola and it was a contamination issue. It wouldn't have mattered. It took me four months to get comfortable in the last seat.

"It's . . . well . . . he's . . ," Bradley said. "Nothing."

Bradley sighed, turned away from me, and took the long way to the seat. I tensed my neck muscles and occupied my mind by mentally reciting the periodic table. I didn't want to see him disinfect my old chair before sitting down. And someone who frequently forgot their deodorant after PE shouldn't be worried about me.

I recited all the elements, but as usual, my brain changed directions on me and fixated on something else: the papers in my backpack. They were probably crumpled from stuffing everything inside. I wrinkled my face to mimic the wrinkled papers.

My neck twitched again. My face scrunched itself up. Another neck twitch. Then a face scrunch neck twitch combo. Great, a new one. I slumped further into the corner and stared at my sneakers.

What grand purpose could switching desks serve? Was she alphabetizing the classroom? Putting us in height order? Maybe it was something completely radical, like arranging us by birthday. While all those possibilities seemed rational to me, they were uncharacteristic of a woman who mixed her pens and pencils and left sentences half finished.

Bradley mumbled something to the boy behind him while Mrs. Frances finished filling the first two rows. Six seats in each. Twelve.

I counted to ten.

She started the next row. Dead center of the room. My neck twitched. My face scrunched. One new neighbor was nothing compared to what the middle of the room would do to me. Being surrounded by other kids' desks, some turned slightly diagonal, pencils left crooked, and wrinkled pieces of paper taunting me, would make my whole body shake. I would have to touch everything. Repeatedly.

I stared at the teacher and resisted putting my finger to my temple like Professor X did in the *X-Men* movies before he learned to implant his thoughts into someone else's mind without all the dramatics. I screamed the words in my head. *Put me next to Abhy again.* The urge to touch his desk should be gone since I already knew what it felt like. And his desk was neat.

I counted to ten, stood straight, then leaned forward hoping she'd call this craziness off. But Mrs. Frances ignored my signals this time too and continued reading names. Spencer, Esther.

Not a middle desk. Please not the middle. An invisible hand squeezed my chest. I tried to suck air in, but none made it to my lungs. One, two, three, four—there would be four desks to touch— five, six, seven, eight, nine, ten.

"Eric." Mrs. Frances pointed to a desk in the third row, three seats back. The room started to spin.

"Abhy," she called.

A tiny bit of air got in. She called more names and pointed to more desks. Each time she filled a desk, the breathing got easier. I was on number six when she called my name. Seven, eight, nine, ten. I could breathe again and even the stale classroom air felt good. I skimmed the back wall on the way to my new desk.

Fifth seat back in the row closest to the door. There was no one behind me, and I was golden if there was a fire drill. All that stood between the door and me was Bob, the classroom skeleton, and a waist-high bookcase filled with magazines, books, and videos from the nineties. The videos were probably fire hazards, but it was a chance I was willing to take for this seat.

I sank into my chair and breathed freely. Oxygen in. Carbon dioxide out. Repeat. Mrs. Frances smiled at me. I nodded back. I had a new love for her. Either she got my mental telepathy messages or she really was observant despite her obvious lack of organizational skills.

My neck twitch went from every four seconds to every two minutes, and the face scrunch showed up every fourth time. I straightened the wrinkled papers in my backpack, pulled out my science notebook, and wrote the date: February 1. Then found the courage to peek at my new neighbor on the left.

Khory Price.

A girl.

My neck twitched faster. Touching a boy's desk was bad, but a girl's? With my place on the social ladder, it would come across as creepy, and I didn't need another label. I already sported the nickname "American Horror Story Freak Show."

I shoved my left hand under my leg. My elbow jerked trying to free it. With my right hand I smoothed the crinkled papers. A difficult feat, but it kept me occupied. My head still bobbed. My shoulder still lifted.

I didn't want to be a jerk and ignore her, but if I looked toward Khory and saw the brown faux wood of her desk, I'd have to touch the place where it attached to the gray metal. My fingers tingled with the idea of running themselves over the seam.

I mind-messaged Mrs. Frances to start class, but she continued to scribble questions on the whiteboard. Apparently our connection was gone.

Against my better judgment, I peeked at Khory Price. She had her left elbow on the desk and her forehead in her hand, and alternated between writing and erasing numbers in an open notebook. The only thing consistent was the sighs.

Her hair slid off her shoulder and covered the wood and metal seam of the desk. Suddenly the urge to touch the wood disappeared, but it wasn't as satisfying as I'd hoped. My fingers still tingled and moved up and down as much as they could trapped under my leg. They had an urge to touch something, and realizing what it was made me wish for the desk.

Her hair. Long and brown, with a hint of red when the sun shone through the window. It was shiny and smooth. My fingers would slip down like on a water-park slide and get lost in the curls at the ends. I ran my right hand through my own hair. It did nothing to satisfy the tingle and probably just made my hair stand up straight. My left elbow jerked to free my hand. I yanked it out and held it back like it was a two-year-old going for candy.

Khory slammed her pencil down and stared at me. "What?"

My cheeks burned. I shook my head and focused on my own notebook and the date. Sixty-five days left.

"Sorry, I'm Khory," she said.

Of course, I already knew that. There were only twenty-two of us in the class. I didn't talk much, but I listened well.

"I'm Troy." That was the extent of my conversation abilities.

"Hi."

Thankfully she didn't want to shake hands or I'd have to free my left hand. If we were both girls, we would have hugged and squealed or made some other noise only dogs could hear. I got away with a nod. She turned back to her desk, frowned at her notebook, then bit her bottom lip. I counted to ten and watched her hair fall over her shoulder and cover part of her face. She twisted the edge of her paper. My left arm lifted a few inches and moved to the edge of my desk. There was no controlling it. It had a mind of its own and stretched out until it was a millimeter from the tip of her curls.

"I hate math," she said. "Or maybe it's just Mr. Nagel. He stares too much and creeps me out. I hate when people stare at me."

I let out a big breath and yanked my hand away just as Khory looked up.

I had him too, but he turned away when I walked into the room. Maybe he thought I was the creepy one. I kept that to myself since I couldn't handle another seat rearranging and fumbled with my pencil. I counted to myself and tapped it ten times on my desk, then leaned back and attempted to seem cool, or not as weird.

"Okay, class. Listen up," Mrs. Frances announced. "Before we start the new section, I want to tell you about a new science summer program. It's a three-week intensive course on astronomy ending with a field trip to New York."

The chance for a trip to New York, even for a school-type program, got people to put their phones down and sit up straight. Except Khory.

She sank in her chair and stared at her desk. A shadow covered her face, one that had nothing to do with the sun streaming through the window.

"You good?" I asked.

Khory turned to me. "Yes. It sounds interesting, doesn't it? I'd love to go, but New York is so far."

"Sure." It sounded like a dream come true, but it conflicted with another, more important dream I had. Summer was almost five months away, and my list would be completed by then.

FEBRUARY 1

After Chemistry and a brief stop at my locker, I started the trek to the back door and the bus lot. One, two, three, four, five, six, seven, eight, nine, ten steps. Bend down. Repeat. Faster and faster each time. I didn't want to walk the three and a half miles home if I missed the bus. My brother was waiting for me.

I climbed the school-bus steps. My favorite seat behind the driver was taken by a short, beefy kid with a trombone, so I scanned the seats for an empty one, or at least one by the window. My neck twitched. Sitting on the end with a seat across the aisle was just like the classroom-desk issue. The urge to touch it, and the person sitting there, would be overwhelming. The thought alone made my fingers tingle.

There was one empty seat seven rows back. I made my way there and slid all the way to the window. I ran my fingers over the empty space next to me, then tapped it ten times. Just as I was about to start another round of tapping, a pair of gray legging-covered legs stopped in the aisle.

"Great," the legging girl groaned.

I yanked my hand back. She flopped onto the seat, swung her legs toward the aisle, and put her back to me. Her long, blonde ponytail teased me. *Pull me!* I grabbed my jacket and pulled it instead. Nowhere near as satisfying.

The bus engine choked, sputtered, then eventually came to life. When we bumped our way to the open road, I took out my phone and opened the List of Ten. I thought about the new seats, Khory, and the astronomy summer program. Could I fit them into the list?

Before high school, my real dream was to have friends and a girlfriend. Someone who would wait at our locker before school and get me in trouble for texting me during dinner. Of course, we would share a locker. But high school was a rude awakening for what the real world had to offer. Hormones brought on a whole new mess of Tourette tics, emotions, and interactions with society that I would have preferred not to have. So what did adulthood promise? More of the same.

I could just imagine Dr. Hardly Qualified's reaction if I'd told him my plan to commit suicide. He'd press his pointer finger to his cheek, which he always did to appear thoughtful while he came up with something to say. Then he'd grab some outdated, dust-covered book from his shelf.

"Hmm, suicide. Depression!"

"I'm not depressed," I would have explained. "Just tired. Exhausted from the whole thing."

"And what do you mean by that, specifically?"

"The Tourette, the OCD, being in constant pain because my muscles won't stop moving and my brain won't stop counting." Even my explanations were on repeat. To a trained professional, it should have been obvious by looking at me.

"Troy, you need to give it time. Close your eyes, breathe in, and count to ten." Then he would have added antidepressants to my current medicine cocktail.

I did give it, and him, time. Ten days. Ten months. Years even. And now that the tenth anniversary of my nightmare life was coming, the significance couldn't be ignored. I was sure HQ wouldn't approve.

I shifted toward the window, as the number of neck twitches and hand squeezes increased, and focused on the rows of trees whizzing by. My muscles ached as I tried to control them, but they quivered from the inside like a million ants scurrying through my body trying to get free. People already thought I was crazy. If my muscles took over, everyone would run away screaming like the zombie apocalypse was here.

I listened to the voices complaining about new semester classes, teachers, and homework as we passed the shopping center where I learned to ride my bike. Almost home. The bus turned into my neighborhood and pulled to the curb. My stop was the first one, two blocks from my house.

I scooted past ponytail girl and started the ten-count-bend-down, pushing away the visual of chewed gum, spit, and dog poop that lived in the floor's rubber tread. A boy behind me sighed. His breath was warm on my neck. Did he think I enjoyed this? My neck twitched. Trust me, no one wanted to get home faster than me.

I leaped off the last step, took a deep breath of cool air, and wiped the sweat off my forehead. When I turned left onto my street, I ran the rest of the way, too fast to slow down when I got to the number ten. I stopped at the door, touched the ground ten times, then disappeared inside.

As soon as the lock clicked, I freed the ants scrambling in my body. My neck twitched fifteen times. An odd number. My hands clenched. Fingernails dug in my palms. My neck twitched five more times, felt the craving, and quickly did it ten more times. Thirty. Even number and divisible by ten. Which left a three. Ten more times. Forty. Four times ten is forty. Searing pain traveled from my neck down my left shoulder blade. An eighty-five out of one hundred on my rate-the-pain scale.

I let out a big exhale and shuffled to my room. Ten steps. Touched the hardwood. Ten steps. Touched the carpet. My fingertips slid over it. Soft. Too soft. I pressed my fingers into it, feeling for the hard floor underneath.

In my room, I collapsed on the floor, letting my body melt into the carpet. I stared at the light-up stars on my ceiling. My fingers ran over the carpet, but that didn't matter anymore. I closed my eyes, thankful to be home just in time. How were strangers supposed to understand that? Of course I had to at least try to explain it before April 6.

I sank deeper into the carpet. Life could be worse. I could have lost an eye, or a leg, or everything I owned in a house fire set by a drug-addicted second cousin, as Dad would say.

"Troy, as a cop, I see despair every day."

Doubtful since he was a captain who worked behind a desk in the part of town where lowlifes were people whose houses only had four-car garages. And what did he know? He didn't live in my body. I would never judge anyone. Actually, I envied people whose lives were worse than mine but who found the courage to survive.

I rolled onto my stomach and made a pillow with my hands. Some cruel joke of the universe gave excruciating pain, a dumpster full of tics, and a number fixation to a sixteen-year-old boy. As if being medicated and pudgy with a few pimples wasn't embarrassing enough. That's why I made the list. I was exhausted.

The only relief was sleep, and right now I would give up my iPhone to get some, but the sound of jingling keys meant I'd have to wait.

"Troy? Are you home?"

I opened my eyes as my stepmom poked her head in the doorway. She scrunched her eyebrows together. "Are you alright?"

"Just tired."

"Are you okay to stay with Jude? I have to leave in five minutes."

"Sure."

I followed her into the family room. She put the baby monitor and a stuffed giraffe on the coffee table, tied her shoulder-length hair in a bun, then loaded up her tactical belt with the handcuffs, gun, and a flashlight. She was a cop who actually saw the dregs of society. That's why she let her muscles peek out of her uniform sleeves.

"He's still napping," Terri said. "There's spaghetti in the fridge for dinner. Your dad should be home around six-thirty."

"Got it."

I dug my notebooks and iPad out of my backpack. After twenty minutes, I had only done two questions, and now had the image of Khory and the way her hair fell over her face burned into my mind. I laid my pencil on the table parallel to my notebook and went in search of last year's yearbook.

Back in the family room, I flipped through it until I found her. Khory had the same long brown hair and huge dark eyes last year. She smiled with perfect straight teeth, and I assumed, if the picture were color, she'd have some version of the pink lipstick she had today.

I sighed, flipped to the index, and scrolled to her name searching for other pictures with her hair falling over one eye or her biting her bottom lip like she did in class.

My fingertips gripped the page and pulled gently. An urge grew in my chest like the beginning of an itch. *Pull harder*, my brain taunted. Then, a second later, *don't rip the page*. Tourette was one big contradiction.

The tingle went down my fingers to the palm of my hand aching for the feeling of balled-up paper. The hand squeeze was a losing battle like all the others. I shoved the yearbook away, sat on my hands, and fell back against the couch. One, two, three, four, five, six.

A gurgling sound came through the monitor. Seven, eight, nine, ten. I got up, and the yearbook fell open to a page of kids making goofy faces at the camera. It was weird how people chose to scrunch up their faces or stick their tongues out when most of my life I tried to avoid doing that. Or avoided cameras altogether because I couldn't.

I went to Jude's room, and my neck calmed down. We did the whole diaper-and-clothes change thing. Not my favorite part of our afternoon party session, but a small price to pay for quality time with my best friend and most trusted confidant.

"How was your day?" I grabbed his Thomas the Train blanket on the way back to the family room. "Mine was fine. Thanks for asking. I met a girl."

Okay, she was assigned to the seat next to me, but I didn't look up anyone else in the yearbook. Or spend half the afternoon thinking about them.

Jude laughed, which I didn't take personally since his eyes twinkled with excitement and not ridicule.

"*Oy. Eeee. Aah,*" he said. Well, that's what most people probably heard, but since I spoke eleven-month-old, it was clear he asked, "Is she cute?"

"As a matter of fact, she is."

I set him on the carpet, gave him his blanket, and took out four blocks and a train with lights and the most annoying music since

18

the eighties. I made it through two more math problems before he derailed the train.

Since we were a lot more interested in science, we watched the videos Mrs. Frances assigned. Jude's smile was the only thing I looked forward to when waking up in the morning. He was a lot like our dad, with his tuft of brown hair and blue-green eyes, while I was exactly like my mom. Brown eyes, solid build under the medication weight, and the disorders.

My parents knew what I had even before they took me to the doctor almost ten years ago. The repeated neck twitches, grunting, and touching were classic Tourette symptoms. And some were the same Mom had.

The doctor, an older lady with black hair and deep lines around her eyes, put me on the exam table and studied me. No shining a light in my eyes or examining my ears. She just watched. My neck twitches increased. I touched her arm. Twitch. Touch. Repeat. Dad reached for my hand while Mom backed up toward the parent chair.

"Of course he has Tourette," the doctor said. "I'm sure you recognized the signs."

I peered around Dad to see Mom collapse in the chair. She nodded and stared at the floor.

"Mommy?"

Dad rubbed my back. "Yes, we did," he said to the doctor. "We just wanted an official diagnosis, so we could move to the next steps."

Those steps turned out to be questionnaires that uncovered my obsessive-compulsive disorder, attention deficit disorder, and anxiety. Then prescriptions for medications that made me feel like a zombie, and finally psychiatrist information that eventually led us to Hardly Qualified.

I put Jude on my lap and gave him a hug. These afternoon hang-outs would help get me through the next sixty-five days.

"So, I have this list of ten things I want to do." I took out my phone and opened to the list. "As you can see, number two is to get my first kiss."

"*Mm, aahshh, oy.*"

"Well it may be shocking for you that I've never kissed a girl, but sadly, that's my reality. So, I want to make it happen, and I want it to be Khory."

Jude reached for the phone. I put it on the couch, slid the yearbook closer to us, and flipped to Khory's last-year picture. "See, she's cute. Actually, she's beautiful."

Why would she want to kiss someone like me? I had nothing to offer except the entire *Star Wars* movie collection on Blu-ray and a head butt if she got too close to my left side. And my impressive academic skills, something she'd know if Mrs. Frances had arranged us by GPA.

"Jude, what is the one and, based on her frustration today, probably the only thing Khory needs that I can provide? Help in math."

Jude turned away from the yearbook and smiled at me.

"I know, genius, right? Now comes the hard part. Asking her."

FEBRUARY 1

Jude and I took a homework break and went on the swings.

"Dinner!" Dad yelled through the back door.

Already? I still had homework and doubted any teacher would accept the excuse of being distracted by a baby or working on a plan to get a girl to kiss me.

I carried Jude across the backyard. We made a game out of the ten-count-bend-down, me counting, then both of us reaching for the ground. His giggle made the compulsion bearable.

We walked into the kitchen, and I plopped him in the high chair. Dad, the taller and more muscular version of Jude, had his uniform sleeves folded at each elbow. He dashed from the microwave to the sink to the refrigerator, banging plates and pots and running water.

I soaped up a towel and squeezed the extra water in the sink. My palm tingled. I squeezed the towel again. Repeat. I groaned.

"Are you washing Jude's hands?" Dad asked.

I took six long steps to Jude, counted the rest to ten, then rubbed the towel over his hands, cleaning the dirt between his fingers. My palm tingled, and the feeling spread out to my fingers. My heart pounded. I couldn't stop it.

My hand squeezed into a fist. Jude's tiny fingers were trapped inside. They rolled over themselves and felt like a handful of stones inside mine. He screamed. I rubbed his hair to soothe him, but my hand squeezed again. I leaped back. My neck twitched. My hands squeezed together. Repeat. Repeat.

"What happened?" Dad yelled. "What are you doing?" He stomped over and snatched the towel from my hand. Did he think I did it on purpose?

"Sorry. It was an accident. I didn't mean to." My body shook. I grabbed my hair and pulled. Harder. One, two, three, four, five, six, seven, eight, nine, ten. Repeat. I moved my hands behind my back.

Dad turned to me. "It's okay. You didn't mean it. Take a deep breath."

Then what? Count to ten and suddenly everything would be better? I shook my head.

"Jude's fine. Don't worry. Sit. I'll get dinner."

I sank into my chair. Dad went to the kitchen and came back with two plates of spaghetti, sauce, corn, and a cup of yogurt.

Forks and spoons tinged against the plates. Dad was like a robot. One bite for him, two spoonfuls for Jude. I sat straighter, divided my food into ten equal parts, and made a barrier for the encroaching sauce with lines of pasta. The corn transformed into crushed bones. What happened? I was harmless. Except to paper and the occasional door I slammed against the wall. But people? Never.

I had a theory about Tourette: the busier the brain was, the less trouble the body caused. So I thought about the homework I didn't finish, which led to chemistry, and then to Khory. There was a big difference between helping someone in math and kissing them, and I had no idea how to get from one to the other. My math skills were above average, but my social skills were definitely an F.

I couldn't even tell if she liked me. As just a person, obviously, but the fact that she wasn't like Bradley, who asked for another seat, and didn't scoot her desk as far from me as she could, were good signs.

"How was school?" Dad asked.

"The same," I said.

"Great."

To Dad, "the same" was synonymous with "great." Unfortunately, things had changed since he first asked that question. Tenth grade wasn't second grade, and the same no longer meant recess, science fairs, and reading time that turned into superpower conversations.

"How's that kid you used to be friendly with? Eric, Evan?"

I sighed. "The one that moved away in fifth grade? Or the one in seventh grade that freaked out when I touched his hair?" The touching tic always got me in trouble.

"Oh, sorry. I forgot about that."

Dad refocused on his food, ripping bite-size pieces of garlic bread from his and handing them to Jude. I grabbed my garlic bread. My hand clenched around it until it was covered in a layer of butter and garlic. Crumbs flew across the table. Jude's eyes went wide. He laughed, grabbed a piece of his bread, and copied me. Then he threw it across the table.

"Jude, don't throw your food," Dad said.

It had to be frustrating to eat dinner with your sixteen-year-old who had table manners as bad as your baby. I wasn't expecting an it-sucks-to-be-you comment, but he could have asked if it was time for my medicine. Or if I needed a napkin.

"So, tell me something that happened in school," he said.

I repositioned my food into their ten groups and thought about asking how to get a girl to kiss you. He's had two wives, so he must know something. But what if he asked for details? Or what if he didn't? I put my head down.

I went over my day again. Freaking out about the new seating chart and ponytail girl were on the tip of my tongue, but all I said was I needed a new spiral notebook.

· · · · · · · · · ·

After dinner I grabbed my notebooks and sat at my desk. I had home-work to finish, but even science couldn't push what I'd done to Jude out of my head. The thought of his tiny fingers inside my hand made me queasy. I pictured Khory and her hair curling at the ends, but my brain kept forcing the bad images through.

I shoved my laptop away and pounded the desk. Again and

again. My chest tightened. I yanked a handful of paper from my notebook and scrunched it up. Repeat. The feeling wasn't the same. My brain wanted his fingers. Those tiny little things I could crush into sand. My neck twitched. I pounded on my chest. Breathe.

Somehow I had to control myself. It wasn't long. The tenth anniversary was too close for me to off myself after an excruciatingly painful day, or a trip to the principal's office because I straightened pencils on someone's desk who preferred them crooked.

I grabbed my phone and opened my list. Number two: first kiss. I clicked on the paper-and-pencil icon, opened a new page, typed "First Kiss," and created another list.

1. Ask Khory if she wants help in math
2. Meet in a quiet place (my house, her house, the library)
3. Find the right situation to kiss her

I clicked back to the original list and ran my finger down the entries. All doable with planning, although some were easier than others. Number one: meeting someone with TS. There were support groups, I just had to find out where. Number three: being pain-free? Now that would take some thought. If I had that answer, all this wouldn't be necessary.

I stopped on number nine: Talk to Mom.

I snuck a peek at my closet. Hidden behind the door was all I had left of her. Our relationship for the past six years fit into a shoebox. Seven cards didn't take up much room.

When Mom first left, the cards came so regularly, I practically stalked the mailman. After school and on Saturdays, I sat on the driveway, then rushed down to meet him.

"What a good helper," he said to me.

I nodded even though helping by collecting the mail never occurred to me. I shuffled through the envelopes, picked out the one with my name on it, and tore open the brightly colored envelope. Then read and reread them. "Happy 10th birthday!" "Thinking of you." "You Graduated!" She'd written my name and signed hers, but that was it. No letter saying when she was coming back. No invitation to visit her. Certainly no plane ticket. Just impersonal messages written by someone else who cranked them out for money.

And after a year, they stopped.

If she'd just written, or called, I could have told her she didn't need to explain why she left. I just wanted someone to talk to. Someone who understood why I had to touch everything, why I grunted under my breath, and how lonely it was when no one wanted to play with you. Instead, I got HQ and the number ten.

When I found her, she was going to give me that explanation. It would have been easy if she'd just done it back then, because now I had a few things to say. She'd know this was her fault. We could have lived with it together, but she never gave me that option. By leaving, she took all hope of surviving.

But I couldn't do it now. I wasn't ready to face those cards. My hands tightened into fists and my fingernails dug into the palms. I dared them to bleed.

I took a deep breath and clicked on the paper-and-pencil icon again. On a new page I made another list: Methods to Die.

1.   Gun

I didn't have to try and buy one or steal one. There was a hand-gun locked in a gray metal box on the top shelf in Dad's closet. I found it by accident when, six months ago, I was looking for a hat. It called to me even then, just a whisper because it wasn't the right time.

But it would be soon.

I stuck out my pointer finger and thumb in the shape of a gun like I'd done so many times when I was little and playing cop. Now I knew there were more uses for a gun. I opened my mouth and jabbed the "barrel" to the roof of my mouth. Placement was the difference between living and dying. I pulled the "trigger." The bullet traveled up to my brain.

Pow!

FEBRUARY 2

Whatever clueless administrator decided we should have four seventy-five-minute classes a day clearly never sat through English with Mrs. King, had ADD, or planned his or her life around talking to a girl.

So, thanks to this A-day, B-day schedule, I didn't have science today and wouldn't talk to Khory until tomorrow. But to get her to kiss me, I needed as much time as possible. All I had to do was figure out her schedule and a way to be in the same hallway as her.

The schedule was the easy part. We both had Mr. Nagel for math. I had him third block, and Khory and I had science together fourth, so that meant she had math first or second block.

Since Mr. Palmer, my second-block Introduction to Engineering teacher, handed out bathroom passes like candy on Halloween, I tried him first. Ten minutes before the end of class bell rang, I was counting and bending across the school to the only possible hallway Khory could take from Mr. Nagel's classroom to the cafeteria.

I got there just as the bell rang and leaned against a locker hoping the owner didn't show up. Someone being freaked out by my bizarre behavior might influence Khory in the wrong way. My neck twitched; I counted to ten and squeezed my hands. I repeated it three times before Khory darted around a group of people hanging out and blocking the hallway. She was headed this way. I put a hand on the locker to steady myself.

"Khory," I choked out, barely loud enough for me to hear. I cleared my throat. "Khory."

She turned toward me and tilted her head. Maybe she didn't remember me. I ran my hand through my hair and thought about letting this chance pass. Face the locker, pretend it was mine, and let her think she was hearing things. But time was running out. I had a sixty-four-day deadline.

I waved her over. She leaned toward a girl with long brown-and-green hair, then stepped toward me.

"I just wanted to say I'm good in math." Math, yes. Conversation, no. "I mean, if you need help."

I cringed as the words came out of my mouth. Would she think I called her stupid? And why did I assume she'd want my help? Khory peered down the hallway, then back at me and smiled.

"I'm supposed to meet my friends for lunch. Come on, we can talk there."

"Okay," I said.

Then I realized what I agreed to. I almost died during the last seat change, and now lunch with a thousand more people? There was a reason I'd picked out my seat at the beginning of the year and did everything except carve my name in the table to make sure no one else sat there.

Just like in Science, I preferred an out-of-the-way place. The back corner. I wasn't completely alone. Riley and Nicholas were near. Not close enough to touch their trays, but close enough to debate DC Comics versus Marvel.

Did her friends have lunch trays? They would have to, or brown bags. Something for me to reach out and touch. I squeezed my hand. One, two, three, four, five, six, seven, eight, nine, ten. Air couldn't find its way to my lungs. One, two, three, four, five, six, seven, eight, nine, ten. Why did I think HQ's technique would work one day?

I forgot what to do. Breathe? Khory moved to my left, closer to the middle of the hallway where people with coordination texted and sprinted past the slow kids. Just as on the highway. I breathed in. Then out. Repeat. We started walking. I focused on ten steps and breathing. When I got to ten, I bent down and touched the floor. The dark spots on the white-and-tan swirly tiles were not part of the design. Whoever invented portable hand sanitizer was a genius.

When I stood, she was still beside me.

"It's okay," she said. "My friends will save us seats."

I gasped. I couldn't look at her. Or talk to her. My neck twitched faster. Talking about it would come. It had to, it was on the list, but right now I stared straight ahead and focused on the path. We made a right turn and went through the lobby. I could see the cafeteria doors. Images of lunch trays invaded my mind. My hand reached out like I could touch them.

I took a breath, but the air didn't get past my throat. I sucked in some more. A drop of sweat trickled down my face. We were at the cafeteria doors.

My regular seat called to me like a brand-new video game. I needed a good excuse to decline her invitation and find comfort in the corner, but everything I came up with was crap. Even I would have told myself I was full of shit.

I followed Khory to the short line for drinks, grabbed a bottle of water for each of us, and paid the cashier.

"Thanks," she said.

She scanned the cafeteria. I held a cold water bottle against my chest in an effort to jump-start my lungs. I was on my eighth round of ten when she pointed to a table in the middle of the room. Of course, the middle. I put the bottle to my forehead and followed her again. This time to my doom.

Khory stopped next to the girl with brown-and-green hair. "Hey, guys, this is Troy. He's going to tutor me in math. Troy, this is Rainn and Jay."

Rainn's love of green didn't stop with her hair. She wore a lime-green blousy-type shirt over a darker green tank top. It wasn't bad. Then she pulled out a green lunch box. That may have been overkill, but who was I to judge? My clothes and lunch box were bland and blue.

She leaned forward and studied me from head to toe. Her nose crinkled, and her lip curled like she'd drunk spoiled milk.

"Hi," Rainn said to me, then shifted toward Khory. "Math tutor?"

Khory hit her arm and turned away from me.

Jay sat across the table. He was black with short hair, pretty much shaved, and a patch of chin hair that made the five sprigs on mine look like Charlie Brown's head. He glanced at me, then down at his food.

My neck twitched nonstop. I stared at my empty seat in the corner. If I ran to the back, Khory would never kiss me.

"Sit," she said.

I sat next to her. Jay shifted in his seat and pulled his lunch bag closer to him. I put mine down, and even though my stomach was rolling like storm waves, I pulled out my sandwich. I needed to keep my brain busy.

"So, what's up, girl?" Rainn asked.

"Same," Khory said. "Mr. Granieri gave us too much homework, as usual. How are things with Diego?"

Rainn sighed. "He's not nurturing my dreams," she said. "Plus, he's a Scorpio."

I knew better than to get in the middle of a boyfriend/girlfriend conversation, especially when I wasn't one hundred percent sure what was wrong with being a Scorpio. I sat back, tempted fate with both hands on the table, and tried to ignore the drama.

"You're a math tutor?" Jay asked.

I didn't know what to say. Technically no, but I couldn't admit I used it as an excuse to get close to Khory. I nodded.

"We're in the same math class."

I nodded again. That meant he'd most likely caught my touching act during class, which was why he pulled his lunch bag closer to him.

Khory mixed dressing into her salad and faced me. "Aren't you going to eat?"

I stared at my sandwich. Ham and cheese with lettuce and tomato on wheat bread. I'd read somewhere that processed foods made tics worse, so I compromised by not eating white bread. And it was rough.

"So, about the math, you should give me your phone number since we'll have to work on it after school," Khory said and took out her phone.

I gave her my number and watched her punch it in then press the green button. My phone vibrated in my pocket.

"Now you have my number, too," she said. "Can you come over after school today? The sooner I learn this stuff, the better I'll do on the midterm."

A girl's number and an invitation to her house all in one conversation? If I wasn't sitting, my legs would have given out.

"Yeah."

I smiled and took a breath. Her hair smelled like coconuts. It bounced around her shoulders as she moved. Then the bubble popped.

"Actually, I can't. I babysit my brother after school." I clenched my hands, and my neck twitched at the memory of Jude's tiny hand in mine. "Can you come to my house?"

Was I crazy? The only girls who came to our house were eight and dumped their dolls to play with a real baby.

Khory stopped eating, fork halfway to her mouth. A piece of lettuce teetered on the edge. Of course she couldn't.

"I'm not allowed to go anywhere after school." Her shoulders slumped, and the sadness in her eyes overshadowed everything.

Jay stared at the table and gobbled his stiff slice of pizza. Rainn frowned. Clearly I'd missed something. For years I'd believed every denied invitation or nearby laugh was about me, but this time I knew it wasn't.

"We'll work something out." She picked up her fork and nibbled on the lettuce.

When the conversation between Khory and Rainn turned back to boys, I pulled out my phone and typed COMPLETED next to the task of asking Khory about math. I wanted to fist bump the air, but settled for a smile hidden behind my disgusting sandwich.

· · · · · · · · · ·

A rare event occurred on this Tuesday afternoon: I finished my homework before Dad got home. That hasn't happened since the day I started Patrick Henry High School. I planned to celebrate with hours of video games, but I couldn't concentrate. I kept replaying today's lunch. And it wasn't an OCD thing. It was a girl thing.

Something about Khory made me feel electric. The way her hair glistened in the sunlight definitely did something to me, but it was more about the way she stayed with my ten-count-bend-down pace and asked me to sit with her and her friends at lunch. And she still wanted my phone number.

I guess we didn't really know anyone. The school was full of different kinds of people: guys and girls who cared about fashion, the drama club, band members, and the random kids who didn't belong anywhere. But really, that was all surface. For the first time I realized it went deeper. Like the sadness in Khory's eyes. And me, as exposed as I was, still hid so much more.

I was a frequent lurker in the online TS groups, so I knew people hid the same things I did. Some probably had their version of the List of Ten. Not that I was interested in sharing. I didn't need to be overwhelmed by talking-me-off-the-ledge comments.

"You have so much to live for." As if they knew anything about my life.

"We're here for you." You don't know me.

"Please talk to someone. Call the suicide hotline." Okay, this one did have a point.

But how could they be "here" when they were faceless usernames floating through the internet? For all I knew, they could have typed the hotline number with a loaded gun in their lap.

They weren't all wrong. I needed someone here. Physically here. To tic along with me, grimace in pain, and fill that empty space that's been growing since April 6.

I opened my laptop, went to the internet, and typed in "Tourette syndrome support groups Richmond Virginia." I held my breath as the blue bar traveled from left to right. How did the groups work? Would we be able to hear each other if we all mumbled or yelled? I may not have met anyone else like me since Mom left, but I've seen enough videos to know there were a lot of tics out there not as quiet as mine.

A list popped up. Richmond, Virginia Support Group Mid-Atlantic Chapter, Virginia Parent Support Groups, Find a local chapter: Tourette Association of America.

I clicked the first one.

The Tourette Association of America logo popped up along with pictures of smiling people. I sighed. I knew it was just a picture, "on the count of three, say cheese," but I could never fake it like that. I scrolled down to the list of services. Social and educational events, donate, youth ambassadors, and support. I clicked on the last one.

A support group, open to everyone affected by TS, met every other Thursday at the main branch of Richmond General Hospital. The next meeting was February 4. This week.

I opened the List of Ten. Under number two: meet someone with Tourette syndrome, I typed the date and address. I would be there.

I closed my computer. Too much stress and planning wore me out. I forced myself up, went to the bathroom to take my medicine, then got into bed and waited for the medicine to kick in and my body to relax. Door closed. Lights off. Goodbye, day.

Then my phone rang.

I jumped so high I practically smacked the ceiling. The only people who called were Dad and Terri. I glanced at the phone. There in big white letters was the name Khory Price.

"Hello?"

"Troy? It's Khory."

My heart skipped a beat. I counted to ten.

"Troy? Are you there?"

"Yeah. Sorry. What's up?" My conversation skills were lame even on the phone.

"Since you can't come over after school and I can't go over your house because my parents are crazy overprotective, can you come over Saturday? After lunch. Maybe one o'clock?"

Overprotective? That was her excuse and why everyone's mood changed?

"Sure."

"Great. I've been reading over the units so I won't seem like a complete idiot."

And I actually paid attention to Mr. Nagel's lecture on trigonometric functions, so I'd be able to help her. "Okay. I'll bring my math book," I said.

"Thank you so much for this," she said. "I'll text you my address so you'll have it. It's in the Thornhill neighborhood."

I could hear her smile through the phone, if that was even possible. I smiled too and sank into my pillow.

"No problem," I said.

"Well, I should go. But you can call me whenever you want."

"Um, okay." Call her? I could barely put two words together around her.

"See you tomorrow," she said.

"See you tomorrow."

Then she hung up.

The red button disappeared, and my screen faded to black. She couldn't have actually meant call her anytime. No, she meant for math only. Yeah, that was it. I was just the math tutor. My neck twitched. I squeezed my hands together. Stress was stress, even if caused by a beautiful girl.

My mind wandered like a dream. In it, we were talking on the phone. It was late. Our houses were dark and quiet. She fell asleep, and I spent the next few hours listening to her soft inhales and exhales.

My hand squeezed the phone and brought me back to reality. A dream. That's all. I opened my notes, went to the First Kiss list, and typed COMPLETED next to number two, the place to meet. Now all I had to do was kiss her.

FEBRUARY 4

Tonight was the support group meeting. I had to leave at six. It was five fifty-seven. My heart thumped harder and my neck twitched faster as the minutes ticked by. I stood by the living room window. Where was Dad? Come on, Dad, you promised. I watched Jude bang plastic cars into each other. I clenched my hands together and fought back the memory and sensation of his hands and hair in my fists. The tingling came anyway. I grabbed my own hair, but, not a surprise, no satisfaction.

The hum of an engine got my attention, and I turned back to the window in time to see the trunk of Dad's car disappear into the garage.

"Bye, Jude, see you later."

He glanced up, gave me a big grin, and slammed the cars on the carpet.

I rushed past Dad in the kitchen. "Math tutoring, remember?"

"Yes, you told me five times," he said. "Where's Jude?"

"Family room. Gotta go." I burst through the garage door. I had eight minutes to get to the bus stop. No bike. Only the power of my two feet.

As soon as the garage door closed, I ran. Past the school bus stop, then up the hill to the main road. If I missed the city bus, I'd have to ask Dad to drive me, which meant a big explanation. Or wait until the next meeting, which I didn't want to do.

Tonight would be the night I met someone like me.

I ran along Elm Lane, my focus on the mall lights in the distance. I breathed in and out, pumped my arms harder, and ran faster. Despite being a little pudgy, I wasn't in too bad a shape, cardiovascularly. Shocking since I didn't go out much.

At the mall, I dodged cars driving through the parking lot and made it to the side of the bus shelter. I huffed and puffed and tried to catch my breath, wiped the sweat off my forehead, and shook out my shirt. Then I checked out the other people waiting with me. They sat on the bench or leaned against the shelter's wall staring at their phones. None of them moved or twitched.

I'd never ridden a city bus, but I knew the issues would be the same as the school bus. Except with complete strangers. My chest tightened as if a giant hand wanted to squeeze the life out of it. My neck twitched faster. I dug my fingertips into my left shoulder blade to ease the shooting pain, but that wouldn't help a seventy-on-the-rate-the-pain scale. I tried to get air into my lungs for the twelve ten-counts it took for the bus to come.

People rushed the doors as soon as the bus screeched to a stop.

Apparently, their dads didn't teach them manners like mine did. I stayed on the side until it was my turn, but that probably meant my chances of getting a window seat in the back were busted.

When it was my turn, I climbed the steps and started down the aisle, my neck twitching and face scrunching. I wrestled the urge to bend down, even halfway. But with each row I passed, and the closer I got to ten, the stronger the itch got until I thought I'd explode.

I bent down and touched the floor. I tried to force in images of a snow-covered ground or my bedroom carpet instead of the unknown blue sticky substance facing me, but even the worst my mind could come up with was better than the judgment on the riders' faces when I stood up.

A few looked away. Some scrunched up their faces like they sucked on a lemon. A lady in a business suit scooted to the middle of her seat. "This seat's taken," she said, then glared at me until I passed her.

No big deal. I tried to convince myself I wanted the back anyway. There were four people in front of me. The hand squeezed my chest tighter as each one passed perfectly good open seats. I counted as I followed them. My muscles tightened as I forced myself to stay straight.

"You okay, kid?" A gray-haired man in a light-blue jacket asked as I approached his seat. "You need a doctor?"

I nodded. "I'm fine. Thank you." At least someone cared.

The last person sat two rows from the back. I bent down, then hurried to the last seat and collapsed into the one by the window. I took a deep breath.

As the bus pulled away from the curb, I stared in the direction of my house. What was the point in meeting people like me? We weren't going to be friends. I wouldn't be around long enough for friends. I spun toward the mall. I wanted to run away, bury myself under my blanket, and call for Mom even though I knew she wouldn't come. That's what I wanted. And needed. And I guessed the next best thing was a group of people affected by TS.

The bus chugged past houses and schools. We passed strip malls, then offices, until finally the buildings towered over the trees. Downtown. We were here.

The second stop was mine. The main branch of Richmond Memorial Hospital. The meeting didn't start until seven o'clock, but with the ride here and the ten-count walk, time was running out. I made the most of the steps and my long legs.

The lobby was a huge room with tan tiles, off-white walls, and brown furniture. An information desk sat in the center with a signboard on the left. It directed TS support group attendees to a conference room on the left along with those looking for prenatal classes and information for elder caregivers. I took a deep breath, then spun around. I couldn't sit in a room full of ticcers. It would be like staring in a mirror. I never did that.

I ran to the right, where another sign directed me to the bathroom. I darted into a stall, sat on the toilet, pants up, and buried my head in my hands. Then I let it all out.

My neck twitched. I dug my fingernails into my palms, leaving deep indentations. One, two, three, four, five, six, seven, eight, nine, ten. One, two, three, four, five, six, seven, eight, nine, ten. I lost count after ninety reps. Then my eyes found the floor. No. I pleaded and begged my brain. This was a hospital, the floor had to be covered with all sorts of infectious diseases.

The large tan tiles did a terrible job of hiding dirt. Circles of dried liquid shone in the light that seeped through the crack where the door and wall met.

Please no, I begged my brain again.

I rubbed my fingertips together. Scratched my fingernails down my face. Tears welled up. The urge was like rotten food churning around in my stomach, then rising to my throat, and when I couldn't force it back down, it spewed out all around me.

My fingers ran across the tile, making sure they hit every circle of dried disease. They were sticky.

After ten counts of ten, I pushed myself up and opened the door. A man at the sink eyed me from the mirror, turned off the water with soap still on his hands, and grabbed paper towels as he rushed to the door.

"I'm good, Sir, thanks for your concern for a fellow human being." Asshole.

It was past seven o'clock, but I scrubbed my fingers for the next ten minutes and prayed the memory of the floor wouldn't set off a cleanliness obsession. When my fingers were red and reeked of antiseptic soap, I ran a wet paper towel over my face, tossed it in the garbage, then grabbed another one to cover my hand before I opened the bathroom door.

My meeting was at the end of the hall, the last door on the right. It was closed. I pressed my ear against it, expecting to hear noises or screams or who knows what. I couldn't handle more than a few seconds of internet videos of ticcers, but it was enough to know anything could be happening inside that room. And these were the people I wanted to meet.

I took a deep breath and opened the door a tiny bit. The smell of burnt coffee seeped through the door crack. A woman in jeans and a sweater leaned against a table addressing about twenty people sitting in rows of chairs.

There were a few older, gray-haired people near the front, and mixed in were people Dad's age in jeans, dress pants, and dresses. They all sat still. Not like me.

But the ticcers were there, scattered throughout. I could tell by the neck twitches and grunts.

I opened the door a tiny bit more for a better view. More people on the right. Neck twitches seemed to be the tic of choice. Ha! As if we had a choice. A man shrugged his shoulders three times quickly, then rested. Then repeat. A woman kept turning to her head to the right, then rolled her head around. Another man sitting toward the back flapped his arms as if they were chicken wings. I couldn't stop staring. Not because it was a freak show, but because I saw versions of myself.

I slid into a seat in the back row on the left, closest to the door. The speaker glanced at me, nodded, and smiled. A few people followed her gaze and studied me. I felt like a circus attraction and would have curled into a ball if I could. I looked down, and my shoulders rounded.

"This week," the speaker continued, "we are going to hear from the Isenhours about the meeting with their son's school administrators."

I glanced up. The eyes were back on the speaker. She sat down, and the woman with the head roll stood up. I uncurled myself.

"We met with David's teacher and the principal. They had been given pamphlets and videos, along with information from the ADA." She turned her head to the right, then rolled it around. "Finally, they agreed to give him special considerations for test taking."

"That's great news," a woman in the front row said.

"Yes, hopefully this will help relieve his anxiety," David's father said. "And to be honest, it will help his classmates, too. David's noises can get quite loud when he's anxious."

As if on cue, a man a row in front of me grunted. Then louder. And then again, until I realized it wasn't just a noise.

"Jerk!" The man bolted out of his chair. "I'm sorry. You know I don't think that. I . . ."

I gasped and sat up straight.

"That's alright, Charlie," the meeting leader said. "You don't have to apologize for anything. Here or anywhere."

The Isenhours smiled at Charlie. If I yelled that at school, I'd be kicked out of class. But here they keep you. My chin trembled. The Isenhours continued.

"David hopes if the situation improves, the kids will include him when they play sports. Our David is quite the athlete. He just doesn't get the chance."

I thought back to elementary school, where my love of books developed. I'd told my teacher I didn't want to play football, kickball, or whatever the game of choice was that day, but I really couldn't handle any more bruises from the other kids whipping balls at me. On the plus side, I was probably the most well-read kid in tenth grade.

The Isenhours settled into their seats, and other parents, grandparents, and ticcers shared their stories.

"I'm failing English Lit class," a blonde woman said. "My dosage of clonidine controls the tics but puts me to sleep. Right in the middle of class." She put her face in her hand. Her shoulders shook.

The man who shrugged his shoulders turned to the woman. "I get it. I've changed my medication three times in a year. The latest one made me dizzy, and I almost wrecked my car."

Arms flapping and always turning your head, they had to have the same muscle issues I did, but they didn't complain about that. And there were no grimaces or lips pressed together. Did I hide the pain that well, too?

A woman on the right stood up. "My daughter is being bullied on the bus. She locks herself in her room. Won't go to school." The woman collapsed onto her chair and leaned against the man next to her. He put his arm around her.

My body shook. I knew all about bullies. And being zoned out by meds. My mind was flooded with fear. Depression. I tried to picture Mom sitting here. She didn't talk about it like they did. If she did, would she have stayed with me?

"Time is about up," the speaker said, "If no one else has anything, we will meet here again in two weeks."

The feelings and tics exploded from my body like fireworks. My neck and back muscles burned. I wanted to say something. I had questions. What other medicines were there? What did they do when someone wiped off their seat before they sat in it? I thought them, but couldn't make them come out.

I dashed out of the building, ran straight to the bus stop, and got on the bus headed for home. With my earbuds in, Shinedown playing loud, and my eyes closed, if anyone stared or had a smartass comment, I'd never know.

The cool air refreshed me on the walk home. Once inside, I fell on my bed and replayed the meeting in my mind, focusing more on the people ticcing than what they'd said. That's what I looked like. I wished I didn't know.

I opened my phone to the list. I loved lists. The organization. The ability to mark "completed." But the numbers were off. I rearranged them so that completed ones would be at the top. The organization made my muscles relax. I sank into my pillow, then checked off number one. Nine more to go.

1. Meet someone else with Tourette syndrome—COMPLETED
2. Get my first kiss
3. Be pain-free
4. Find a babysitter for my baby brother
5. See the space shuttle
6. Talk about Tourette in public
7. Give away my Tim Howard autographed picture
8. Drive a car
9. Talk to Mom
10. Commit suicide

FEBRUARY 6

I woke up in a wave of neck twitches and stomach flutters. Saturday. I was going to Khory's house. Step two. The next one would be the kiss.

At noon I got dressed in jeans and a black sweatshirt and told Dad I was going to tutor someone in math. I bolted out the door before he could ask who the person was. It had been a long time since I'd gone to someone's house, but he'd probably get the wrong idea. Khory wasn't really a friend, and I didn't have time to explain. Or even make up a lie.

I rode into the Thornhill neighborhood, my neck twitching in full force. Would I have to meet her parents? What if they were like the lady on the bus? *Just relax, you're one step closer to the goal. And you're spending time with Khory.* I felt stupid giving myself a pep talk, but it calmed me. I took a deep breath, turned onto her street, and stopped in front of her house.

Like most of the other houses around here, hers was a two-story brick. But unlike the others, someone here obviously had a love of gardening. Or they paid well for it. The grass was green and the bushes were lush, even though it was winter.

I parked my bike on the sidewalk, glanced around to make sure no one was watching, then began the ten-count-bend-down up the driveway to the brick walkway. A shortcut would have been better, but that meant tromping on the grass. I was sure that would revoke my invitation, especially because I snuck a feel during a bend-down. It was real.

There was a green tree in a pot by the front door and a welcome mat with bright yellow flowers that actually made me feel welcome. Almost like I should be there. I pointed my finger toward the doorbell.

"Hey, Troy!"

I spun toward the voice as a silver Mazda pulled into the driveway and parked. The passenger door flew open, and Khory jumped out. She looked amazing in jeans and a white sweater, and if I had the guts, I'd have complimented her. But I didn't.

"Sorry I'm late," she said.

She reached into the car and pulled out a black duffel bag and a pillow with a purple pillowcase. When I dreamed about us lying in bed talking on the phone, I pictured a white pillowcase like mine. This was so much better.

"I stayed at Rainn's last night. It's the only place my parents let me go. I told Mom you were coming at one, but she made me go to the store with her on the way back." Khory walked toward me as the car pulled into the garage.

"It's okay, I just got here."

She fumbled with the front door, pillow, and bag. I reached to help, and my fingers glided across the soft pillowcase. My hand tingled and clenched the edge. A door across the house slammed, and keys jingled. I yanked my hand back.

"Khory?" A woman called from across the house.

"Come on. You have to meet my parents. It's okay. Most of the time they're not too bad."

She smiled and tossed her hair over her shoulder. Wasn't she worried about her parents seeing me? How can she act like it's normal to have a kid come to your house, touch every knot in the wood floor, and run a finger along the grain? My feet wouldn't move.

Khory grabbed my wrist and pulled me toward the kitchen. "Don't worry."

Sure, what did I have to lose? Except my dignity and the ability to face her in school on Monday. At least I didn't trip over the doorstep, so there was that.

I glanced around the entryway. Living room on the right. Office on the left. Stairs in the center. The house was nice. Everything matched as if all the decorations were from the same store. We walked down a hallway toward a kitchen table, and I stopped at a series of pictures in black frames. A nice even number of six. They were photographs of Khory at different ages, from a few years old until about nine or ten. The weird thing was, there were two of her in each picture. Two Khorys. I glanced at her. She stared at the pictures. Her mouth turned down.

"My mom's a photographer," she said. "She always made us pose for pictures."

Us. Not trick photography. Was her sister still at Rainn's? So Khory just came home for me—I mean tutoring?

We went to the kitchen where a woman who I guessed was her mom pulled pots from a cabinet and vegetables from the refrigerator. She was the complete opposite of Khory. Shorter and heavier with blond hair so short it was almost boy-like. But fashionable like a TV actress. Her pale skin told me she wasn't the gardener in the family.

"You must be Troy," she said. The only similar features were their eyes. Hers were just as dark with the same touch of sadness.

"Yes, ma'am."

"Khory tells me you're helping her with math."

"Yes," I said.

"Enough small talk, Mom. We've got work to do." Then to me, "Come on."

We went through the kitchen to the dining room. It had the typical big table surrounded by a lot of chairs, and a cabinet filled with breakable glass. At least they were evenly spaced. I took the seat farthest from the cabinet.

Khory put her pillow and duffel bag on a chair, then pulled out a yellow spiral notebook and sat next to me. Through the window I saw a man in gray pants and a long-sleeve shirt. Her dad was obviously the person from whom she got the dark hair.

I grabbed my notebook from my backpack and opened to my notes. "So I thought we'd review the last unit since it's the basis for this one."

"Sure," she said. "Exponential and logarithmic functions. I'm not too bad at those, but you're right, a review is a good idea."

She tucked her hair behind her ear, and I noticed little pink heart earrings. Pink like the lip gloss she wore the other day. My eyes were drawn to her lips. They looked soft and smooth like her pillow. My lips and fingertips ached to touch them.

"Okay, so exponential functions are written like $f(x) = b$ to the x power. You know b is the base and the x is the exponent, right?"

Khory nodded.

"As an example, let's say there's an exponential function with a base of 2."

She leaned close to me, angled my notebook toward her, and read my notes. Her hair brushed my arm and tickled it.

A clang came from the kitchen like a pot dropped on the counter. "Oh, my God!" Mrs. Price said.

Khory and I flinched. My elbow jabbed her arm. Did her mom think we were too close? I scooted to the left almost a whole seat away.

"Mom, everything okay?" Khory asked.

She looked at me, her head tilted. I shrugged.

"Maybe she dropped a pot," I said.

"Yeah." But her eyes stayed on the kitchen doorway.

The back door slammed, and we spun toward the noise. Her dad sprinted to the counter and took the phone from her mom. He held onto it like life support.

"Yes, Detective Lee," Mr. Price said.

Khory gasped.

"Burglary?" Mr. Price asked. Then silence. "Oh, I understand. We are so grateful."

Khory leaped out of her chair.

"Is everything okay?" I asked.

"Shhh." She put her hand on my arm, scooted her chair back, and went to the kitchen.

My arm tingled where she touched it, like the nerve endings came to life.

"Monday," Mr. Price said. "We'll be there."

He put the phone down and pulled Khory to him. He hugged her like he hadn't seen her for years. I bowed my head, stared at my notes, and counted to ten.

"Troy, you have to go," Khory said. "Sorry, we can work on this next week."

The shadow was back, but there was more this time. It wasn't the sadness in her eyes, and not really a twinkle, but a spark. Of anger.

I stood up and scrunched my face. "Okay. I hope everything is okay."

"Yes. It is. Thanks."

I shoved the notebook in my backpack and thought about saying something like goodbye or thank you to her parents. Through the doorway I saw Mr. Price with his arms around his wife. His eyes were closed. She leaned against him as if she would collapse without him, which was probably true because her whole body shook.

FEBRUARY 8

I should have texted Khory on Sunday to find out if she was okay. What happened at her house on Saturday was just weird. I had no idea what to do or what to say, and I wasn't the invade-your-privacy type. So this morning I scanned the halls for her before and after every class, but I may have missed her, since a tenth of the time I was focused on the floor.

By lunchtime I had pretty much given up. I stuffed my books in the locker, repacked my backpack with science and math books, and grabbed my lunch bag. Then started the trek toward the cafeteria.

"Hey." Khory's friend Jay was by my side. "*Uh,* Khory told me you're helping her in math. I hate to ask, but do you think you could help me with a couple things before our Pre-Calc quiz? I know its last minute. It will take five minutes. Ten tops."

Did he realize the quiz was today, right after lunch?

"*Uh,* sure. We can do it now." I moved closer to the lockers and stopped to take my backpack off. I expected my stomach to start gurgling on cue, but no matter how loud my stomach yelled, I was so sick of ham and wheat bread, it would never be appetizing.

"Great." Jay tilted his head. "But not here. We can go over it while we eat."

Cafeteria? Middle of the room? I could feel the air being squeezed from my lungs. My legs wobbled as I slung my backpack over my shoulder. But Khory would be there. Was seeing her worth the risk of having a full-blown anxiety attack? I smiled to myself. Of course it was.

We walked down the hall toward the cafeteria. I tightened my leg muscles and got away with two bows instead of full bends, but as I counted the third round of ten—one, two, three, four—the urge grew. Five, six. It started at my waist. Seven, eight. And traveled up my body and into my arms. Nine. My fingertips tingled. My body leaned forward. My arms stretched out toward the ground. I willed the floor to come to my hands. I know that was stupid, but I desperately didn't want to meet it at its level. My arms reached further. It was coming. I couldn't stop it.

Ten.

I stopped, bent all the way, and let my fingertips touch the cool floor. I stood up and pretended like it was completely normal.

I took giant steps to catch up with Jay, who hadn't slowed down to wait for me, and caught the tail end of him complaining about logarithms. Not wanting to make a bigger fool of myself, I mumbled, "yeah, that sucks," as if I'd been there the whole time.

Jay sighed, and I continued counting. We had a long way to go.

From the corner of my eye, I saw Jay glance at me. His eyebrows were scrunched together.

"Dude, I'll run ahead and save us seats," Jay said. "You know it's crowded in there."

He sped off with a quick flick of his hand. My muscles relaxed; I got to ten and touched the floor.

The lunch line was pretty short by the time I got to the cafeteria. I searched the middle tables. Jay was alone with an empty seat next to him. No Khory. I scanned the back corner where Riley and Nicholas sat. Why did I agree to help Jay? I sighed and headed to the dead center of the room.

Jay held an uneaten wrap in one hand, a pencil in the other, and stared at his open math book like he was burning it with laser eyes. His eyebrows were still scrunched together. I sat down and forced air into my lungs. Oxygen in. Carbon dioxide out. Repeat.

"I can't get this inverse thing." He stabbed the book with his finger because obviously his heat vision wasn't working.

I glanced at the empty seats across from us, then pulled the book toward me and read the examples. "Let's see. Okay, I can explain this."

I dropped my sandwich, pulled a pencil and a spiral notebook from my backpack, and opened it to a blank page. I drew a right triangle, labeled the sides, and wrote an equation: sin C = 6/10, or 0.6.

"Since we know the sin of C, we use the inverse sin function to find the angle," I said.

"Okay," Jay said.

We worked out a few problems. After five minutes, he felt comfortable enough to take a bite of his food.

Rainn blew to our table. With a green scarf and the green streak in her hair, she was like a tree in a tornado. Her lunch bag flew into mine, and she landed in the seat across from Jay with a thump.

She leaned forward toward him. "Did you talk to Khory?"

"No. Why?"

"They caught the guy. That's why she's not here today. She went to the police department. It's all so surreal."

Jay opened his mouth, but nothing came out. The wrap dropped from his hand. I turned to Rainn. She covered her face with her hands. I looked back at Jay.

Someone say something!

"How," Jay whispered.

Rainn uncovered her face. "DNA. He's been living in Florida or Georgia. Somewhere south. They don't know much, just that he's in jail there for something else."

"Burglary," I said. "I heard part of that."

They turned toward me. "I was at her house Saturday working on math. Her dad was on the phone with a detective." My cheeks grew warm. "I wasn't listening. She told me to be quiet so that she could hear."

"So what did you hear? I bet her dad wants to kill him." Rainn put a hand on her forehead. "I can't even imagine how Khory's feeling right now."

"I don't know. I didn't understand what they were talking about," I said.

"You don't know about her sister?" Jay asked.

I shook my head. "I saw pictures at her house. Khory and her sister. I just thought she had a different schedule."

"Where'd you go to elementary school?"

"Richmond Park."

"That's why. I live a couple houses down from them, and we've been friends since second grade, so I was around when it happened. Khory had a twin sister, Krista."

Had? "Was Khory the girl that was almost kidnapped? Her sister. She was the one who didn't escape."

Jay nodded and slumped toward the table.

I did remember. We were ten. Some crazy guy drove up to their front yard and tried to take them. Got them in the car, but one got away. Khory. They found her sister later, but it was too late. Dad had to know, being a cop, but he never mentioned it. Maybe he figured I was safe since I stayed in my room most of the time. I took back everything I'd said about his job. No drug dealer, robber, or rapist was worse than a guy kidnapping a kid, doing who knows what, then killing her. I was frozen again and still couldn't enjoy the stillness. At least the tics had respect for the dead.

Then the tics came back with a vengeance, so fierce I couldn't hold them in. My neck twitched. I squeezed my hands so tight there were fingernail indentations in my palms. They were deep.

"It's sad," Rainn said. "She had finally let it go. As much as she could, I guess. But when I talked to her Saturday night, she was so angry."

"Well, what do you expect?" Jay asked.

"I know. I just hate it when she talks about death. Why are there crazy people like that out there?" Rainn grabbed her lunch bag and stood up. "I can't eat."

She left Jay and me sitting there. He moved his food around but didn't eat. I thought about death. On your own terms is one thing, or even old age, but like that? It made me nauseous. My neck twitched, and a shooting pain traveled down my back. My face scrunched up, which made my cheeks sore. The pain easily rated a seventy.

The people around me stared and pointed.

"Dude, did you stick your finger in an electrical socket?" a muscular kid three seats down asked. His friend twitched and shook, and everyone laughed.

Jay glanced at me, then put his head down. What did I expect? I was just the math tutor. And since our tutoring session was over, I grabbed my lunch bag and fled.

· · · · · · · · · ·

61

I spent the rest of the afternoon trying to think of the right thing to say to Khory, but all I came up with was *sorry* or *things will be better now*. Lame. Lame. Lame. I was already established as a non-conversationalist, and if I were her, I would tell me to mind my own business because I clearly didn't understand. And I knew all about people not understanding. I'd been wishing for someone to understand me for the past six years. That's why I had to say something.

As soon as Terri finished her instructions for Jude, dinner, and Dad, I sat on my bed, pulled out my phone, and texted Khory.

ME: Rainn told me about your sister. I'm really sorry.

I pressed the arrow and fell back on my pillow. Done. My neck twitched ten times. I squeezed my hands. The phone vibrated and tickled my palm. I sat up, saw Khory's name, and pressed the green Accept button.

"Hello?" Why did I answer like a question?

"Hi, Troy. It's Khory. Thanks for the text. Rainn told me you guys talked during lunch."

"Yeah. I'm, *uh*. I don't know what to say."

"I don't know either. It's so weird," she said. "I wanted to tell you that's what the phone call was on Saturday. I didn't mean to shove you out."

"It's okay."

"I'd still like to get that help in math. Do you want to sit with me at lunch tomorrow?"

"Sure," I said. Except I wasn't, because today I'd been humiliated out of the middle section and I doubted she would want to sit at my table in the back corner.

"Great. And thanks for talking to me. See you tomorrow."

"Yeah. Okay. Bye."

I had to focus on the fact that she invited me to sit with her at lunch. Again. I smiled and watched the screen fade to black. Lunch tomorrow. The only time I'd get to see her.

We might work on math, but I was sure the main topic of conversation would be the guy. And Khory's sister. Especially if Jay and Rainn were there. I didn't want to be left out, so I grabbed my laptop and scoured the internet for stories. I found a bunch of articles, all with the same smiling faces that hung on the wall of her house. Below the pictures were details of what happened.

I knew the basics, but did I really want to know more? The OCD pull was strong. It made me want to read every word. Every noun, adjective, and verb. I was the one person who couldn't skip extra-long setting descriptions or the word said in novels no matter how hard I tried. And I tried hard.

But once I read the articles, the details would be stuck in my brain forever, making a comeback whenever the time was wrong, because that's what these disorders did. They tortured me, invaded my thoughts, took over. I fought against my brain and muscles and closed the tab. I didn't want to look at Khory and see the details. I knew enough to understand part of the shadow that covered her face.

I thought of her loss, and the tingle I felt when I stared at her lips and hair now felt heavy like a brick. Technically, Mom's disappearance wasn't permanent, but it was brutal. Her slinking away in the dead of night was like the pain of someone being ripped from you against your will. Like a claw reaching into your chest, pulling your heart out, and tearing it to shreds.

Hardly Qualified said I wasn't the only kid who lost a parent and that I had to figure out a way to accept that Mom was gone. Well no shit, but that didn't make it any less painful.

After that session, I had a hard time falling asleep. When I finally did, I fell into a nightmare and the cold, dark lair of a monster. He was big, twenty feet tall, with red-and-brown slime dripping from his mouth. When the slime fell, it formed a sour-smelling pool at my feet. That's when I realized it was the blood and guts of all the moms who had disappeared.

That nightmare plagued me for years, until I was old enough to know it wasn't real. At least not for me. I didn't need to read the details of what happened to Khory's sister to know the monster in my dreams was her reality.

FEBRUARY 9

Khory marched down the hallway in the fast lane. She was hard to miss even if I hadn't been searching every corner of the school for her. And today it wasn't just her hair or smile. There was a fierceness about her. Basically, a "get out of my way, I have places to go."

I certainly wouldn't be the one to stop her. My tongue-tied-slow-walking self couldn't do that on a normal day. I grabbed my lunch bag, books for Pre-Calc and Geography, and started moving in the slow lane toward the cafeteria.

When I stood up after one bend-down, a whiff of coconut lingered around me. I inhaled and my head spun.

"Lunch, right?" Khory asked. "I brought my math notebook."

I stared at her and thoughts swirled in my brain. The monster from my nightmare. The math tutor. And the kiss.

"Yes."

I took a breath, focused my attention straight ahead, and started counting. She grabbed my arm and pulled me forward. For a second, I forgot what number I was on.

We hung close to the lockers. She took ten steps with me, waited like last time, until, finally, we were in the cafeteria and on our way to her regular seat.

I longed for the comfort of the back corner, but I had to focus. The list. Math tutor. First kiss. Even without those, I couldn't say no to her. She was different. No one else moved at my pace and made me forget what number I was on. And she was beautiful.

Jay and Rainn were already at the table. This time, there was no squirming in seats and no head-to-toe inspection. We sat. Rainn, Khory, then me. Jay turned away from me and stared at the table.

Rainn gave Khory the full-body inspection, touched her hair, and rubbed her arm. "You're looking better than this morning. Have you been doing your breathing? Remember, breathe in, count to ten, and breathe out." Her arms floated up as she inhaled and floated down as she exhaled.

"Hmph," I mumbled.

"What?" Rainn asked.

"Nothing. Sorry. I didn't mean anything." I dug into my lunch bag and pulled out my sandwich.

"You don't believe in natural remedies? Well, I don't believe in medicating every problem away."

Has she seen me? Did I look like someone who's medicated everything away? She may not have a name for them, since explaining myself was not my strong point, but there was no way she, or anyone, could miss my tics. My body moved more than a toddler on a sugar overload.

Khory seemed just as interested in my answer. Could I do it now? I should. Knock out number six by telling them about the Tourette?

My neck twitched as I formed the words in my brain: Tourette syndrome. I squeezed my hands together and felt my body heat up. I hated those words, the bizarre behavior they represented, and mostly that they belonged to me.

"Someone told me to do that once," I said instead. "It didn't work. At least not for me. Everyone's different." I put my head down. Please let this be over.

"It is possible they didn't teach you right. The breathing, it has to come from the diaphragm. Most people just inhale as far as the lungs," Rainn explained.

I nodded. I couldn't remember how HQ said to breathe, but knowing him, it was wrong.

"I'll be happy to teach you. It really works. Right, Khory?"

"It does. Most of the time," she said, then sat up straight. "Look, I did a lot of breathing yesterday. And crying and screaming. But that's done. He's in jail, so I want to focus on something different for a change."

There was that look I saw in the hallway. The spark of excitement. Determination.

She leaned forward, hands on the table. "I've been thinking about this and decided it's time to get out in the world. Aren't there things you've always wanted to do? Places you've always wanted to visit?"

Now she was talking my language. I was tingling, and it wasn't tic related for once. Make the most of your time here. Fulfill your dreams.

"I'm going to make a list of all the awesome things we do. I'll call it Krista's List. It'll be like a bucket list in reverse, because this one will keep growing. I owe it to her to make the most of my life. What do you say, guys?"

"I love the idea!" Rainn clapped her hands together.

"Sounds cool," Jay said. "You have to put the Vomit Comet on the list."

Khory, Rainn, and I stared at him. Really? Something named Vomit should be on a to-do list? I'd hate to see him drunk.

"Oh, my gosh. You guys don't know about it?"

We shook our heads.

"It's not really called that. It's Gravity Redefined. There's a company with a plane that simulates being in space. I guess some people barf, and that's how it got its nickname."

Space. Like a real astronaut. My whole body tingled.

"Can anyone do it?" I asked. With my luck there would be an age or disability restriction.

"Yeah, I guess so, but it's like five thousand dollars," he said.

My shoulders slumped. Figured it'd be a money thing. Why

was everything so damn expensive? No way I'd be able to save that kind of money.

"Well, I don't know if we can make that happen," Khory said.

"I know, sucks right?" Jay asked.

He had no idea. Being an astronaut instead of just seeing the space shuttle would have been the ultimate number five. I bit into my sandwich. My hands squeezed and smushed the bread. They watched me. I wiped my hands on a napkin, then nodded, smiled, and did just about everything but stand up and cheer about the list. Hopefully that was enough to fool them into thinking I was excited, too.

"Great! So let's start with a movie. I haven't seen one in the theaters in years," Khory said. "I don't even know what movies are out."

"There's a new Ryan Reynolds movie. I've been dying to see it," Rainn said.

Jay moaned and shook his head. "It's a love story. Count me out."

"I'm thinking about getting back together with Diego, so you won't be the only guy," Rainn said.

Clearly I wasn't invited. That's right, I was just the math tutor. And I should have been okay with not being included, because Tourette and movies don't mix, but a teeny part of me hoped I was wrong. I put my head down and focused on making my sandwich appear somewhat edible again.

"Really? And he agreed? He's an idiot for letting you string him along. Or do the stars tell you to treat him like that?" Jay asked. "Just do me a favor and remember other people will be there."

"Jay, remind me why I'm friends with you," Rainn said.

"Come on, guys," Khory said. "This is a new beginning. How about hanging out at the mall instead? You're coming too, right, Troy?"

With a big gulp I forced down a piece of sandwich. I was happy for her. After what she'd been through, Khory deserved to experience as many things as possible. And I wanted to be around her, even if that meant stepping out of my comfort zone and playing along.

"Sure," I croaked.

I put my hand in my pocket, grasped my phone, and desperately clung to my list that had an end.

· · · · · · · · · ·

It was one of those days when everything seemed to go my way. The girl of my dreams wanted to hang out. I made it to the bus in time to get my seat behind the driver. And the girl with the ponytail already claimed her seat far, far away from me.

Then reality hit. My neck jerked and got stuck in the tilted-to-the-left position. The kid behind me snarled, daring me to stand up for myself and say something instead of just breathing banana-scented hot air toward him. The only thing worse would have been an uninvite for this weekend. "Sorry, we decided we don't want to be seen with you in public. Actually, we're not sorry."

I guess I expected the text to come, because I stared at my phone the entire bus ride. Accept yourself, HQ constantly told me. That was probably the best advice he'd given me in our twelve months together. Unfortunately, he didn't tell me how. If he had, maybe I would have been able to explain the concept of Tourette and medication to Rainn and cross another item off my bucket list.

But Rainn mentioning medication during lunch did give me an idea. I opened my phone to my Methods to Die list and added another one.

1. Gun

2. Pills

It was a good idea to have a backup. What if Dad's gun was moved or he was home sick and I couldn't get to it? I couldn't wait until the next day. It had to be April 6. Ten years. I squeezed my hands together and counted to ten. Repeat. "It's okay," I told myself. But it really wasn't. It had to be ten.

The bus finally got to my stop. I ran home and went through the regular routine: tic explosion, Jude's monitor on the table, and Terri announcing tacos for dinner. Yum. I dropped my backpack in the family room.

Terri took forever to pack up. A cop should always be ready to go, just in case there was an emergency, but by the time she clipped everything on her gun belt, the robbery would have been over and someone would be lying dead on the ground.

"Bye, Troy."

"Bye," I said for the fourth time.

Her car door slammed. The motor started. I leaned over and

stared out the window. She backed out of the driveway and stopped. A car passed. The garage door closed. She finished backing up and drove away.

I exhaled, got up, and went to the bathroom where I kept my medicine bottles. Clonidine for Tourette, melatonin for sleep, and Lexapro for OCD and anxiety. The cocktail that was supposed to get me through the day.

I picked up the clonidine bottle and squeezed my hand around it. Tighter. Then repeated with melatonin and Lexapro. I moved the bottles around in my hand. They fit perfectly.

Each label was kind enough to list their most common side effects, and lucky for me, they all had the one I was hoping for: drowsiness. How many would I need to take to put me to sleep permanently? I opened each bottle. They were full. I was sure that would work, but could I stop taking them for the next fifty-seven days? My neck twitched. My face scrunched up. I pounded the countertop.

No one wanted to see the real me. I didn't even want to, which was why I never looked in a mirror. Feeling it was plenty. But if I hid a few pills every week, I'd still have enough for my daily combination and get refills sooner. Refills meant one hundred and twenty pills. I rolled my shoulders back and poured two out of each bottle. Six. One more from each. Nine. I took out one more Lexapro, ripped off squares of toilet paper, and wrapped the pills inside. Then I shoved the package in the back of my toothbrush drawer.

I got back to the family room just as Jude's voice sang through the monitor. I jumped up. There was so much to tell him.

"Do you remember the girl, Khory, I told you about?" I asked and lifted him out of his crib.

Jude smiled and spoke in the language only I understood. "Yes, the pretty one from the yearbook."

"Well, we are going out Saturday night. Okay, it's with other people, but she invited me out with her friends."

I smiled so big my cheeks hurt. Jude reached up and stuck his fingers on my teeth. Yeah, this was a new expression for me.

We went to the family room, and I put him on the floor with his toys. I pulled out my homework. Chemistry first. Jude tossed his toys to the side and crawled toward me. I showed him my diagram of an ion. He reached up, and I moved my notebook out of the way. Then he put his hands on the table and pulled himself up.

"You're standing!" I said. "I can't believe you're standing."

I grabbed my phone and pressed record. He held onto the table and bounced up and down. I pushed my books away and bounced with him. He collapsed on the floor but got right back up.

At lunch Khory said we should make the most of our time here. That's what I planned to do. I'd miss a lot of Jude's life, all the big events, but I would always have this. I put him on my lap, and we watched the video. He giggled and screamed and reached toward the table to do it again.

I texted Dad and Terri the video. Imagine when he took his first steps! I sighed. I wasn't going to see that.

But I'd make sure he had a babysitter who sent Dad and Terri videos so that they didn't miss anything. Not a nanny who plopped him in front of the TV and searched the house for things to steal. A good one who played with him and taught him about science. They had to know he loved rockets.

FEBRUARY 13

When I saw Khory in Chemistry yesterday, she didn't say anything about going out on Saturday. So when I woke up this morning, I was convinced being silent was her way of ditching me.

I didn't want to wait two days to see her again, but I was okay with not going out. I had things to do at home. A whole list of things. I picked up my phone and started a new list: Babysitter. I typed the requirements.

1. Take him to the park
2. Read to him
3. Knows CPR

That last one was mandatory. There were the girls in the neighborhood who liked to play with Jude, but they were young. They probably still needed babysitters themselves.

How about someone from school? The only people I knew were

Riley and Nicholas, and I didn't really know them. Then there was Khory, Rainn, and Jay. That was it.

My phone vibrated. A text.

KHORY: Still available tonight?
ME: Yes

I was thrilled she couldn't see me grinning like an idiot.

KHORY: Good. Taco Bell at 6 then movie.
ME: OK.

My smiled faded. Dinner was not okay. It would be the cafeteria all over again. And movies were even worse. My neck twitched. Ten times. Twenty times. My face scrunched up. Then my hands. Repeat.

There was a reason I hadn't been to a movie theater in years, and not because there weren't awesome ones to see. It was brutal being the only kid who didn't see the new *Star Wars* movie when it came out, but it was easier to pretend I did than explain why I didn't. Ticcers didn't go to the movies, at least I didn't. The urge for that one tic was so overwhelming, no amount of self-control, lame breathing techniques, or medication would help.

A movie was going to ruin my little fantasy. In it, Khory wouldn't just be my first kiss, she'd actually like me, and we would go on a date. Of course, once we went to the movies, it would all explode.

Still, I couldn't help but dream. I closed my eyes. Khory and I were at the movies, sitting next to each other sharing sour gummies.

"I'm so excited about Mrs. Frances's summer program," she said.

"Me too. My dream career is to be an astronaut."

The idea of floating in space made me as lightheaded as she made me. But then I landed with a crash when the tic formed in my brain. It was a word that pushed everything else out. I squeezed my hands and pressed my lips tight. If I said it once, I wouldn't be able to stop. I opened my mouth just enough to shove a few gummies in.

The word was now an image in my mind. A device, black with different-colored wires. The letters. My throat made a guttural sound. It was coming. Like a fire working its way up to the roof ready to be expelled in a verbal explosion of inappropriate words and phrases.

"BOMB! BOMB! I HAVE A BOMB!" I yelled.

People screamed. Most fought their way to the exits. A few lunged toward me and tackled me to the ground. They beat the shit out of me and held me down until the police came. And no matter how hard I tried, no explanation in the world could fix it.

"I have Tourette syndrome," I said. "Shouting words like that is a tic. I can't control the stupid things that come out of my mouth."

"Shut up!" The guy pinning me down said.

"I'm the most nonaggressive kid you've ever met. Just ask Justin who pounded me in fourth grade."

And then the police came and took me away.

I opened my eyes and was back in my room. My door and

windows were closed. I put my head down and mumbled *bomb* over and over. Ten times. Deep breath. Exhale. Repeat. I shook my head to stop the tears that were coming.

I couldn't go. I needed an excuse for canceling. I had to babysit Jude. I had too much homework. We were having quality family time. They all sounded fake. There was always the truth.

"I have Tourette syndrome, and no matter how hard I try not to, I will yell the word *bomb* in a crowded movie theater. There's the possibility you'll be shot just for being next to me, and I can't put you in that kind of danger."

My face burned with humiliation at having this disorder. Canceling with a lie was the only answer.

But after a shower, late lunch, and two episodes of *Arrow*, the best excuse I came up with was wanting to binge-watch a TV show I'd already seen. Maybe Jay and Rainn would convince her not to invite the math tutor. "We don't want to talk math on the weekend, so what could he possibly have to say?" I rolled over on my bed, let my head sink into the pillow, and started a third episode. I could lie here all night.

My phone beeped. I crossed my fingers for the uninvite.

KHORY: Rainn's house after dinner. No movie.
ME: No movie?

I sat up. That changed everything.

KHORY: Dad won't let me.

The number one reason why texting was better than calling: she couldn't see me leap off my bed and punch the air with my fist.

ME: Sorry.

KHORY: It's ok. See you later.

I turned off my computer, put on jeans, changed my shirt four times, and went to tell Dad I had plans tonight.

I didn't know what to say. Who would have thought telling your dad you were going out with friends would be hard? Actually, it wasn't him I was worried about. It was twenty-questions Terri.

She dropped her phone on the table and jumped out of her chair. I stepped back, afraid she was going to hug me.

"That's great. Who are they?" Terri asked.

"Just some friends from school." One question down, nineteen to go.

"Like who? Boys, girls?"

I stared at Dad and drilled my eyes into him. *Help me out here, please.* But he smiled and crossed his arms. Gee, thanks.

"A kid in my science class and some people I eat lunch with," I said.

Vague, but there wasn't time for details. It was a fifteen-minute walk to the mall, but it would take me thirty. I put on my jacket.

"Well, that sounds like fun," Terri said. "Do you need money? How about we drive you?" She reached for her keys.

"I could use some money, and thanks, but I don't need a ride."

It would have saved me a lot of time, but if she saw Khory, she'd assume I liked her, which was true, but then she'd want to talk to her.

I took the twenty-dollar bill Dad handed me, shoved my phone and house key in my pocket, and left before she had time to ask the remaining sixteen questions. I sang along to "Renegades" by X Ambassadors, and between the music, counting, and bending, my brain was too busy to really focus on the possibilities for disaster that waited for me at Taco Bell. None of which had anything to do with the food.

FEBRUARY 13

I made it to Taco Bell in twenty-five minutes without having an anxiety attack, but my chest tightened at the sight of the restaurant. I moved to the side, hid in the shadows, and gasped for air. I ticced until my whole body ached. Dinner wasn't a good idea either. The people. Food trays. But the urge to spend time with Khory was like a tic itself. I couldn't say no. I needed to be near her.

Mrs. Price's Mazda drove up and pulled to the curb. I stepped out of the shadows as Khory and Rainn climbed out of the back seat. Khory slammed the door as if a hurricane had blown through, yanked Rainn by the arm, and practically dragged her to the restaurant.

"Don't let them bother you," Rainn said. "They let you go out. Take some deep breaths, and let's have a good time."

Khory inhaled while I counted to ten and exhaled. Her shoulders dropped, and she smiled. I definitely didn't have the right technique.

"You're right," she said. "I'm out. We're going to have fun."

"Hi." I said. Baby steps. Going out first, conversational abilities next.

"Hey, Troy. I'm glad you came," Khory said. "Is anyone else here?"

"I don't know. I just got here."

I moved in front of them, grabbed the door handle, and pulled it open. Khory nodded toward my hand on the door and smiled. "A gentleman. Thanks."

I followed them inside and over to the counter where Jay stood with a big muscly guy I assumed was Diego. He was nothing like the animal-loving cartoon character I watched as a kid.

"Go, Diego, go," I mumbled.

Diego spun to me. "Like I haven't heard that one before."

He scrutinized me and curled his lips. "You must be the tutor."

I stared at my shoes. My shoulders hunched over. Great way to start the night. I pressed my lips together to hold in any other stupid comments and a possible whimper. Khory put her hand on my arm and pulled me toward a different register.

"I'd like two beef hard tacos and a Diet Coke, please," Khory said to the tall pimply cashier.

"I'll have the same. But a regular Coke." I would have added another two tacos or maybe a chicken wrap, but the less I ate, the less I'd barf up if things didn't go well tonight.

When our food was ready, we filled our drink cups and took everything to a table. I sat between Jay and Khory since I knew them best, and I didn't think Go Diego Go would appreciate me invading his personal space. Khory's hair brushed my shoulder, and my hand tingled. I wanted to feel the softness between my fingertips, but I

82

was trying to stay away from the freak show label. I shoved my hand under my leg and pressed down as hard as I could.

"Jackson, do you guys know him? He's a running back on our football team," Diego said. "Anyway, he got a VR machine. It's awesome. I'm saving all my money for one."

Rainn turned to him and pressed her lips together. I wasn't sure if she was upset that he was talking video games or that he would be spending money on one and not on her.

"I've seen those virtual reality games. They're pretty cool," Jay said. "Can you imagine being in the middle of a first-person-shooter? That would blow my mind."

"I have one. The VR machine," I said. Dad wasn't fond of the first-person-shooter games, too realistic for his taste. But he was fine with games like Batman.

"Dude, you are so lucky," Jay said. "What games have you played?"

"Can you interact with other systems?" Diego asked.

Who knew the way to make people like you was to talk game systems? Diego leaned in closer and apparently forgot I compared him to a whiny cartoon character. Was I now the math tutor and VR connection? My hands clenched and unclenched. I guess it wouldn't hurt to just talk. I tempted fate and let my hands rest in my lap.

We talked video games, and Khory and Rainn seemed interested. To a point. After we finished our tacos and drink refills, Rainn huffed and crossed her arms. Then huffed again.

"What?" Diego spun toward her.

"You're ignoring me." She sighed and pouted.

Diego put his arm around her shoulders and pulled her to him. That was enough to make her happy, because she turned to him and kissed him. Mouth open, her tongue poking in his mouth. I sucked air through my straw so I wouldn't mumble the word *whipped*.

Still, I couldn't help but stare. The compulsion was too strong. I tried to turn away, but that just gave the urge power. Like peeking at the test of the kid sitting next to you or staring at your history teacher's chest because her shirt was too low. I waited for them to call me a pervert, but they were too wrapped up in themselves to notice me. Literally. His arm was around her shoulders, and she was nestled in his armpit. Their faces were tilted toward each other, they'd smile, whisper things I'm sure I didn't want to hear, then kiss, open mouth, tongue, everything.

Khory nudged me. "They wouldn't seem so cute if you heard the fights they've had."

That was cute? My stomach didn't think so. His tongue in her ear wasn't mixing well with the two tacos I just ate. But a part of me wondered what it would be like to be Diego and have someone want to be that close to you.

I studied Khory. Her hair tucked behind her ear revealed a silver earring with a blue stone that matched her sweater. Why didn't she have a boyfriend? Because her parents wouldn't allow it? She smiled at me, let out a sigh, then played with her napkin.

Sometime between slobbery kisses and blue earrings, the conversation turned to what movie we'd rent at Rainn's house. But based on the titles being thrown out, guys for action, girls for comedy, I figured we'd end up sitting on the couch staring at one another for two hours.

We tossed our garbage, got our coats on, and walked out.

"Where's your car, Jay?" Khory asked.

"What? Oh, it's in the shop. No heat. Guess we're walking."

Khory wrapped her coat around her and looked toward Rainn.

"It's fine," Rainn said. "We can call my mom."

Khory shook her head. "No. Let's walk. Taco Bell and walking home from the mall without parental supervision. Two things I've never been able to do."

Rainn lived in the neighborhood across the street, a ten-minute walk for them. I tried to keep up, counted the steps, and stared at the sky. But this was a new sidewalk. It was probably like every other one in the city, but what if this was the one that felt different? I bent all the way down. My fingertips touched the sidewalk and slid across the hard, pitted concrete. It was the same, but it felt good.

Not a surprise, I fell behind the group. What a way to ensure your place as an outsider. Khory slowed down and stayed at my pace. Just like she did at school.

"I don't know why we picked Taco Bell," she said. "The food is disgusting."

85

"Yeah. It's kind of like school food," I said in between bend-downs. "Nothing against the cafeteria workers, but they aren't gourmet chefs."

She laughed. "You're right. So why do we insist on eating it?"

"I don't know. Maybe to spite our parents by eating complete garbage with no redeeming nutritional value?"

She laughed. I couldn't believe we were having a conversation about food that I actually ate at a restaurant. I wanted to punch the air and jump up and down.

"Oh, I was supposed to call my parents when we left the mall." She pulled out her phone and pressed a number from her recent call list. "We're almost at Rainn's house . . . . to watch a movie. . . . I told you, five of us. . . . Ok. I love you too."

She hung up and shoved her phone in her pocket. "I don't get to go out much like this. They're overprotective. Because of my sister. Mostly we just hang out at Rainn's house or mine."

Even in the dark I could see the shadow coming. It wasn't just her eyes but the way she frowned and tilted her head down. I hated that look, so I said the first thing I could think of. "I don't go out much either." And, because I couldn't stop myself, I added, "This was my first dinner out in about three years."

As soon as the words crossed my lips, I knew it was the biggest social mistake ever. Telling the girl you like that you're a social outcast, even if she could guess it herself, was like showing up on the first day of high school in SpongeBob SquarePants pajamas. Just brilliant. I bent down to avoid her eyes and let the coarse ground satisfy my fingertips.

"Sometimes it's easier to hide at home, isn't it?" she asked. "That way you don't have to worry about strangers."

I stood up straight and nodded. Not only did she get me to go way outside my comfort zone, but she was also the first person to understand what was in my head.

. . . .

We were only five minutes behind everyone else. Not bad, considering my track record, but this was the one time I wished it were twenty. Being alone with Khory felt comfortable. And I was never comfortable around other people. Part of it was the darkness that hid my neck twitches and face scrunches, but also the connection we seemed to make. We had something in common. Okay, hiding at home, but I wasn't one to question.

I followed Khory into the house and was immediately assaulted by bright colors. Blues, yellows, and of course greens. The front door was like a portal to a tropical island. It warmed me after being outside in the cold. We went through the dining room to the kitchen where she introduced me to Mrs. Levine, Rainn's mom.

"Very nice to meet you, Troy." She inspected me from head to toe. Didn't I already go through this with her daughter? My neck twitched. My face scrunched up. "I may have something for you to help you relax. We'll talk sometime, I'll do an analysis."

I nodded to be polite, but I was pretty sure I had just agreed to have my aura read.

"Khory, I heard they caught the man. I am so relieved." Mrs. Levine pulled her into her arms and squeezed.

"Thanks, Mrs. Levine," Khory said gently pushing away. "We're going to find Rainn."

"Oh, sure. They're in the basement."

I followed Khory down a set of stairs off the kitchen to what was clearly the entertainment center of the house. A humongous flat-screen TV decorated one wall, with a media cabinet underneath overflowing with movies, video-game systems, and games to go with them. Across from electronic heaven was a cream leather couch and two matching recliner chairs. It's like I died and heaven was a man cave.

Jay had already claimed a recliner, Rainn and Diego cuddled in one corner of the couch, and Khory flopped in the other. That left either the recliner farthest away from Khory or the middle of the couch. The middle had too many opportunities to reach out and touch someone, and in this case, one side would end with a beating and the other with humiliation.

The happy alternative was a denim-blue beanbag that I pulled to the corner of the couch by Khory. I leaned against it and stretched my legs out. My butt would be asleep in ten minutes, but it was a sacrifice I was willing to make.

Jay grabbed the remote and flicked on the TV. "We decided on *Hunger Games*. Since you guys were late, you didn't get to vote."

Seemed like a good compromise. The girls could watch Liam Hemsworth, and the guys liked the action. Of course, Jennifer Lawrence wasn't bad either.

Diego turned the lights off, and the movie started. I sank into the beanbag, and pain stung the left side of my neck and down to my shoulder blade. I hadn't realized how much my neck twitched on the walk here, but with the pain being close to a seventy-five, it must have been out of control. I took a deep breath and rolled my shoulders back when I exhaled. Another useless Hardly Qualified tip: deep breathing with the shoulder roll. Maybe I should have had Rainn or her mom teach me their techniques.

I focused on the movie, Katniss talking to Gale, catching dinner for her family, and then the line that made everyone want to be a kickass kind of person, or at least pretend they were: "I volunteer as tribute."

Khory leaned down to me, her breath warm with a hint of mild salsa. "I'm going to be like her. She doesn't hide. She makes things happen. I know it's just a character, but doesn't her bravery inspire you to do something great with your life?"

Yes, and that's what I was doing. Just like Katniss, I would make things happen. Ten things.

FEBRUARY 14

My idea of fun apparently consisted of burping up tacos and having a sore butt from sitting on a hard floor. That's what I did last night, and it was one of the best nights of my life. I don't know what the rest of the group thought, but at some point, I felt less like a math tutor and more like someone who belonged there.

I took a deep breath, hoping to catch even a tiny whiff of coconut that lingered on last night's clothes. It may have been my imagination, but I smelled it. The connection Khory and I made last night wasn't an illusion. At least not for me. She got me. Understood my need to stay home and made me forget I had to hold my tics in.

The only things she couldn't do were take away the pain and stay. Just like Jude, she would have a life and wouldn't have time to wait for me to catch up. I'd be left by myself, ready to snap a ligament, break a bone, or bleed.

But that wasn't going to happen. I went to my closet and gazed at the box where I kept Mom's cards. A blue Nike box high up on the top shelf. My neck twitched. I squeezed my hands together. My face scrunched up. Repeat. I counted six sets of ten and hadn't even pulled the box down.

The first card from Mom was for my elementary school graduation, three months after she left, and the last for my eleventh birthday. That one came with an autographed picture of Tim Howard, the soccer player with Tourette syndrome. Was that supposed to mean something to me? Was a picture supposed to replace her?

I'd kept them close the first few years, because they reminded me of her and what I thought was our happy family. I was sure she'd come back. She needed me. Back then I believed there were no other people like us.

Mom had a neck twitch like I did. And she mumbled. "Can you speak louder?" people asked, because they assumed she actually had something to say. Sometimes she'd repeat it, no matter how unintelligible, or sometimes she'd scream.

At home she lined up her shoes by the front door, each one touching the next. A complete contradiction to my obsession to separate things. My needs consumed me, and when she left the room, I'd spend the next few minutes moving them apart. Close enough so she'd think they touched, but far enough that I almost saw the air swirling between them. We should have kept them in our rooms like Dad asked, but that wouldn't have solved the problem with cereal boxes, cans, and books.

When she blinked, I blinked harder. She begged for quiet; I stood outside her door and shrieked. I shouldn't have been surprised she left. I drove her crazy. But she was the adult and should have sucked it up, stayed, and taught me how to survive. Instead she taught me how to give up, and as soon as I found her, I'd tell her that. Then I'd say goodbye. The other thing she didn't do.

I took the box down and collapsed on my bed. I meant to throw the cards away, but every time I got close, I wondered if one day she'd come back and ask about them. I pulled out the autographed picture and stared at the soccer player in action. I'd heard he was a good guy, cared about kids and other people with TS, so I didn't want it to go to waste. Someone would appreciate it, and I thought of just the right person. I tucked the picture inside an empty folder and wrote David Isenhour on the front. I'd give it to his parents at the next TS support group meeting, then check another item off my list.

Back to the box. I sorted, shuffled, and studied the cards and envelopes. Maybe I missed something back then. Postmarks: July 28, September 16, April 1. All of them from New York City. No return addresses. Nothing new. Just the same pile of wasted paper.

I went to my desk and opened my laptop. "Google, please find Jennifer Hayes in New York City," I said as I typed.

Barely two seconds later the results popped up. Turns out there were a lot of Jennifer Hayes's living in New York City. Over eighty-five thousand results according to the number under the search bar. Of course, there were a lot of duplicates and random people thrown in, like Eddie and Charles Hayes, whoever they were, and the actress Jennifer Hudson.

This wasn't going to be as easy as I thought. I had fifty-two days left to complete nine more items and would spend half that time searching the records. I sighed. That left Dad.

I hoped to enlist Dad's help only after I'd found her, for a plane ticket, but I didn't have a choice. Good thing it was family dinner night. I needed Terri on my side.

She wasn't my real mother, but she tried her best. She bought my school clothes and took me to more doctor's appointments than Dad. Twenty-five to four, I counted. Of course she was the one home during the day, but I know she cared.

I walked into the kitchen and smelled stuffing. Unfortunately there would be chicken or pork to go with it. Jude was in his high chair, hands washed, and ready to eat with Dad next to him.

"Troy, help me with these," Terri said.

We carried the plates from the kitchen to the table. I sat across from her and cut my chicken into bite-size pieces, separated them into ten groups, then added peas and stuffing. Should I just say it? Dad, where's Mom? Or should I wait for an opening like, hey your mom called today. Although he never said that, so I could be waiting a long time.

My neck twitched ten times. My face scrunched up. Repeat. I squeezed my hand around the fork, and the peas rolled off. Why couldn't we have vegetables you could stab with a fork? I scooped up the peas again and made it to my mouth this time.

"Terri, pass me a napkin. Jude stuck his hand in the yogurt."

Dad moved the yogurt and spoon from the high-chair tray. "Terri, napkin please."

I glanced at her. She stared at me, her eyebrows scrunched together. I wanted to scrunch mine too but settled for whole face scrunches. And neck twitches and hand squeezes.

Without taking her eyes off me, Terri passed Dad a stack of napkins. "Is something bothering you, Troy?"

To people who understood Tourette, a major increase in tics was a dead giveaway for stress and nerves, and based on the shooting pain down my back, that's what gave me away. It sucked to be so transparent, but on the bright side, this was the opening I needed.

"I want to find Mom. It's been six years since I've talked to her. The last cards she sent were five years ago from New York City, and I googled her name, but there were way too many to search through. Eight-five thousand results." I took a breath.

Dad froze, napkin halfway to Jude's face. He turned toward me, eyes wide. He opened his mouth, then closed it. I probably should have mentioned the part about duplicates and celebrities.

"Troy, your dad doesn't know where she is," Terri said.

"She's right." Dad rested his hands on the table. "I don't know. She hasn't contacted me in five years."

When she sent me a birthday card and the picture of Tim Howard. My neck twitched. I counted to ten.

"Listen, I would never say anything bad about your mom, but she had a lot of problems. If she wants us to know where she is, she'll call or send a letter." Dad turned away from me. Was it because I had the same problems?

I pushed my plate away. "I get that, but I still need to find her."

"What's so important that you need her now? We have a happy family here. If you have questions about girls or, um, health, we can help you. Terri may not be your biological mom, but she loves you."

"He's right. You can talk to me about anything. If you didn't already know that, I'm telling you now."

Yeah, anything except the one thing I need to know about. What did I expect? Dad still thought things were "great." I sighed, pulled my plate back, and dug into my dinner.

"I think you should focus on the life you have now," Dad said.

The life full of pain, anxiety, and the damn number ten? No thank you.

"Please. She's my mom. I know you have access to all kinds of super-secret-privacy-invading databases. Just a quick search."

"I can't do that." He turned to Terri. "Neither of us can."

· · · · · · · · · ·

Technically, Dad didn't forbid me from searching for Mom, he just said they wouldn't help. Fine. I'd do it the old-fashioned way. Back to the internet.

"Hey, Troy, can we talk for a minute?"

Terri stepped into my room without knocking or being invited and closed the door behind her. Her eyebrows were scrunched together again. She pulled out my desk chair and sat down with her hands in her lap. That meant serious business. I backed away and leaned against the closet.

"Your dad's giving Jude a bath, so we have a few minutes. I don't know if he would be happy with me sharing this, but I think you need to understand his side. With your mom."

My chest tightened. "I don't need to know why she left. I just need to know where she is now."

"It must have been painful, tragic, when she left. I can't even imagine. And I'm sure you have questions, but try to see this from your dad's point of view. Your mom didn't just leave you, she left him, too." Terri rolled the chair closer to me. "He lost his wife. A woman he was madly in love with."

What? If we had been outside, a bug could have flown into my mouth. She was talking about another woman her husband loved.

"Don't look so surprised. I knew he had a family before I met him. And he was honest with me. He told me about her, the Tourette, and what happened right before she left. One day he had a wonderful family, and the next he was a single man with a child he wasn't sure how to raise."

That day came back like a tornado. Dad met me after school instead of Mom. He never picked me up. His eyes were red and puffy, and I didn't get it at first. I was ten and more concerned with video games, superheroes, and using all my energy to keep myself together at school. I completely missed his grief.

After we got home and I'd let out the tics I'd been holding in all day, he'd told me.

"Mom left. She loves you more than anything in this world," Dad said. "But she thought it would be best if I raised you."

I was one hundred percent sure he'd say she was dead. But she chose to leave. My tics came back full force. The neck twitch, hand squeezing, wrist twisting. At one point, I bent my finger back so far it should have broken. I wanted it to break. And what I remember most about that day was learning that Mom wasn't dead but wishing that she was.

"Raising kids is tough, especially one with special needs." Terri's voice brought me back to the present. "He is doing the best he can. And about your mom . . ."

I stood up straight. Yes?

"I honestly believe he doesn't know where she is."

"But—"

"He's moved on, and trying to keep in touch with someone who wants to remain hidden is just too painful for him." She stood up and crossed the room. "You should think about that, too. I would love if you could focus on the family you have now. I will never be a substitute for your mom, but I'm always here if you need me."

I nodded, squeezed my hands together, then stared at the floor.

Terri put her hand on my arm and let it rest there for a minute. Her hand felt heavy, and my arm tingled where she touched. I wasn't sure if that was the Tourette talking.

"Thanks," I said.

She left the room and closed the door with a soft click. I went to my bed and lay down. I may have been a lot of things, but I wasn't a jerk. I knew I had a decent family and that Dad tried as hard as he could. But what could he do when he couldn't understand?

Okay, I had no idea what it felt like to have a wife leave me, but that didn't change the answers I needed to get. Actually, it added to them. When I found Mom, I would get the answers for Dad, whether he wanted them or not.

I opened my phone and added another sublist: Mom.

1.   Dad and Terri—No

2.   Internet—in progress

I put my phone on the night table and went to the bathroom to take my medicine. Back in my room, I crawled under the covers and wished my list was complete.

FEBRUARY 16

The comfort of the cafeteria's back table called to me, but I couldn't fight the urge to peek at the one in the middle. Rainn's green hair streaks stood out in the sea of other girls' pink and purple ones. And Khory, well, she was mesmerizing.

"Hey, Troy, you sitting with us today?" Jay snuck up from behind, his lunch bag slung over one shoulder.

I glanced toward my regular seat. Empty. Riley and Nicholas leaned toward each other. It didn't look like they missed whatever comment I'd contribute. I turned back to Khory. She and Rainn faced each other instead of the table, backs straight. Rainn had her hand on Khory's arm like she was trying to control a tree branch in the wind. They seemed deep in a conversation too, but I bet they weren't debating DC Comics versus Marvel, although that could get pretty intense at times. So it was probably one of those girl issues I didn't want to know about, or a boy. I gasped. Were they talking about me?

I didn't want to know but followed Jay to the dead center of the room and sat next to him. The girls looked up and shifted to face us. Khory smiled at me. I sighed, smiled back, and tried not to do anything stupid, like blurt out "I love you!"

"What's so serious?" Jay asked. "Wait. If it's about what some guy did or did not do, I don't care."

Rainn glared at Jay. "It's about *the guy*. He's coming back to Richmond."

It was clear the guy was Krista's killer by the way disgust dripped off each word. I knew from the article headlines his name was Steven Wesley, but they never used it. Did they do that for the same reason I never said *Tourette* out loud? The same misguided belief that if I never said it, it wouldn't hurt so bad?

The word *Tourette* bubbled in my throat to taunt me. I swallowed as if that would push it back down where it belonged. It snuck up again. Guttural. I let out a noise, which sounded like the letter *m*. I bowed my head and fumbled with my sandwich.

"He's in Florida, but he's being brought back here to face a judge." Khory gripped her lunch bag. "We're going to speak. My family. And me. I'm going to speak for Krista."

Jay shoved his lunch to the side and leaned across the table. "What are you going to say?"

Khory slouched. "I'm not really sure. I have time to think about it, write it out maybe, but I want him to live. It's not an anti-death-penalty issue or a religious thing. I don't want him to roam

100

free and torture society, but think about it, if he gets the death penalty, it's done for him. It's a waste."

"He is the worst part of humanity. Because of him, Krista didn't get to live. That's the waste," Jay said.

Khory sighed. "I know, but I just feel everyone has good deep inside. And bad, yes, but if he were put in different circumstances, like jail, he could pull out the good.

I never would have used *jail* and *good* in the same sentence. Jay, Rainn, and I glanced at one another. Jay's mouth hung open. Rainn shrugged.

"You have to focus on the numbers," Rainn said. "Khory and I researched him and based on his birthday, *the guy* is a seven. The symbol of the philosopher. On the positive side, he is introspective, but thoughtful."

"And on the negative side?" Jay asked.

"Well, he may be secretive and pessimistic," she said.

"Great. So he sits and thinks about what he did for the next fifty years? I'm not seeing how that's going to help anyone," Jay argued.

"*Ugh*, you don't understand." Rainn sighed and dug in her lunch bag.

"I get it," I said. It just slipped out. I pressed my lips together, more shocked than anyone to agree with her, and that I did it out loud.

"You believe in numerology?" Khory asked. "I never would have guessed."

Jay nudged me. "Dude, don't encourage her. I thought you'd be on my side with all this breathing, mystical stuff."

I took a bite of my sandwich to avoid blurting anything else out. After HQ sadistically planted the number ten in my brain, I had to do something while hiding in my room. I read about processed foods, astrology (I'm a Leo, by the way), and numerology. I thought it was all crap, but I couldn't deny the numbers.

Based on my birthday, I'm a seven too. It freaked me out back then because it's an odd number, and now Rainn just used it to explain a child killer. But the definition and how it determines my future fit. Especially my connection to the number ten, which meant *completion and fulfillment.*

Rainn sat up straight and folded her hands on the table. She beamed. I guess she never had backup before, and apparently she'd take anyone. I wanted to tell her not to get carried away. I still thought the breathing in and out to the count of ten was bullshit.

I shrugged. "So, Khory, what do you mean him dying would be a waste?" A clear get-the-attention-off-of-me subject change.

"I just think everyone has something to contribute to society. Who knows, maybe *the guy* was a lawyer or teacher. He can use those things in jail," she said.

"Yeah, he can teach others to commit crimes. Or as a lawyer, he could teach them to get away with it," Jay said. "Sorry, Khory, I don't get it. But at least he'll spend the rest of his life paying for what he did."

"And if you don't have anything to contribute?" I asked. I thought about Jude and his hand being crushed in mine. Him being safe from my tics would be an added benefit.

"Numerology and fortune-telling. Interesting," Khory said. "Well, everyone has a choice, don't they? To be good or bad, productive or a slug?"

"Sure," I said, but I didn't believe it.

For someone who knew firsthand how a bad guy could ruin your life, Khory had an incredibly delusional view on life. What if you didn't want to live? Even though you could contribute a lot to society. What if you chose not to?

"Well, I think Khory is really brave," Rainn said.

"I'm trying. Hey, it's something else I can add to the list. Facing your fear. Yeah, that's it."

Khory took out her phone. I wanted to take out my own list and type updates, or at least read it again, but ours couldn't be compared. And as excited as she was to add to hers, I was just as anxious to cross things off mine.

· · · · · · · · · ·

I clicked on links and read internet pages until my finger was sore and my eyes crossed. It was just as if Mom had disappeared. How could that be when everything was everywhere? I thought I'd die of boredom way before April 6. So much for Principal Brooks's lecture that what you put on the internet will be there forever. Either he lied or Mom never turned on a computer. Or she never existed. No. Every neck twitch and hand squeeze reminded me of how real she was.

I put a pillow behind my back and leaned against the wall. For me, the internet was for school, video-game research, and a few other things like finding TS groups. But social media? Never. The last thing I wanted to do was take pictures of myself and post them for the world to make fun of. Maybe Mom was the same, which meant I needed to research a more old-fashioned way of keeping pictures and memories. The photo albums in the family room.

My phone beeped just as I picked it up to add to my list. It scared the hell out of me. And when I saw the name, my heart pounded.

KHORY: Do you feel like tutoring me this weekend?

Really? She had to ask if I wanted to spend time with her? Even for tutoring? Good to know I wasn't obvious like a drooling love-sick puppy.

ME: I can help.

I hit Send. The phone rang. I pressed the green button.

"Hi." *Ugh.* One day I'll amaze her with a great conversation.

"Hi. Is it okay that I called? Sometimes it's easier than texting," she said. "I know, who would say that, right?"

A smile ran through my entire body. She was nothing like the girls who took selfies every time they changed desks. "I won't tell anyone."

"So, the whole numerology thing . . . Rainn's pretty happy she has someone on her side."

"Well, you know, I wanted to help her out," I said.

"So, did you really figure it out? What number you are?"

"Yeah. I'm a seven. But not like *the guy*. I mean, I wouldn't hurt anyone." I squeezed my hand.

"I know that."

I listened to her breathe. I wasn't sure what to say, so I breathed, too.

"What made you look into it? Was it for the Tourette?" she asked.

I gasped. My chest tightened. Of course she knew what I had; it wasn't like I could hide it. But she said the word. It sounded just as bad as me saying it. I took a breath. A little air got in. Then another. More air. Repeat.

"Troy? Sorry. That was kind of nosy."

"Yes." One step at a time. "I mean no, you're not nosy. It's . . . I have a thing for numbers." Breathe. "Well, just the number ten."

I exhaled. Wow. That was more than I've said about the TS and OCD out loud in five years. Hardly Qualified would have slapped his leg and demanded I take this opportunity to explain my disorders.

But I figured Khory would rather hear about the causes of the agricultural revolution than the history of Tourette. Even I didn't care about Georges Gilles de la Tourette, the associated disorders, and the unknown genes, unless it would make them go away.

"So what do you do for the Tourette?" she asked. "Wait, I'm being really nosy now. You don't have to answer. Let's talk about something else."

My hand squeezed the phone. My neck twitched five times. Only five times. I moved it five more to equal ten.

"Medication. I take medication." *Phew.*

"I haven't met anyone else with it. Have you?" Khory asked.

Mom sat across the kitchen table from me. Her neck twitched. Mine twitched in response. I reached out and touched her plate. She studied me; her frown deepened with each tic.

"Mommy, what's wrong?"

"Nothing." Her neck twitched again. Faster.

"You hate it, don't you? When I touch your plate."

"Of course not," she said. "It's just who you are."

"Crazy. That's what everyone at school says I am, because they don't do that. Or make weird faces."

Mom reached across the table and held my hand. "You're a very smart, special boy. Don't believe what they say. They don't understand Tourette. But we have each other, right?"

Wrong. She left a year later.

"I went to a meeting," I told Khory.

"Like a support group? I used to go to those. They helped, you know, make you feel connected. Or at least not as alone," she said. "But there wasn't anyone like me. There's no twin-of-kidnapped-girl support group."

"I actually wondered about that."

"Yeah? Maybe I should start one, but I'd probably be the only member. OMG, I've never talked about it like this. Most people see me as the dead girl's sister. Even Rainn sometimes. But you don't. I could tell that when we first met."

Was it confession time? Could I say the same to her and not humiliate myself? If I did, I'd just avoid her at school. Except for science. And if she approached me in the hall. I was so damn slow I couldn't outrun a 105-year-old man. But I had to tell her. It was like a compulsion, except this one I didn't want to fight.

"I don't talk about it. Ever. My dad doesn't even know about the meeting," I said.

"Thanks for sharing with me." I heard the smile in her voice and smiled back. "Listen, my mom's calling me for dinner, but if you need an excuse when you go to a meeting, you can tell him you're at my house. I'll cover for you."

That was a great idea, especially because I hadn't come up with another excuse.

"I will. Thank you."

"Anytime. See you at school tomorrow."

FEBRUARY 18

Five fifty-five. Dad wasn't home. He knew I had somewhere to be and had to leave at six, but he probably thought going to Khory's wasn't a time-sensitive issue. And if that's where I was going, he'd be right. But it wasn't. There was a TS meeting tonight.

I started the eighth round of ten and was on the ninth round when headlights illuminated the driveway. Five fifty-nine. Way too close. I put my phone in my jacket pocket and met him in the garage.

"Jude is in the family room. I changed his diaper and gave him a snack about an hour ago. A small one," I said before Dad even made it to the kitchen. "Sorry, but I have to go. See you later."

"Okay, don't be too late. It's a school night."

"I know." I walked out the door.

When I was two houses down, I ran like I was actually meeting Khory. All the way to the bus stop. Excitement and fear of missing the bus propelled me forward.

I made it, jumped in line behind five other people, then found a seat by the window in the last row. My neck twitched, but it was more like background music than in-your-face heavy metal.

Trees, houses, and buildings flew by. If only tomorrow would. It would be torture to sit through another day at school knowing being alone with Khory waited at the end. I leaned my head against the window and pictured her smiling with the pink lip gloss. I sank into the bus seat, and my hands rested on my legs. Just the thought of kissing her made me weak. Breathe in. Breathe out. The bus pulled over at my stop. I thought about staying on, riding it for the next hour and enjoying this new feeling, but I had to get back to reality.

I got off and walked toward the seven-story hospital building. One, two, three, four, five, six, seven, eight, nine, ten. I bent down and touched the sidewalk. The grittiness felt good on my fingertips. I dragged them across the ground in front of me, then stood up and counted again.

"Hi. I'm Susan."

I turned to my left and stared into brown eyes that were tired and helpful at the same time. They belonged to the meeting's host.

I rolled my shoulders back. "Hi. I'm Troy."

She didn't offer to shake my hand. Maybe because I just scraped them across the sidewalk coated with chewed gum and dirt. Clearly I didn't have a germ obsession, but maybe she did.

"The bathrooms are disgusting," I blurted out, my TS brain overriding my filter. Normally I wasn't a blurter, but I seemed to do this a lot lately. If this was a new tic, would I say inappropriate things in front of Khory? Or to her? I shivered.

"I know. I try to go at home or hold it until I'm about to explode."

I nodded. Why didn't I go before I left?

"I'm glad you came back. Are you here alone?"

"Yes." I glanced at the hospital in front of us. "My parents couldn't come. Is that okay?"

"Of course. We have reading material up front if you want to take some home to them. And they're welcome whenever you're ready."

When I'm ready? Was it that obvious?

We walked into the hospital and turned left at the information desk. The meeting was in the same room as last time. Susan went to the front, and I took a seat in the back.

The smell of burnt coffee was back, along with a few people from last time. The husband and wife whose son was doing better in school, the man who called him a jerk, and the guy who flapped his arms. There were people I didn't recognize from last time, some with TS and some not. At least not that I could tell. There were all sorts of tics that ran through your brain and tormented only you, like crazy or inappropriate thoughts that could be so macabre they're better left in your mind.

"Good evening everyone. I'm Susan. Just a reminder, we have pamphlets up here in case anyone's interested. And coffee and cookies in the back."

Everyone turned toward the refreshment table, but no one got up. A few people turned to the front, then back to the table a few times, but it wasn't because they were contemplating an after-dinner treat.

"After our last meeting when Frank and Rita discussed their success with the Americans with Disabilities Act in their son's school, I printed out some basic information." Susan picked up a stack of papers and waved them in the air. "I'd like to start the discussion tonight. For those who don't know, my son has Tourette, obsessive-compulsive disorder, and sensory processing disorder. He is happily married and has two wonderful children. My grandson, his oldest, was just diagnosed with Tourette. Of course, we already knew." She took a deep breath and let it out slowly. "Not the best news, but we are confident he'll have a better time of it than his dad. We know more now, medications are different, and there are alternative therapies."

Was she crazy? A better time? Compared to what, the dark ages?

I scanned the room. People nodded. As the leader of this so-called support group, it should have been obvious things still sucked. This was my second time here, and I knew that. My hands squeezed into tight fists. The only thing we knew for sure was that it was genetic. And one more thing, her son was selfish for having kids in the first place.

My hands squeezed again, daring my fingers to dig right through my palms and draw blood. I opened them and shoved them under my thighs. I counted, cursed HQ, and closed my eyes.

111

Sometime during my episode, she stopped talking. The conversation moved around the room.

"Hi, I'm Jo."

Jo sat on the aisle with a golden retriever at her feet. She waved her arms in the air and her leg bounced. It stopped, then bounced again. She waved her arms in the air again. The dog sat up, nuzzled her hand, and rested his head in her lap. Her leg stopped bouncing.

"This is B-B-Blane," Jo said. "He is a therapy d-dog. He knows when my tics are about to get out of c-c-control and calms me d-down. That's his j-job. It's amazing how in tune he is with my emotions already, and we've only been t-together t-two weeks."

The room was quiet as she talked. No one sighed or moaned. Everyone waited patiently like a woman taking fifteen minutes to tell a five-minute story was completely natural. Maybe that's why Susan called this a safe group. We understood each other's disabilities and didn't judge. Except me. I'd called her son selfish. I bowed my head.

She finished at seven fifty-five. No one else volunteered to share or ask a question. Our lives were too complicated to sum up in five minutes. I sighed and said a silent thank you to Miss Therapy Dog for taking so much time. Not that I would have talked anyway.

Susan gave us a reminder for the next meeting, then everyone stood to leave. Because of my seat choice, I was the first one out. I stood against the wall and waited for the Isenhours.

I opened the folder and stared at the picture. Nope, hadn't

changed from an hour and a half ago when I left the house. Or five years ago when Mom sent it to me. Man, that was a disappointing mail day. I thought she'd sent a letter about how much she missed me or filled with questions about my life. Did I like my teacher? Were kids being nice to me? Did I have friends? No, no, and no. She probably knew the answers already, so why ask?

I still didn't get why she'd thought I'd want a picture of a stranger, even one with Tourette. It was as useless as the face staring back at me in the mirror. It couldn't answer questions, reassure me that life didn't suck, or that my head wouldn't be permanently bent to the left. I slammed the folder closed, hoping it would bang like a door. What a disappointment. I would have thrown it across the hallway, but it would have fluttered to the ground like a dying butterfly.

Finally they came out. I stepped away from the wall and shoved the folder in Mr. Isenhour's hands.

"This is for David. You said he likes sports, so I thought he would like this."

Mr. Isenhour dropped his wife's hand, opened the folder, and smiled. "David mentions him a lot. He's a great role model."

There was that role model thing again. I opted for the polite response, which meant trying to change the subject. "I'm Troy."

"I'm Frank." He stuck his hand out to me, then tilted his head to the woman on his right. "This is my wife, Rita."

Rita did the head turn. I did the neck twitch. Frank stood with his hand still out. I shook it.

"I'm Troy," I said again.

"Nice to meet you," Mr. Isenhour said. "Are your parents here?"

I shook my head. "They had to work."

"*Uh huh,*" the wife said.

Were my lying skills fading? I did so well with Dad.

Mr. Isenhour held the folder to me. "Thank you very much for this, but we can't accept it. It must mean a lot to you."

I squeezed my hands tight. In frustration and as a way to not take the folder back.

"It doesn't mean anything to me. I've had it a long time, and it's been in a box." I shifted my feet. *Go ahead, say it. That's why you're here. Rah rah, cheer cheer. You can do it.* "It brings back bad memories."

Mrs. Isenhour nodded. Her eyes drooped. Maybe she had a bad role model growing up and wanted to be different for David.

"I'm sorry to hear that, but we really couldn't," she said. "Someone must have gone through a lot of trouble to get that for you."

Yeah? Well, Mom should have saved herself the trouble and stayed. Now who would I give this to? I couldn't leave it for Jude. The last thing he needed was a reminder of his dead brother. My neck twitched ten times. How would I cross it off the list? My neck twitched again. I counted over and over.

"David. He's nine," Mrs. Isenhour said. "We like to share what we learn, especially when it comes to the school system. A lot of people with disabilities have a hard time getting consideration. We also come to hear good news about other kids. It gives us hope for a happy future for him."

Was that a hint or something? Did she think I had good news? I would have if they took the picture, and I could check something else off my list. But their idea of good news and a happy future was probably a lot different than mine. Anyway, she had Tourette and obviously made her decision a long time ago about risking her son's future. What could I possibly say to make things better?

I glanced toward the bus stop. "I, um, I have to get the bus home. I don't want to miss it."

Mr. Isenhour handed the folder back to me "Can we drive you home?"

"I should take the bus. Nothing personal. My dad wouldn't want me to take rides from people I don't really know. He's a cop. Kind of obsessed about it." He also wouldn't want me riding the bus downtown by myself at eight-thirty at night, but he never specifically told me not to.

"Of course. Your dad is right," he said. "It was nice to meet you, Troy."

"Thanks. Nice to meet you, too."

I got to the bus stop just as it pulled up and found a seat by myself. My hand squeezed together. I wanted to scream at Tim Howard, who looked so damn athletic and well adjusted. My hands squeezed again, and I fought the urge to crumple the picture all the way home.

FEBRUARY 20

Dad and Terri came out of the bedroom all dressed up, suit and dress kind of dress-up. Tonight was their anniversary. They were going to dinner, then to do whatever grownups did when they had a free at-home babysitter. A movie? Dancing? For Terri's sake, I hoped they stayed away from the dance floor.

"Jude had his bath, and he'll be ready for bed soon," Terri said.

Got it. I've done this before. Story, bed, and don't forget his turtle. My hands ached to shove Dad and Terri out the door.

"Thanks, Troy. Try not to play video games all night," Dad said.

No problem. I had other plans. I brought Jude to the family room and took out blocks and a train for him to play with while I updated my list.

Mom:

3.   Photo albums

4.   Dad's room

The door into the garage closed, and the car engine started. I scanned the photo albums on the shelves. It was easy to pick out the ones of my family. My first family. Pre-Terri and Jude. There were four, all dark blue and the same size. Consistent. Organized. Based on Mom's choices, Terri's rainbow albums would have offended her sense of order. I know they offended mine.

Headlights beamed through the window. The motor from the garage door groaned and squeaked and finished with a thud. I pulled the photo albums off the shelf. Four chances to find a clue about Mom's current location.

"Jude, do you want to see old pictures of Dad?"

I sat next to him, put the albums on the floor, and opened book one. There were trip pictures from New York City, the Grand Canyon, and Europe. Obviously pre-me. Mom and Dad stood next to each other holding hands and smiling. They appeared happy, but vacation pictures never showed the horrors of real life.

Jude patted the pictures. "Yes, that's Dad. You can't miss him with the same hairstyle and same clothes. Probably the exact same. And the lady next to him is my mom."

"*Do gee ya*," Jude commented.

"Yes, I do look like her." She had wavy brown hair like mine and brown eyes that had no sparkle.

I opened book two. My debut.

"There's me. Bald, big brown eyes, and no teeth."

"*Go ya ya ah.*" Jude showed off his four teeth.

I flipped the pages. Pictures of Dad and me, me in my crib, and a few with Mom. She held me in her arms, snuggled with me on the couch, and in bed. Did her brain fight her like mine fought me? Was that why she looked sad in most of the pictures with me? *Tourette: a genetic disease with a fifty percent chance of passing it on.* Percentages were practically the first fact you read on every website. Knowing that, why even have a kid?

A picture on the next page seemed to answer that question. Mom curled next to me on a white sheet, a sliver of her wood headboard visible at the top of the photo. Her eyes were closed and her lips soft. No squeezing or tightness. Just the happiness of being with your baby enjoying the stillness of sleep.

Jude rubbed his eyes and snuggled with his blanket. I sat him on my lap, and we flipped through the pages. Mom, Dad, and I posed with animals at the zoo, stood in front of the Empire State Building, and were soaked from head to toe in front of Niagara Falls.

But sometime after my fifth birthday, things changed. My face became distorted. My school pictures ranged from nonexistent to bizarre. I'd managed to be sick on a few picture days, but on those occasions when I was trapped in the photographer's chair, I focused hard to stay still. That translated into wide eyes and lips pressed together. Those who didn't know better would have thought I'd just been chased out of a funhouse by a clown with a knife dripping blood.

I slammed the book closed.

"Bedtime, Jude."

I carried him to his room. "What should we read tonight? How about *Oh, the Places You'll Go!* by Dr. Seuss." For Jude's future.

When he was tucked in the crib with his turtle, I went back to the family room and opened album three. I held my breath as I flipped each page. Would the clown jump out? Or worse, me?

I scanned the pages faster for signs of Mom's previous life. Letters, souvenirs, reunion pictures with childhood friends. Nothing. Not even a glimpse of my grandparents.

My grandfather died before I was born, and Mom did tell me something about my grandmother. What was it? That they didn't speak? I wasn't even sure my grandmother knew I existed. There was an emptiness like part of me was missing.

I grabbed my hair and pulled like it would yank out a deeply buried memory of my grandmother and bring it to the surface. An image, a city, even the mention of death. Nothing. Just like the photo albums of the family after my ninth birthday.

· · · · · · · · · ·

Eight thirty. Dad and Terri were probably still on appetizers, which left me hours to search their room. There had to be something there about Mom in case of emergencies. What if I died, wouldn't he want her to know? Would she want to know? I sighed.

I stood in the master bedroom doorway and glanced around. Except for the pile of clothes draped over the chair in the corner, the dresser and night tables were clean. Now where to start? The laptop.

Would they leave it out if it had a clue to Mom? Was this a reverse psychology thing? I couldn't distract myself by trying to psychoanalyze adults.

I moved to the dresser, turned on the laptop, and logged in with Dad's password. It was only supposed to be used in emergencies, like if my computer broke. I assumed he meant for homework, but he never actually defined *emergency*, and to me, this was life or death.

The background picture loaded. It was of me pushing Jude on the swing. I didn't know Dad took it, but it made me smile. Focus! Did I take my medication this morning? My neck twitched.

I read the folder names and started with the obvious one: Troy. Please no more insane-looking pictures. I crossed my fingers, wished for something good, and double-clicked.

Documents. Generic school information, a PDF of a Tourette syndrome brochure, and a letter to Principal Brooks explaining what TS was. Dad clearly plagiarized from the national website but added a note of his own requesting special consideration if I was late to class, needed to be excused, or pissed people off.

I closed the folder and went through the other ones just in case he tried to be tricky and hide something there. But this was Dad. He was clear-cut, a right and wrong kind of guy. All I found was a copy of Jude's birth certificate and birth announcement. Boring kid. But I wanted to be like him.

I shut the computer off, put it back on the dresser in the exact spot, and went to his night table. I took everything out, cards from

Terri, iPhone batteries, and condoms. *Ugh*! I wiped my hands on my jeans. Besides visuals I could never erase from my mind, there was nothing. I shoved everything back in and went to the closet.

Both sides had blue uniforms, but the left side had dresses and pastel-colored shirts. The right side, much smaller, had suits and dress shirts. I started with the built-in shelves straight ahead. They were filled with winter clothes, and I ran my hand under each sweater and hat. Then patted down the hanging dress shirts, suits, and uniforms. Nothing.

The shelf that ran above the hanging clothes had shoeboxes. I counted twelve. Not divisible by ten. Thirteen, fourteen, fifteen, sixteen, seventeen, eighteen, nineteen, twenty. Did Dad keep cards in a shoebox like I did? My heart raced.

I ran to my room, grabbed my desk chair, and brought it to the closet to stand on. The boxes on Terri's side were filled with high heels and sandals, just as the descriptions said. On Dad's side, I opened box after box. Dress shoes. Hiking boots. The next box was lighter. Nikes, size 9.5, blue and black. Cards were light. Papers almost weightless. I pulled it down and lifted the top. Empty.

I searched the floor for the shoes. They were there, one turned on its side underneath a flip-flop. I squeezed my hands together and fought the urge to straighten them. I counted to ten. Squeezed. Counted. Repeat. I hopped down, lined up the sneakers and flip-flops, then climbed back up. The only thing left was the gun box.

I stroked the metal. My finger traced the lock. I reached across the closet, grabbed the key from the opposite shelf, and rubbed it between my fingertips. Smooth. Cool. I stuck it in the lock. Turned it. The lock popped open.

The semiautomatic pistol rested in gray cloth. A box of ammo next to it. I took a deep breath, wrapped my hand around the black grip, and lifted it out. It fit like the pill bottles, but solid. Firm. Absolute.

It would be so easy to do right now. I raised the gun to my head and closed my eyes.

"*Aaaayyyyy!*"

Jude? I spun around and wobbled on the chair. I gasped and yanked the gun away from my head. Jude couldn't be here when I did it. What if he saw me? After. His dead brother bleeding on the ground, head missing, brain splattered on the wall. I shivered, closed the gun box, and put the key back.

"*Ayyyaaaa!*"

"I'm coming," I yelled.

I jumped down, carried the chair back to my room, then ran to Jude.

"Did you have a bad dream? It's okay, I'm here. I'm not leaving yet."

I lifted him out of the crib, gave him a hug, and brought him to the rocking chair. We sat and rocked. I rubbed his back until he stopped crying and fell asleep.

"I'm sorry," I whispered. "Sorry I have to leave you."

I wiped the tears from my face and closed my eyes.

FEBRUARY 23

Khory leaned against the locker next to mine. The girl who used it was going to be pissed when she smelled coconut instead of cigarettes and coffee. Khory smiled. My body felt weak. She had to stop being so damned breathtaking with that long smooth hair, or I'd collapse right there.

"I looked for you during lunch," she said. "You were all the way in the back."

"Yeah, I've been neglecting Riley and Nicholas. We had crucial video-game info to discuss." Woo-hoo! That was me being all witty and clever.

She giggled.

"We haven't talked lately. I thought you might be avoiding me," she said.

I tilted my head. "Why?"

"All those questions last week. Maybe they were too personal." Her cheeks turned pink like a smiley emoji.

My chest tightened when I thought about how easily she said

Tourette. I couldn't talk about it now. Not here, not yet. Actually, I'd prefer to just stand here and stare at the way her hair fell over the right side of her face. And how her eyes accepted whatever they saw in me.

"No, it's fine. This just isn't a good place to talk about it. And lunch, I didn't know I was invited."

"You're always invited," she said.

I wanted to ask if the invitation was as a math tutor, but I was happy in my little fantasy that she invited me as a friend. I closed my locker, leaned next to her, and watched people pass by. And Jay strolled up.

"Am I interrupting something?" he asked.

I sighed. "No." Unfortunately.

"You going to Math?" he asked.

"Yeah."

"Okay. See ya there." He knew better than to wait for me.

"I've got to go, too. See you in a little while," Khory said.

She pushed herself off the locker and walked down the hall. I stared at her until the bell rang, then started the ten-count-bend-down to math.

As much as Mrs. Frances was cool with my issues, except letting me organize her desk, Mr. Nagel was annoyed by them. I tried not to take it personally when his glare followed me from the door past two rows of desks to the second seat from the back, or eight steps from the door. He scowled as I fell into my seat, counted to ten, and scrunched up my face to match his.

On the positive side, he craved order, so there was no urge to straighten or fix anything. If he just accepted my OCD, I would have been his favorite student.

I pulled out my notebook and pencil while Mr. Nagel started the new lesson on solving basic sinusoidal equations. *Ugh!* At least it didn't stress me out like Jay, whose legs had been stretched out when I first got to class but now were tucked under his desk. He leaned forward and gripped his notebook.

Since Mr. Nagel "strictly forbade the use of cellphones in this class, with the only exception of there being an active shooter on the premises," I opened to a blank page in my notebook. I didn't have time to waste on math. There were only forty-three days left.

1. Meet someone with Tourette syndrome— COMPLETED

2. Get my first kiss—IN PROGRESS

3. Be pain-free

That would take more research and maybe a relocation to farther down the list. My current meds clearly weren't enough, but there was Rainn's mom's offer to do something. Color my aura? Then there were the people at the TS meeting. Had they ever wondered what being pain-free would be like? But more importantly, had they found an answer? Maybe they discovered a new medication or some ancient inner peace thing. Breathe in, breathe out. Count to ten. Rainn said use my diaphragm. I couldn't remember where my diaphragm was. I tried it again. Still nothing. I kept writing.

4.   Find a babysitter for Jude

I had no clue where to look since the neighborhood kids were out. Maybe Khory would know. *Bam,* I just gave myself a conversation starter.

5.   See the space shuttle—ASK DAD TONIGHT

Seeing the shuttle was my one peek into the career I would have strived for. But the thought of going to the Air and Space Museum, with thousands more people than a Taco Bell and city bus put together, made me dizzy. I told myself it didn't matter what people thought. People were idiots, and after my list was complete, I'd never see them again.

So why did I care?

I tapped my pencil ten times. Counted to ten. Nothing worked. The invisible hand squeezed my chest tighter. Damn Hardly Qualified. What were you good for? I squeezed my hands together and closed my eyes.

"Mr. Hayes."

My name floated around my head like a dream.

"Mr. Hayes."

Smack. My eyes popped open. Mr. Nagel stood in front of my desk.

"Were you sleeping in my class?"

"No, Sir."

He glanced at my paper as all the air left my lungs. If I tried to cover it, he'd snatch it and read it aloud to everyone. He was a jerk like that. I hoped his upside-down reading skills were as crappy as his social skills.

He stared at the notebook, then peered up at me. If mind texting didn't work with Mrs. Frances, it had no hope with him. I tried to fool my neck twitch by daring it to stay away from my shoulder for sixty seconds. Only an asshole would stare at me that long. I crossed my ankles for luck and prayed he didn't stop me on an odd number.

One, two, three . . .

I counted. I started the second round of ten when he cleared his throat. "Please continue working on your math classwork."

I nodded. He tromped back to his desk. My body relaxed, but that presented another problem. It had only been eleven seconds, but it felt like my neck had been still for eleven hours and had to make up for lost time.

A shooting pain traveled from the base of my head down my neck to my shoulder blade, where it stopped and dug itself in. We're talking a rating of ninety at least. I rested my forehead on my hand and focused on the paper. With my head turned down, maybe no one would notice the tears.

"Busted." Jay came up to my desk after the bell rang. "Were you writing a note to Khory?"

I tilted my head. "What? Oh, no. Why?" I swung my backpack over my shoulder and headed for the door.

"I thought it was a love note or something," Jay said. "You guys are going out, right? Just tell me so I'm not the guy who sits between two couples making out."

I froze outside the doorway with my mouth hanging open. Was it that obvious I liked her?

"She wouldn't . . . she doesn't like me."

"You're clueless, dude. You practically drool on her. And she likes you, too. I've been friends with her and Rainn for so long, I know more about girls than girls do." He shivered. "Sometimes it has its advantages, but most of the time, no."

Were there signs for the average guy to know if a girl liked him? If so, I completely missed them. Now, if they were the "get away from me" kind, I would have been all over that.

I felt like floating as we moved down the hallway. At eight steps I moved to the wall. "Jay, wait. What do I do?" My neck twitched. Numbers swirled in my brain. "You have to help me."

"Dude, come on. Ask her out. Kiss her," he said. "I gotta go. Geography. Mrs. Hill is crankier than Mr. Nagel."

He left me alone in the hallway with those terrifying choices. My only defenses were twitching, scrunching, and counting.

Khory was deep into a novel by the time I got to Chemistry,

but she glanced up and smiled. Her eyes twinkled. Mine squeezed closed. Please not a new tic. Not now! Damn stress. I was already a pudgy teenager with more disorder abbreviations after my name than Stephen Hawking had honorary degrees. I didn't need to add anything else right before I asked out the girl of my dreams.

I sank into my chair while Mrs. Frances struggled with the smart board and tried to talk. She wasn't talented enough to do both.

"Class registration cards for next year go out on March first. Remember the astronomy summer program when choosing your science."

I pushed my feet into the floor to keep from leaping up and straightening the crooked display.

"Troy, did you hear me?" Mrs. Frances asked. "The summer program. I hope you are thinking about it."

"Yes, ma'am, I am," I said.

How could I not? But the astronomy program I'd miss and Khory liking me were too overwhelming. The shooting pain in my neck was back.

"Is everything okay?" Khory asked.

"Yes." I swallowed, then took a deep breath. "Do you want to study Saturday? Then do something. Out. That night?" Tongue-tied again.

"Out? On a date?" she asked.

Damn. Did Jay want me to make a fool of myself? Because I just did. I squeezed my hands together and fumbled with my notebook.

"Never mind."

"Yes, I want to go out with you." She brushed her hair from her face. Her cheeks were pink.

I smiled, nodded, and tried to act like going on a date was a normal thing for me. But inside my body was supercharged. It made my legs weak, and I was grateful to be sitting, or I would have fallen on my face.

. . . .

Dad scrambled around the kitchen. Took preshredded lettuce, precut tomatoes, and cheese from the fridge. Taco meat from the microwave and shells from the oven. He trekked back and forth to the table.

As we sat and stuffed tacos, Dad and I went through the regular conversations: work, the same, school, the same. Except it really wasn't. I took a big bite so that my smile wouldn't creep through. I wasn't ready to share, but I had to swallow sometime.

"What's the smile for?" Dad asked.

"So, there's this girl," I started. That sounded like a movie line.

"And . . ." Dad prompted.

"Nothing big. I'm tutoring her in math, and she's in my Chemistry class." My hand squeezed the taco shell and shattered it. No big deal. Taco salads were good, too. I wiped the meat and cheese off my hand.

"Is she the girl you went out with a couple weeks ago?"

"Yes. And some of her friends. We may go out this Saturday if that's okay." I mixed in a few sprigs of lettuce to make it an actual salad.

"Of course. I'm happy you're making friends and going out. Before you met her . . . what's her name?"

"Khory," I said.

He tilted his head. "Khory. Well, I hated how you stayed home most of the time."

"I took Jude to the park," I said in my happy voice, as if the Tourette and hiding at home were jokes. Apparently they bombed, because Dad shook his head. He was right, my life was not funny.

"You know what I mean. It's not healthy to stay home all the time. You should go out and have fun." He sighed and stared at his plate.

Of course I should, but we both knew I wasn't a regular kid. Really, what mentally stable person would make a bucket list at sixteen?

"Okay, how about this for going out? I want to go to the Air and Space Museum. It's not too far. We could probably do it in a day."

His head jerked up, and he smiled. "Wow, all or nothing for you. Why there?"

"I like space. Jude likes space."

He nodded. "The Air and Space Museum is a great idea. We'll look at the calendar to see when your next break is. We can make a weekend of it."

"Thanks."

I ate with a new passion. The space shuttle. I pushed away the thought of people staring, pointing, and laughing. At me. Instead I replaced the scene with my own visual.

A humongous warehouse, cement floors, and an open ceiling. The kind where you can see the air ducts and metal frames. And in the middle was the shuttle. A thick gray rope surrounded it to keep people at a safe distance. No touching, climbing, or vandalism allowed. Because it was my fantasy, the room was empty. Visitors hadn't made it here yet, so there were no little kids running around and no families taking selfies. It was there. Alone.

An American flag stood to my right just inside the warehouse doors. The slap of my sneakers echoed in the room as I stepped toward the shuttle. There were goosebumps on my arms. My hands opened and reached toward the gray rope, but they grabbed air.

"Troy? You okay?"

I opened my eyes. My body warmed. Good thing it was Dad. I wasn't interested in a repeat of today's math class.

"Everything's great. I was just dreaming of seeing the shuttle."

Dad grinned. "It's going to be a great trip."

"Yeah." My hands crushed another taco. Good stress.

· · · · · · · · · ·

Today was another one for the this-can't-be-my-reality list. A date. The space shuttle. No way! I tried to focus on my homework, but that was not going to happen.

It wasn't wrong to have fun while I checked items off my list. Even date. I'm pretty sure that's what this thing with Khory was. I'd asked her out, and she'd said yes.

My hand squeezed around my phone. Did that give me an open invitation to call her? I did have a reason, a legitimate question. Of course I couldn't tell her why I wanted to know, and maybe I'd be lucky and she wouldn't ask. *Ha!* I doubted it, but I texted her anyway.

ME: Random question. How can I find a babysitter for my
    brother?

KHORY: I can ask some friends. Why?

Lame, lame, lame! Why didn't I think of an excuse first?

ME: Just curious

And then a quick change of subject.

ME: Have any math questions?

KHORY: No. It was easy tonight.

Then my phone vibrated, and her name popped up.

"Hi," I said.

"Hi. I still need math help though. You are coming over on Saturday, right?"

"Of course."

"And we're going out Saturday night?" Khory asked.

"Whatever you want. I'll let you decide." But please don't say a movie. I should have said no movie. "What's on Krista's list? Maybe that will give us an idea."

"Well, let's see, there's bungee jumping, but I really don't want to do that. I'll have to think about it. What would you put on the list?"

"List? I don't have one."

"I know. I meant if you added to mine. Just for fun."

My hand squeezed the phone. One, two, three, four, five, six, seven, eight, nine, ten. Lists weren't a game for me.

"Oh, right. Well, I don't know."

"Come on, okay, how about this? If you could do one thing, what would it be? Like your deepest dream."

My list? My deepest dream? That would be number ten. Or live happily ever after with Khory like the couples in romance movies. My neck twitched. I couldn't say either of those.

"Um . . . see the space shuttle," I said. A small lie, which, shockingly, was easy to tell.

"I bet you're excited about Mrs. Frances's astronomy program."

"Yeah." And if things had been different, I would have begged Dad to let me go.

"Well should we add seeing the space shuttle to the list?"

"Sure," I said. A twinge of guilt pinched my heart. A girl who wanted to live for two people would never understand me giving up my one life.

FEBRUARY 27

Just do it.

Jay's words spurred me on like the slogan splashed across the TV screen. She likes you, he said. I questioned the word of a guy who sat by himself Saturday night, but she did agree to go out with me.

So today I was going to kiss her. It was time. And it was on my list.

Why was I such a scaredy-cat? As I rode my bike to Khory's house, I raised my hand in the air and tried a pep talk. "Troy! Be confident. Face your fears. This is not the time to hide." It came out more like a lecture, and now I was scared of myself and Khory slapping me in the face.

I dropped my bike on the sidewalk, careful of her Dad's pristine yard. How did he get each blade of grass exactly the same height?

"What are you thinking about?" Khory asked from the doorway.

"Nothing," I lied. Telling her I was obsessed about grass height might ruin my plans for today.

She tilted her head and squinted her eyes but met me on the walkway and led me inside.

"My parents went to the store, so it's just us. But they said they'd be home soon."

Was that her way of saying not to try anything or to do it fast? My hands squeezed together. She couldn't know what I planned. I didn't tell anyone. Girls were so confusing. Life would have been so much easier if I was home playing video games.

I dropped my backpack on the dining room table next to her laptop, followed her to the kitchen, and leaned against the counter. She took two glasses from the cabinet and filled them with water. She grinned like she had a secret, and I could have sworn her hands were shaking. My neck twitched sixty times in sixty seconds, so my eyes were probably bouncing in their sockets making everything seem shaky.

I was nervous enough about being alone with her and now terrified my hand-squeeze tic would break the glass. What if it was a family heirloom passed down from her great-grandmother or her dad's favorite cup from his one and only trip to Disney World?

We went to the dining room, and I put my glass in the center of the table, hidden by my backpack. I hoped my brain would forget it was even there, but suddenly I was parched.

During my "should I touch the glass or not" internal debate, I took out my notebook and a pencil. Khory flipped through notes in hers. I leaned on my right arm and studied her. Her eyes moved quickly across the pages taking in the numbers, letters, and equations. She sat up straight, completely engrossed in math. I liked math, but come on, it wasn't that exciting.

My legs bounced ten times. Ten left. Ten right. I switched to the hand-squeeze tic before the bouncing annoyed her. Open, closed. Open, closed. Repeat.

She leaned over her notebook, and her hair fell over her face. As if I didn't have enough problems already. From the first day I met her, the hair was my downfall. She pushed a lock behind her ear, revealing the blue earring and a twinkle in her eye.

"I thought you focused," she said.

I'm pretty sure I never told her that. Not with my ADD. She put her pen down and turned to face me. Her lips were together, but her eyes were bright.

"I'm going to find a new tutor," she said.

I picked up my pen and scooted closer to the table. "Okay, fine. I'm good now. Just a minor distraction. Your hair." I cleared my throat. "I thought you had something in your hair. It's good though."

But I still couldn't focus. I was obsessed with something else. And I knew better than to argue with an obsession. It wouldn't rest until it was satisfied. Screw the math.

I shifted in my seat and grabbed her hand. Her eyes opened wide. Don't think. Don't analyze. Don't obsess. Just do it. Thanks Jay. *Ugh.* Don't think about Jay. I stood, halfway, because the table jammed into my stomach and blocked my way. I leaned toward

137

her, and the arm of the chair dug into my hip. I pushed the pain to the back of my brain, which let self-doubt move to the empty space up front. The obstacles of solid wood were a clear sign to abandon the idea.

So there I was, half standing with no logical explanation. She didn't move. Not toward me or away. I stood there for what seemed like ten rounds of ten, but then I realized I wasn't counting. Me, not counting. *Huh.*

I moved my face as close to hers as I could and just did it. My lips brushed hers. They were soft and smooth. With a hint of strawberry.

My first kiss.

My insides were twitching like crazy, and my body was warm from head to toe like electricity was coursing through me. I opened my eyes. Khory stared at me. Her lips parted. Not frowning, not smiling.

She closed her mouth and rubbed her lips together. My shoulders sank. Was it the ham sandwich I had for lunch?

Khory scooted her chair back and turned toward me. She smiled. Okay, that was better. A smile wasn't the action of someone disgusted with me. I knew about that. I'd studied peoples' reactions toward me since I was six. I could teach a class. The Emotional and Physical Reactions to Meeting Troy Hayes. I could give myself an honorary PhD.

I slid my chair back so I wouldn't stab myself again. We leaned in. She tilted her head a little to the right, and I did the same. Weird what pops into your mind at times like this. Like how awesome it was we bent our heads to the right or I may have neck-twitch-head-butted her with my left side.

We moved closer. Our lips touched. Harder this time. Definitely pressure. If the first kiss was questionable, this one definitely qualified as real. Real enough to taste the strawberry.

I pressed my lips harder, fumbled for her hand, and felt her fingers. Mine brushed over hers. Her skin was smooth, and my fingertips craved the feeling. I pressed harder.

A door slammed. Khory jumped back, grinning under the hair that partially covered her red cheeks.

I froze, not wanting to put more distance between us, but I wanted to be invited back again. I took a deep breath, and the twitching slowed down.

"Khory?" her mother asked. Keys clanked on the kitchen counter.

"In the dining room," Khory said.

She flashed me a warning smile and refocused on her notebook. I shifted toward mine.

"Hi Troy. Are you guys making progress?" Mrs. Price asked.

Yes, yes we were. I almost screamed that I just kissed the most beautiful girl but caught myself just in time. Instead I gave myself a mental high five.

· · · · · · · · · ·

Because Khory's parents thought we didn't do anything more

139

exciting than study earlier today, they gave the okay for us to go on a date. Of course, the phrase "go out on a date" was open to interpretation. Khory hoped it meant a restaurant, then a movie, but her parents defined it as a home-cooked dinner and Netflix.

" 'We'd like to get to know Troy a little better, that's all,' " Khory said, imitating her mom's squeaky voice.

I got it from their point of view, but from mine, it felt like an interview. The idea sent me into a tic frenzy. Besides being at a table with new people and their plates, her parents would study me, quiz me, and most likely ask about the Tourette. I could ignore them, but what if they pushed? And then a crazy thought, what if I talked about it and checked another item off my list? That idea sent an electric-shock-type pain down my left shoulder blade all the way to my butt. Who would have thought me kissing a girl would have been easier than telling someone, who probably knew anyway, that I had Tourette?

"They said if we ever want to go on a real date, we have to do this first," Khory said. "But I'm sure, then, they'll come up with another excuse to keep me home."

Khory was upset and tried to convince me, and herself, that tonight would be fun. I already decided I'd do whatever her parents asked. Their daughter had gotten me to stop counting by just being herself. I knew I couldn't let her go. Yes, I'd have to at some point, but that time wasn't now.

When I got to her house, the kitchen table was set for four, one on each side. Two plates to touch. I stared at it. My neck twitched. I had to make it through this.

"Hello, Troy, I'm Hank, Khory's dad." Mr. Price stuck out his hand. I turned from the table and shook it.

"Hello, Sir."

"Please, call me Hank."

I nodded, but that wouldn't happen. We sat at the table, Khory to my left, and Mrs. Price to my right.

"It's almost like a real date," Khory said. "Just pretend this is Stefano's Pizzeria, my parents aren't sitting across the table, and we're not eating orange chicken."

That got the look from her dad. You know, the one that said, "Do you want to lose your phone?"

I didn't argue. This was my idea of a perfect date anyway, hanging with the girl you really liked without worrying about offending strangers or having them think you were a psycho. Well, except for the interview.

"So, tell us about yourself," Mrs. Price said.

Let's see, I was in tenth grade, I offered to tutor you daughter in math so I could get to know her, and was extremely grateful you didn't let her go to movies. Oh, and I wanted the Los Angeles Dodgers to win the World Series. They were due.

"Khory and I have Chemistry together. I prefer astronomy," I said. Was that the kind of thing she wanted to know? Really, I had no experience.

"Yes, Khory did tell us that," Mrs. Price said. "And what do your parents do?"

"They're police officers." I thought the short versions would be best. The one that didn't involve a runaway parent, divorce, and remarriage.

"Well, we'd love to meet them," Mr. Price said.

"See what a great guy he is? A police family. It doesn't get any safer than that," Khory said. "Please, enough of the interrogation. I still need his help in math."

She winked at me and smiled. Her lip gloss was replaced by the shine of orange sauce from the chicken.

I focused on my own chicken and listened to her parents talk about gardening, photography, and Khory. They liked to talk more than they liked to ask questions, which helped me relax. Unfortunately, not enough to forget about Mrs. Price's plate and the pieces of rice balancing on the edge. I sat on my right hand and ate with my left. Not easy, especially with the hand squeeze, but I didn't want to mess things up.

After dinner Khory and I cleared the table. She washed the dishes, and I dried. Mr. and Mrs. Price went upstairs and gave us a little privacy.

"Do you think they like me?" I asked.

"Of course they do. How could they not?"

Khory leaned over and kissed me. Right here in the kitchen

with her parents one staircase away. My neck twitched. She laughed. Then I laughed, too.

After dishes, we rented *Passengers*, because who isn't a Jennifer Lawrence fan? We sat on the couch; I was in the corner, and Khory was next to me. She scooted even closer to me and covered us with a big red-and-white blanket. Even someone as socially stupid as I was knew a clue when it curled up next to you.

Khory focused on the movie, which turned out to be mostly Chris Pratt. While I waited for Jennifer to wake up, I ran my left hand along Khory's thigh. Then up the side of her body. Her sweater was soft, and I imagined her skin silky like her hair. My hand slid higher on her body and skimmed the side of her breast. Her arm moved away, pulling the blanket to her neck and giving me complete access.

My neck twitched and my face scrunched. My brain fought with itself. One part pushed my hand to squeeze while the other part craved the smooth, soft caress and the tingle of newness. The light side fought the dark side. One, two, three, four. . . . My hand moved up and down like it was acting out the "Itsy Bitsy Spider" song. Five, six, seven. The dark side was winning.

Three seconds before my hand clenched and groped her like a pervert, I forced it away and rested it on her thigh. Eight, nine, ten. The urge took over, as if I could stop it. I made a fist that rested on her leg.

My mind was like a tornado. Thoughts swirled around and made me queasy. Did she think I was scared? Could she feel the tic coming? Should I say something? What do you say in a situation like that? Sorry, the TS part of me wanted to squeeze your boob because it was completely inappropriate. But don't worry, I fought the urge. Your boob is safe. Was that insulting or complimentary? Or creepy. Did I say *boob* too many times?

I let out a big breath. Even my own thoughts exhausted me sometimes. *Could you just calm down for even a second?* I screamed inside my head. No, no I can't.

· · · · · · · · · ·

Mr. Price drove me home, and as soon as the garage door closed, I did a little dance. I didn't even know my body could move like that. I tapped my feet and spun around, then skipped to the bathroom. I was supercharged. I went the next step with Khory without getting smacked in the face. Wow, the feelings that zoomed in and out of my brain were just as intense as the ones that lurked in the darkness. If only I could keep the good ones. Bottle them, then chug it or pour it over my body.

What did Khory see in me? Literally. I snuck a peek in the bathroom mirror. Longer than the five seconds it took to wet and pat down any hair sticking up, and check for pimples.

This time I studied my face. Three sets of ten so far. On the plus side, I wasn't ugly, and by that I meant I looked like most high school guys. Not counting the three-tenths of a percent who shouldn't be wasting their time at PH High because they were destined for TV commercials about new school supplies.

On the negative side, the more I stared at myself, six counts of ten now, the less my average looks mattered. No one would see my chocolate-ice-cream-colored hair or the makings of a mustache. It was human nature for your eyes to be drawn to movement, which meant my neck and shoulder first. And how would anyone notice I was currently pimple free if my face was all scrunched up? I turned away. Ten sets of ten were all I could take.

I took my meds, then crawled into bed. My body was heavy, almost too heavy to move, even for me. My eyes closed, and Khory smiled at me. Did she see past the movement? I thought I knew the answer. And if I was right, it would make it very hard to leave her.

MARCH 6

"Can I tell you a secret?" Khory asked Saturday morning.

I loved that she wanted to talk first thing in the morning after watching episodes of *The Office* with me until eleven o'clock last night.

"Sure."

"I've never had a boyfriend before."

I grinned. "I'm your first?"

"Yup." I could hear the smile in her voice, and just as it always did, it warmed my body.

"Can I tell you a secret? Although it's pretty obvious," I said.

"You only want me for my math skills."

I laughed. "Shouldn't I be the one to say that?" I asked.

"Oh, yeah, right. The truth is, I just keep you around because you're a really good kisser," she said. "So promise you'll keep doing that, or I'll have to do something drastic like fail math tests."

"You wouldn't do that, would you?"

I wasn't sure if this was what boyfriends and girlfriends did, but the words rolled out of my mouth so naturally.

"Of course not. Hey, can I tell you another secret?" she asked.

She breathed heavily into in the phone like something sat on her chest and she was trying to get air in. My heart stopped. Her smile was gone. And even though I couldn't see her, I knew the sadness and shadow had taken over.

"I don't know why I made up Krista's List, because I'm too scared to do any of it." She let out a big exhale. "Phew. That felt good to admit."

I thought it was her parents who were scared to let her out. I never guessed she was, too. She seemed so brave, like Katniss.

"What about talking in court and bungee jumping and going on trips?"

"Well, I talk a big game. I am working on a speech, but I don't know if I'll read it. And trips? I doubt I'll even go away to college. The University of Richmond is right here, and if I stay close, it'll make my parents happy." She sighed. "Okay, enough of me. It's your turn to tell me a secret. A real one."

Just like that spill my secrets? Boyfriend or not, you can't just ask someone to do that like you're asking which movie they want to see on Friday. Plus, I had so many, which would I choose?

I thought about my List of Ten and the last ten years of my life since the diagnosis. There were so many things. I took a breath, then let it out. My neck twitched. My hand squeezed together. Another inhale and exhale. Neck twitch. Hand squeeze. Repeat. I wanted to do the sequence ten times.

"Troy? You don't have to answer."

"No. It's fine. Here goes. I used to see a psychiatrist. When I was younger. After my mom left." Inhale. Exhale. Neck twitch. Hand squeeze. Did I ever tell her Mom left? "Dr. Hadley Quentin, but he was so clueless, I called him Hardly Qualified."

She laughed. "Hardly Qualified, I like that."

"He was the one who suggested the counting to ten and breathing. I blame him for my number ten obsession," I whispered. The invisible hand creeped toward my chest.

The silence was heavy. Was that too much? Did she think I was a psycho and now she'd break up with me? My biggest achievement in life was being someone's boyfriend for eight days. At least it was an even number.

"I saw one, too," she said. "I blamed myself for what happened to Krista. And before you tell me that's stupid and I was just a kid, I know all that. In my head I know it, but the heart doesn't heal as quickly."

"The only smart thing HQ ever told me was to acknowledge what I felt. No one can take your feelings away, but some people can teach you how to live with them." HQ wasn't a complete idiot.

There we were, two messed up people. Neighborhoods away. Experiences completely opposite, but somehow we connected. I listened to her breathe, and a new fantasy started to form. Khory and I stayed together. She made me forget to count. And we both lived happily ever after. The most important part being *lived*. Could it come true?

· · · · · · · · · ·

Was an arranged dinner between your parents and your girlfriend's parents a common event or just a necessity when one set of parents suffered the loss of a child and desperately held on to the other?

Of course, Dad and Terri understood why the Prices would be overprotective. Not only did they remember what happened to Krista, they had also helped in the search for her. Everyone did. Terri told me there was nothing worse than losing a child. A sharp pain went through my chest. I didn't want them to go through that, but I wasn't completely sure my fantasy of happily ever after with Khory would save me.

I stared at the clock. Two hours left. I focused my energy on neck twitches, face scrunches, hand squeezes, and getting just the right feel of the carpet on my fingertips until that no longer satisfied them and I moved to the hardwood floor.

"Calm down, Troy. Everything will be fine," Terri said. "Why don't you put that nervous energy to work and dust the family room?"

Not what I had in mind, but any distraction would save me from tearing a ligament in my neck and spending dinner in the emergency room. So I kind of straightened up the family room, put Jude's toys in the toy box, and fixed the pillows on the couch. Then I swiped a damp rag over everything horizontal. One hour and forty minutes left.

I took a shower and let hot water pound my neck and back and soothe my muscles. I went to my room and spent more time than I'd like to admit on my clothing choice. Of course, Mr. and Mrs. Price had met me a few times already, but tonight was the make-or-break of meetings. The one to decide if Khory could come to my house. The one Khory and I called the final answer.

"So, Captain and Officer Hayes, why should we let our daughter go to your house after school and on weekends. Why can we trust you to keep her safe?"

"*Uh,* hello, we're cops? We *protect* and serve. We have guns. How are those for reasons?"

"Yes, yes! She can go to your house any time. She can even spend the night."

Ha! That was a fantasy I didn't dare dream. But, just in case Khory was allowed to see my room, I made sure it was neat. The books were on the shelves neatly organized by author, and my clothes were in the drawers and not sticking out. I even took out my trash and had time to change my shirt again, this time to a blue button-down one, before the doorbell rang.

Terri got to it two seconds before I did and waved me back so that she could open the door.

"Hi. I'm Terri, please come in."

Khory was so pretty I felt like an astronaut in space. Terri nudged me. I came back to Earth and moved out of the way.

"Thank you for inviting us tonight," Mrs. Price said. "I'm Helen, this is my husband, Hank, and our daughter, Khory."

"Nice to meet you. Clark, Troy's dad is finishing up Jude's bath. He's our eleven-month-old."

Khory and I followed them to the kitchen. "Excited?" I whispered in her ear.

"Freaking out," she admitted. "I hope my parents don't say anything embarrassing."

I actually expected Terri to swing the door open and greet them with "what a relief it is to meet you. We never thought Troy would have a girlfriend, and to be honest, we thought he was making you all up." Understandable, but still, it was a thought better kept to herself.

Dad came down the hallway with Jude bathed and in pajamas. I took him so Dad could do adult stuff like handshaking and drink offering. And when everyone met and we all had drinks, we went to the family room so Terri could cook and talk at the same time.

Khory and I sat on the floor with Jude, a toy rocket, and blocks. He smiled at her and held out a block.

"I told you she was pretty," I said to Jude.

Khory turned red. She took two blocks and tapped them together. Jude smiled, laughed, and held out the fourth block.

I leaned back and studied them. Jude scooted to her and maneuvered himself onto her lap. He obviously loved her as much as I did. And Khory was a natural. Talking baby talk and making stuffed animals dance. This was a match made in heaven.

"He really likes you. He doesn't share his blocks with just any-one." I bolted up. The best idea in the universe had just hit me like a shooting star. "Remember when I asked about a babysitter? Well, maybe you can be the one to babysit him."

Khory looked up at me, eyes wide. The shadow had crept across her face.

"Are you okay?" I asked.

She took a deep breath and gave me a smile, but the twinkle she came in with was gone.

"I don't know much about babysitting. I'm not good at taking care of anyone."

Jude shoved a stuffed animal at her. He disagreed, but I knew this was about Krista and now wasn't the time to get into it.

We played with him, stacking blocks and watching the rocket blast off, and I caught pieces of our parents' conversations.

"Tourette syndrome," Dad said.

"Oh, yes, we are very sorry about your daughter," Terri said.

I didn't know if Khory heard, but adults talking about me when I was in the same room never ended well. That's how I ended up with HQ.

Thankfully, Terri announced dinner before our parents got to the really embarrassing stories, although they could have been sav-ing them for dessert conversation. I leaped up and scrambled to grab the seat between Khory and Dad, since they wouldn't be offended if my hands invaded their space.

During dinner, the conversation moved to the mundane. Mr. Price's job as a computer science professor and Mrs. Price's as a stay-at-home mom.

"To watch over me," Khory whispered.

Of course, they talked about Dad and Terri's jobs. Where they worked, how long they'd been police officers, and how they felt about the way society viewed them. Dad and Terri were awesome. They answered all the questions and told a few stories about crimes gone wrong, like the guy who left his driver's license in the car he had stolen. Mr. and Mrs. Price smiled, laughed, and even stopped eating. Who knew law enforcement could be so funny or that Dad was so entertaining?

Then Dad and Mr. Price turned to the topic of sports. Both loved baseball and the LA Dodgers, and war movies, but only if they portrayed actual events and weren't heavy on the love story.

I put my hand on Khory's leg. "Everyone's having fun."

· · · · · · · · · ·

Khory and I cleared the table after dinner, left our parents in the dining room, and snuck out to the patio. The weather was on my side tonight, not cold, but chilly, so when we sat on the couch, Khory scooted close to me for warmth. I rubbed her hands between mine. I loved Richmond in March.

"I'm glad our parents met. Your parents are nice. Hopefully this means I'll be able to come to your house."

"That would give us more time for tutoring, even if you don't need it anymore."

"I said *parents*, but Terri's your stepmom, right? You never talk about your real mom."

I studied our hands, fingers intertwined. It was nice having someone to talk to. I trusted her and knew she would understand. The guilt of losing someone was a special kind of pain.

"She left a long time ago. But I'm going to see her." Another secret revealed. I felt lighter. "My dad doesn't know. And I don't want him to. Not yet."

"He doesn't want you to see her? Did she, *uh,* how do I say this, did she do something bad?"

"It depends on how you look at it. She left us, but it was because of me." I let her hands go and clenched mine. "She couldn't deal with me and everything. The thing is, she has all this stuff, too. She doesn't understand. . . ." My voice started to shake. Some boyfriend. A blubbering idiot.

Khory rubbed my arm. "What doesn't she understand?"

"That I need her to explain all this to me. Tell me how to live like this. The pain, it's . . ." Everything was rising to the top. The pain in my hands and neck, the pain in my heart for being the one who drove her away. They were rising up to one hundred, the top of the scale. I got up from the couch and paced the yard. Khory followed me.

"I can't begin to understand what you go through. I watch you, and I'm amazed at how you keep going. Happy, funny, really cute." She grabbed my hand and turned me toward her. "But I know about the guilt. I told you that. What I didn't say was that when I jumped out of the guy's car, Krista didn't. I should have gone back to get her. Or stayed with her. But I ran away. See, it really is my fault."

I wrapped my arms around her. We stood in the middle of the yard, the patio light too far away to light our faces, but I knew hers was filled with torment just as mine was.

"If there's anything I can do to help you get to your mom, let me know. I can't have a reunion, but you can."

A razor-sharp sword stabbed me through the heart and not because I sent Mom away. It was because once I found her, it would be the end. Khory could not be a part of that.

I hugged her, then led her behind a tree where the patio light couldn't find any part of us. I kissed her. The softness of her lips and the coconut smell of her hair made me weak. Our lips moved and my tongue found hers. It was warm, moist, and eager. And it took all my pain away.

MARCH 7

The sun was annoyingly bright for a Sunday morning, and it forced
me to keep my eyes closed as I shuffled from my bedroom to the
kitchen. I slammed into the doorway, collapsed into a chair, then
made a pillow with my arms and put my head on the table.

"Good morning," Terri said. "Sleep in a little late? It's almost
eleven o'clock."

"Yeah, long week."

"Your dad and I are going to take Jude to the park. Do you want
to go?"

I peeked out the window. Royal-blue sky. I couldn't deny the
beauty, even though I wasn't into nature. But I had work to do in my
search for Mom, which required a house to myself since Terri was
clear I should give up my search.

"Thanks, but I have homework. And then I thought I'd go to
Khory's."

"Okay. Girlfriend over brother. You don't have to explain. Just
make sure you get your homework done first."

"I will."

After Mom left, Dad packed up everything she left behind and put it in the basement's storage closet. A tingle ran through my body at the thought of finding a buried treasure. It woke me up a little more. I ate breakfast, then played on my phone until they finally left.

Our basement wasn't creepy like the ones in movies where cobwebs hung from the ceiling or the furnace was alive, but it wasn't the entertainment Mecca like Rainn's either. It had finished walls like hers, but the couches were older, the ping-pong table had a layer of dust, and the bookcase was filled with outdated magazines and trophies from Dad's college baseball days. Our basement was the perfect place for a life that didn't exist anymore.

I went to the closet at the far end of the room and opened the door. My neck twitched faster, and my heart beat harder.

"We'll send them to her when she gets settled," Dad told me when he first brought the boxes down here.

"I can bring them when I visit," I said.

His face changed. I could still see it. The smile with lips parted but teeth clenched together. Back then I read it as "sure, that's a great idea," but now I knew it meant, "Oh, you poor sucker. You keep telling yourself that lie."

I lied to myself for the first year or so. Until the cards stopped coming. Then I begged Dad to take me to her.

"I can't," he said. No explanation. Just "I can't."

I stomped my feet and kicked and pounded the walls. At eleven

I had regressed to toddler temper tantrums. How could Dad keep us apart? But after what Terri said, I understood he was too busy managing a special-needs son, working, and convincing everyone, mostly himself, that things were still great. He didn't have the time to worry about a woman who didn't want to be worried about.

I flicked on the light. The closet was filled with boxes. The ones in front were marked "Toys." I peeked in and found my old Legos, Matchbox cars, random trucks, and action figures. All of them saved for Jude when he stopped putting everything into his mouth. I pulled those boxes out and looked at the ones farther back. There had to be fifteen more marked "Halloween," "Christmas," and "Financials." The stuff you keep for the IRS in case they pick your name from the Triwizard Cup for your spot in the audit process.

I dragged those out and found what I was searching for stuffed in the back corner. The ones marked "Jennifer." My neck twitched for ten rounds of ten. I crossed my fingers and hoped for pictures of a favorite city, letters, or information on her parents. I was pretty sure her mom was still alive. Maybe she went there. Did my grand-mother know about me? Wouldn't she want to see me? I thought about finding her too, but I didn't have any more room on my list.

I sighed and ripped open the first box. Jeans, flowery dresses, and lots of black shoes. Stuff only good for Halloween costumes or donations to Goodwill. I pushed the box to the side and tore open the next.

"Yes!"

This was what I needed. I pulled a photo album off the top and flipped through it. There were a few pictures of Mom when she was young, like in middle school and high school, but it was mostly filled with pictures of other kids and what adults called memorabilia. Ribbons. Cards. Tickets.

I put the album to the side, dug deeper into the box, and pulled out birthday, anniversary, and condolence cards. I read through a few and realized they were about my granddad. My body tingled. One step closer. I carried the box out of the closet, dropped it on the floor, then shoved everything else back in. Hopefully I got the order right, but I doubted anyone would go in here until it was time to stick the lawn scarecrow into the ground.

I carried the box upstairs, put it on my bed, and took everything out. Photo albums. Cards. Yearbooks. Letters. I opened another album. There weren't many pictures of her in this one either, but it did show a side of her I didn't know. Besides a few pictures of other people, it was filled with awards. Math. Writing. Honor society. I smiled. She had the same idea I had—hyperfocus on studying to keep the mind and body from going crazy. I flipped through the pages. She had awards in just about everything.

I went through the cards next. Most were from Dad. I tossed those aside, afraid I'd read something that would add to the disgusting condom visual already cemented in my mind from the exploration of the night table. And why torture myself when they wouldn't give any clue to where she was now? They lived together, and supposedly were happy, until their twelfth anniversary. By the thirteenth, I had been diagnosed.

I finally got to the condolence cards. There weren't many. A few from neighbors, Dad's coworkers, and names I didn't recognize. Then I came across the clue that was better than finding plans to the Death Star. My grandfather's obituary.

Steven James Montgomery, of Schenectady, New York, died in 1998. He was an Air Force veteran, then had a thirty-two-year career as an accountant. He was survived by his wife, Margaret, and their daughter, Jennifer Montgomery Hayes.

Mom. I squeezed my hands ten times, dropped the paper before my hand crumpled it up, then opened my laptop and searched for Jennifer Montgomery in Schenectady, New York.

· · · · · · · · · ·

I scrolled through eight pages of Jennifer Montgomerys. A huge difference from the eighty-five thousand results I got before. The basic information told me nothing, but for the bargain price of $5.99, I could find out anything. No wonder this world had such issues. Any criminal with a credit card could find out a person's entire life history, but for someone like me, a law-abiding citizen who just wanted to find his mom, it was as out of reach as a $599.00 report. It sucked to be sixteen without a credit card.

Would Dad and Terri notice a tiny little charge to Findanyone.

com? Of course. They were cops. One phone call would incriminate me, and my technology would be taken away forever.

There had to be a way. I searched other websites and scrolled through the pages until my eyes crossed. I slumped over my desk and mindlessly clicked on the Page Next button. Again. Again. For ten rounds of ten easily.

Until a name caught my eye. Jennifer H. Montgomery. Did the *H* stand for Hayes? I crossed my fingers, clicked on her name, and hoped for something current and, more importantly, free.

The blue bar traveled from left to right.

A new screen popped up. Across the top was the name Jennifer Hayes Montgomery. Farther down, places she had lived. They included Schenectady, New York, and Richmond, Virginia.

My neck twitched. My face scrunched. Every nerve in my body came alive. I scrolled down further. A phone number and this year's date. I clicked on the number. My leg bounced as the new page loaded.

There it was. The number and the name Margaret Montgomery. My grandmother. It had to be them. I didn't believe in coincidences. Like when someone laughed in your direction, they were definitely laughing at you. I opened my phone and the sublist for Mom, then typed the number, date, and website.

Ten simple numbers. Of course, ten. All I had to do was call it. It sounded easy, but then what? Would I tell her everything? If I did that on the phone, she'd never agree to see me. And I needed to see her. One more time.

My stomach churned. My neck twitched. I squeezed my hands together. One simple call to see who answered, then hang up. No talking. No stories. Just to make sure the voice was hers.

I pulled up the phone keypad and put in the first few numbers: 518-875—Wait. Did she have caller ID? Everyone did today. She'd know it was me, or Dad, since the phone was in his name. Maybe she'd see that and not answer.

Khory said she would help. She would figure out what to do. I put Mom's box in the closet, got dressed, and jumped on my bike. The houses and trees were a blur of red and green. A drop of sweat tickled my face as it ran down my cheek. I turned onto Khory's driveway, dropped my bike, careful to not touch the grass, and wiped my face.

She opened the door. I raced up the driveway and stood in front of her panting and shaking.

"What's wrong?" she asked.

I shoved my phone at her opened to Mom's number.

"Whose number is that?"

"My mom's."

She gasped. "You want me to call and see who answers?"

I nodded.

"Are you going to talk to her? Do you know what you want to say?"

I shook my head. "I can't talk. Not yet."

She rubbed my arm. "It's okay. I'll just ask if it's her. Maybe pretend I'm a salesperson or something."

"Good idea. Could you put it on speaker so I'll know if it's her voice?"

I grabbed the doorway. What if I didn't recognize her voice? It had been six years, and I was just a kid when she left. But who doesn't recognize their own mom's voice?

"Are you sure you want to do this?" Khory asked.

"Yeah."

She led me to her room for privacy but left the door open so her parents wouldn't freak out. The furniture was all white, and except for a few bottles of perfume, the tops of her desk and dresser were clean. No distractions or urges to straighten. She was my dream girl. I sat on the bed and stroked the purple comforter that matched her pillow. On the wall above her headboard was a bulletin board with notes, cards, and pictures, including the one Rainn took of us last week. Khory looked beautiful, as usual, but I had a Tourette smirk. Random pictures with smart phones wasn't something I thought about before I had a girlfriend. I leaned over, unpinned it, and put it facedown on the night table.

"Are you ready?" Khory put her phone on her dresser with mine next to it, and turned it on speaker.

I walked to the dresser, counted to ten, and nodded. She put the numbers in her phone. It rang. Once. Twice. I crossed my fingers and silently pleaded with Mom to pick up on an even number. Three.

"Hello?"

Odd. Shit.

The voice on the phone sounded almost childlike. A kid who had answered her mom's phone. Everyone always questioned whether she was the Mrs. Jennifer Hayes and not her daughter.

It was her. I grabbed the dresser.

"Hello, ma'am. I'm Janet from Democrats for a Better America. I'd like to send you information on our organization. Would you like to provide your address?"

"I'm sorry, but I'm not interested. Thank you." She hung up.

Khory pressed the red button, and the call ended. She turned to me. "Was it her?"

"Yes," I whispered. "Good idea to try and get her address."

I cleared my throat and took a few breaths, but the invisible hand skipped the foreplay and went right into squeezing the air from my chest. I stumbled backward to the bed and collapsed. My stomach was in knots. I took a breath, just enough to get some air in and not die. I counted to ten. Out loud.

"One, two, three, four, five, six, seven, eight, nine, ten. One, two, three, four, five, six, seven, eight, nine, ten."

I was on round six when Khory sat next to me and put her hand on my leg. I took another breath, deep, faced her, then leaped up.

"I gotta go." Freaking out was a trait I preferred to do on my own.

"Wait." She grabbed my arm and pulled me back to the bed. "It's okay. Hearing your mom's voice after all this time is pretty weird."

I nodded, but it wasn't okay. My neck wouldn't stop twitching and was already past an eighty on the pain scale. My brain couldn't think of anything except numbers. Ten. Always ten. Calming techniques that didn't work, ages with bad memories. I grabbed my hair and put my head down. Make it go away.

"I really have to go. Thanks for helping." I bolted out of her bedroom, down the stairs, and out the front door.

Halfway home my phone beeped.

KHORY: I love you

Tears filled my eyes. I pulled over onto the grass and texted back.

ME: I love you too.

And I did, but that didn't seem big enough to describe how I felt about her. I guess those words hadn't been invented yet.

MARCH 7

I rode my bike into the garage, dropped it on the ground, and yanked open the door to the house.

"There you are. Dinner is in thirty minutes," Terri said.

I gasped and jumped back. I was so lost in my own mind, I forgot they'd be back from the park. Terri opened the freezer, took out a bag, and put it in the microwave.

"You okay?" she asked.

"Yeah, fine," I said.

She tilted her head and opened her mouth. Of course, she had more to ask, but I didn't have time for twenty questions. They could all be summed up in one answer anyway: life sucked.

I fell on my bed in a fit of neck twitches, hand clenches, and face scrunches. I pulled my hair and bent my fingers back. Break, damn it. Do it. Break. My head felt like exploding. I grabbed my hair again and buried my face in the pillow, but none of it would stop. I was definitely at one hundred.

I closed my eyes and focused on the softness of Khory's hands.

Her lips. I took a deep breath hoping for coconut, but all I got was the scent of sweat. Even like this she loved me. Why couldn't Mom?

I'd recognized Mom's voice right away. Too bad I wasn't on that old game show about how many notes to name the song. My game was how many words to name the voice from your past. I got it in one. Did I win a prize?

The voice was the one that used to ask me about school and if I wanted to go out and play. Today it didn't have the edginess she had when my tics invaded hers.

I swung my arm toward the night table and sent my clock flying. It landed with a thud on the floor. My shoulders relaxed. I opened the drawer, took out a hardcover book, and threw it against the wall. My neck twitch slowed down.

My door opened. "Troy, dinner," Dad said.

I wiped my face and smiled. What was that dumb thing adults said? It's hard to be mad if you have a smile on your face? That was bullshit. Just like everything else they said. I faced Dad. His eyebrows were scrunched up.

"Anything you want to talk about?" He gazed past me and scanned my room.

I followed his gaze to the clock and book on the floor. So my room was messy for the first time in my life, big deal.

"No." It was the truth. He'd find out soon enough.

The smell of steak met me in the hallway. It smelled great, but I wasn't hungry. Unfortunately, that was never an excuse to get out of family meals when we were all home. Jude sat in his high chair with a pouty face. Even at eleven months, he knew his mom was a good cook, and it sucked not to get any of the real food.

"How's Khory?" Terri asked when we were all at the table.

"Good," I mumbled and cut my food into ten pieces.

"Anything going on at school this week?" Dad asked. "Wednesday is a teacher workday, remember."

"Yeah," I said.

"I can tell something is bothering you," Terri said. "Did something happen with Khory?"

My fingers crawled close to Dad's plate. Then closer. They touched the edge, then scooted back across the invisible line that delineated everyone's personal eating space. I peeked at him. He alternated between eating his food and making sure Jude didn't throw his across the room.

"Everything's fine." I stabbed a piece of steak and stuffed it in my mouth. As I chewed, my hand crept out again.

Touch.

Back.

Touch.

Back.

"Tell us about your other friends," Dad said. "We'd like to meet them."

"Not much to tell. There's Khory's friend, Rainn, her boyfriend Diego, and Jay, a kid in my math class."

I picked up my steak knife to cut ten more pieces. Slice. Back and forth. Slice. Repeat. The motion felt good. My hand turned like it had a mind of its own and tried it on my left arm. Lightly like a feather. Slice. Back and forth. Slice.

I stole a peek at Dad. He glanced up at me. Eyebrows raised. I dropped the knife. Usually the urge came before the tic, but this just happened. I stared at the knife, hoping for an explanation, but it just taunted me. The slicing felt good, and I knew it would feel even better harder.

I drank some milk, stabbed green beans with my fork, and stuffed them in my mouth. I focused on Jude, happily eating yogurt and puff cereal, and relaxed enough to pick up my knife again. This time I felt the urge, the itch that builds and screams to be scratched. I put my hands under the table and scratched the itch. With the knife. Ten times. Each one harder.

Dad leaned around the table and yanked the knife away. Then he grabbed my arm and examined the marks. There were three red lines, no blood or broken skin. My neck twitched. I should have paid more attention and made it an even number. Dad got up and tossed my knife in the sink. Terri pushed her plate away, pulled mine toward her, and cut my food into bite-size pieces. I sighed and leaned back in my chair.

"Can I be excused?" I asked.

"No," Dad and Terri said that the same time.

"What's with the knife thing? Is that a new tic?" Dad asked.

I cringed at the comment. We didn't talk about it. But I nodded.

Dad took a deep breath. "Are you sure that's what it is? Were you thinking about slitting your wrists?"

"What? No, I wasn't doing that," I insisted. "I couldn't help it."

"We should look at your medication. Maybe change the dose," Terri said. "I can make an appointment for you for this week."

Slitting my wrists? Up my medication? My fingers tingled. I wanted to pull out my phone and add to my list. Methods to die number three: slit my wrists.

"Sure," I said.

We finished dinner, and I escaped to my room. I'd heard of people who ticced and hurt themselves. And others who cut themselves on purpose. They claimed it relieved the pressure that tried to suffocate you. I wanted the pressure to stop, the urges, the stress, but I needed someone to tell me how, someone besides a quack whose treatment ideas came from an obscure comment in a book published in 1950.

"Troy?" Dad called and knocked on my door.

"What. I'm doing homework," I said, then spied my backpack on the floor across the room.

I leaped toward it when my door opened. Dad scanned my room and lingered again on the clock and book on the floor.

"I wanted to make sure you were okay," he said. "If there's anything you want to talk about, I'm always available."

Great offer, but he wasn't qualified either. Talking wouldn't take the pain away.

"Thanks. I'm good. Really," I said.

Dad stared at me, studied me. "Okay. Don't stay up too late."

He closed the door. My fingers traced the red marks on my arm. They tingled. Tickled. Like someone had rubbed a feather on my skin. I had to scratch it. Do it, the urge whispered. It will feel amazing. I went to my desk, rummaged in the drawer, not caring that I mixed up the pens and notecards, and pulled out a pair of scissors. I traced the marks with the blade, gently at first. I didn't want to break the skin.

But it was like the feather. A tease. I pressed harder. And harder. It hurt, but I could breathe. A drop of blood seeped out after another pass with the blade. I squeezed my hand open and closed. My veins bulged, and another drop of blood bubbled out.

This was a new side of me. A bad one. Worse than the side I already hated. If you asked someone who always frowned if they liked being that way, I bet they'd say no. Even Darth Vader didn't fully accept the dark side, which was why Luke was able to turn him back. Maybe he just forgot what the good side was like. I didn't want to forget. I wanted to be happy and enjoy the time left on this Earth, not be murdered by the dark side.

It wasn't time yet. I focused on the big blue vein that ran up my arm. Long ways. That was the way to do it. Quicker to bleed out and harder to fix. I'd go to sleep and never wake up. After I completed one through nine.

I opened my desk drawer to put the scissors back. What if Dad didn't believe I was fine? Would he take all the sharp objects out of the house? I moved to my clothes drawers to hide the scissors. No, too obvious. The closet? Also obvious. I went to my bed, lifted the mattress, and placed the scissors in the middle. I retucked the sheets, straightened the blanket, and counted to ten.

Then I twitched, squeezed, and scrunched until I collapsed on the floor from exhaustion.

MARCH 8

I woke up sweaty and in my clothes. The light was off, the shades were closed, and somehow the clock had made it back on my night table. With the alarm set. It buzzed and pissed me off. I rolled over. Pain shot through my neck and back. The muscles in my forearms ached. I closed my eyes and sank into the pillow. The smell of sweat engulfed me.

It was so tempting to say "screw school" and go back to sleep since I wouldn't be using Pre-Calc or Chemistry much longer, but my OCD fought me. I got up, took a shower, and trudged to the bus stop.

Wedged between the bus window and a short kid with a poster-board project bigger than he was, I pulled out my phone. Khory had sent several texts after I had bolted from her house. Usually I sprang to the phone when her face popped on the screen, but the Troy she knew hadn't been around last night.

Today was a new day, which meant it was closer to April 6. I couldn't waste my time being whiny and pitiful, and I refused to let the dark side get me too soon. I grasped the light and texted Khory.

When I got to my locker, she was there. She leaned against it, her attention divided between her phone and the hallway. I counted faster. Walked faster. Until I was close enough to grab her hand.

She smiled at me, but there was sadness in her eyes as they searched mine. My neck twitched, and my hand squeezed hers. Hard. I dropped her hand.

"Sorry. And sorry I didn't call you back." I glanced around the hallway. No one paid attention to me, and if they did, they kept their distance. "It took me by surprise. Hearing her voice. I didn't think I'd freak out like that."

"Are you sure you want to see her? Maybe it's better if you don't."

"I have to," I said. She'd understand if I explained how it fit into my list. Actually, she probably wouldn't. I tried a different way. "You know how you want to speak at *the guy*'s hearing? Why is that?"

"To get things off my chest. To tell him what he did was not just to Krista, but to the rest of us," she said. She nodded. "Ah, I get it."

"Maybe by the time I see her, it will be easier." Doubtful, but I had to end it.

Ms. Migloski wasn't as strict about our phones, so in Spanish, I researched how to get to Schenectady. I had three choices: a plane, a train, or a bus. My neck twitched at the thought of being squished next to strangers, and an urge to flap my arms tingled and grew. Would they make a scene when I touched their tray tables? My hand reached out to touch the back of Riley's seat.

But a plane was the fastest way. I typed in routes. Richmond to Schenectady. Round trip. The progress bar moved like sludge. Then the prices came up.

"Oh, crap!"

Ms. Migloski stopped midsentence and stared at me. Oh, so Riley can spend the entire semester watching *Parks and Recreation* and you don't care, but I say one word that's not even bad, and you notice that. Maybe I should have said it in Spanish.

· · · · · · · · · ·

Hundreds of dollars for a plane ticket? That was insane! It was bad enough to be stuffed in a tiny space, but to make me pay for the torture? My chest tightened. Breathe. Oxygen in. Carbon dioxide out.

I pulled out my phone and added to Mom's list.

5.   Plane ticket $500

Dad would be pissed that I found Mom, so I doubted he'd buy me a ticket to see her. I needed money of my own. Looking back, iTunes gift cards may not have been the best payment idea for babysitting Jude, but who knew I'd want real money one day?

What did other kids do for money? I could ask for cash instead of gift cards. Now that I had a girlfriend, I'd want to buy her a birthday present or dinner. Dad and Terri would understand, but there was no way I could raise five hundred dollars in a month.

That left things like washing cars, cutting grass, and walking dogs. Picking up dog poop wasn't my idea of a fun afternoon, but it couldn't be any worse than a baby's, which I did for free. Or almost free. And money was money.

Okay, step one, make a list of jobs. Check. Step two, flyers. After Terri left for work, I brought my laptop to the family room and opened a blank document. Let's see, how about hardworking kid needs money to complete items on his bucket list? In other words, help me raise money to die. I thought about that for a few minutes. Going for sympathy might get more phone calls, but the suicide hotline wasn't the type I wanted.

I went for simple and straightforward: hardworking teenager interested in earning money. I listed the types of jobs I'd do, added my name and phone number, and scanned it for errors. I double-checked the phone number, saved it, and pressed Print. Then Cancel. Rechecked the phone number. Then finally printed forty copies.

Jude woke up as the printer finished.

"Hey, how about a little ride in the stroller?"

He reached out to me, and I lifted him out of the crib. After a diaper change and a snack, we were on our way.

"So, I may be gone a little more on the weekends," I explained as we strolled to the far end of our neighborhood. The farther away, the better. Dad or Terri seeing me wash someone else's car would lead to an extremely uncomfortable conversation.

"I'm hoping to do some odd jobs to raise money. I'm going to see my mom."

"*Ay wa goo ay*," Jude said.

"No, we have different moms. Mine lives in New York. But your mom is awesome, and I know she loves you. And me."

I sighed, pushed the stroller, and placed folded flyers into the bottom slot of each mailbox. Then I calculated how many piles of poop I'd have to pick up to raise $500.

MARCH 9

Jay honked his horn. I put my jacket on and shoved my phone into the pocket.

"I know you don't have school tomorrow, but I have to work and I don't want to be up all night worrying about you," Dad said.

"I won't be late."

"Why don't you have your friends hang out here tonight?"

"Well, we already made plans to go to Rainn's house."

Then Dad gave me a look. I didn't know that one, but assumed it had to do with trust. The cop wanted to know if he could trust me. Now that I thought about it, a dad would have the same question. Neither of us was used to a socially active son.

Jay honked again. I opened the front door.

"Sorry. Another time, Dad. I promise."

"Make sure he's not in a rush to get there. You know how I feel about teenagers and cars."

As if I could forget. He'd told me the stories. Repeatedly. A kid talking on her phone ran head-on into a truck. Steering wheel, engine, and the truck's front fender smashed into her chest. Or the one where a boy took a corner too fast and swerved into a tree. He survived, lucky him, but the front passenger was thrown from the car and his body was found wrapped around a guardrail. Bones weren't supposed to bend like that, Dad had said. Those were just a couple reasons he wouldn't let me drive. Tourette was the other. And because of the stories, I almost agreed with him. Almost. Which is why it was on my list. I nodded and closed the door behind me.

"Hey, Jay." I slid into the front seat. "Did you hear the news? Khory's parents met mine, and she's allowed to hang out at my house."

Jay pulled away from the curb nice and slow like Dad would have wanted and didn't pick up speed until we were a few blocks away. Then he glanced at me, the message from his smirk clear even in the dark.

"I'd be happy to give you some tips. I mean, if you need."

I laughed. "Tips? Who's the one who sits in a chair alone Saturday nights?" I asked.

"Gotcha." He flipped the satellite station. Nineties rock wasn't cutting it, I guess.

The truth was I needed all the help I could get. I was freaking out already. What if she wanted to do more than kiss and a little feel under the blanket? What if I had an anxiety attack and passed out?

I took a deep breath and scanned the dashboard. The radio displayed blue numbers and letters, and the buttons below were backlit in the same way. Jay's 2012 Mustang was a lot cooler than Dad's 2015 Toyota Camry. Still, I looked past the bright lights and knobs controlling volume, bass, and speakers and zeroed in on the emergency brake. I became obsessed with the one thing that could cause an accident. One yank and we'd jolt to a stop, which would be pretty destructive at forty miles an hour.

My brain and hand worked together. My palm tingled and longed to wrap around it. I shifted closer to the door and sat on my left hand. My elbow jerked trying to get free. I sank my weight onto my hand and tried to refocus by making small talk, but, being the lame conversationalist I was, my mind was a complete blank. I stared at the radio's volume button and told myself it would be awesome to blast AWOL Nation, but even that didn't shift my interest from the emergency brake.

What kind of sick joke was this disease? Taunting you with the most inappropriate and dangerous actions. Was this Mother Nature's way of killing off the weak-minded by having them cause fatal accidents? And if that didn't work, just have them kill themselves?

"Yo, Troy, you in there?" Jay swatted my arm.

I turned toward Jay. He was smiling, totally oblivious to the fact that my brain was planning to wreck his Mustang and kill us both.

"Have you ever smoked pot before?" Jay asked.

"*Huh?*" That refocused my brain. Why couldn't he have asked that earlier?

"Oh, damn! Your dad's a cop. Forget I asked." He focused straight ahead, shoulder blades squeezed together, hands suddenly on ten and two, just as in driver's ed.

I laughed. A throw-your-head-back laugh. My muscles relaxed, and my neck stopped twitching.

"What?" He stole a look at me, then eyes quickly back on the road. "What?"

"All of a sudden you're a proper driver. Are you now an *A* student? My dad's a cop. So what? I'm not going to make a citizen's arrest."

Jay eyed me, his head tilted. His shoulders dropped, and he went back to driving with one hand.

"Does that mean you smoke?"

"I never have."

I'd read about it though. People in the TS chat groups swore by it. It relaxed their muscles and slowed down their tics.

"What does it feel like?" I asked.

"Oh man, you're so relaxed. Like you could stare at the stars forever." He sighed. "Except Rainn. She gets horny. Don't tell Diego I said that."

I spun to him. Him and Rainn? I never would have thought that. My body started to tingle. What would it do to Khory? My fingertips rubbed together imagining her silky hair and soft body.

"Open the glove box," Jay said.

I did and pulled out a plastic bag with pot and rolling papers inside. It seemed I was going to find out.

· · · · · · · · · ·

Rainn's mom pointed to the basement. "They're watching a movie. Pizza will be here soon."

"Great Mrs. Levine. Thanks," Jay said. He winked at me and mouthed *munchies*.

"Thank you," I said.

Khory and Rainn were deep into a movie where the girl cries, the guy realizes he fucked up, and they live happily ever after. Movies like this poison girls' brains. Reality is not like this at all.

"We should have gotten here sooner and picked a different movie," I said.

"No, this is perfect." Jay nudged me. "Khory will be so upset when the boy dies, she'll need you to comfort her."

"You've seen this movie?"

"Unfortunately. It's what happens when your best friends are girls."

I had a lot to learn about the whole girlfriend thing. I sat on the couch next to Khory, and Jay plopped into the chair next to us and pulled out his phone. "I really need to get a girlfriend," he said.

Soon after the boyfriend died, Diego came down the stairs with three boxes of pizza and dropped them on the coffee table.

He glanced at the movie, then curled up next to Rainn. My cheeks warmed, my neck twitched, and I put my head down. Diego and Rainn apparently never learned the word discreet.

When the movie was over, Rainn unwrapped herself from Diego and passed out paper plates for dinner.

"Wait. I thought we could go for a walk first." Jay pulled the plastic bag out of his pocket.

"Sure." Diego grabbed the pizza boxes, and Khory and I followed the group out.

"Mom, we're going to eat outside."

Mrs. Levine nodded without taking her eyes off the TV and Dr. Oz. Khory handed me napkins, and she and Jay grabbed a few cans of soda.

We walked to the corner, made a right, went down the street for a few minutes, then uphill to a wooded park. Smart move to hand me the napkins. After the ten-count-bend-downs, the sodas would have been extra shaken.

We turned into a park, which was really a forest with a few worn paths. The only light was from the moon, and even that was dim. We stuck to one path and crunched on dead leaves as it led us deeper into the woods until the trees cleared and we stood in front of huge rocks. It was like the Stonehenge of Virginia.

Diego put the pizzas on a short rock, then climbed the bigger ones. I climbed up behind him to the top. It was corny, but I spread my arms, lifted my head, and let the cold air settle around me. For a second, I felt free.

Jay put the drinks down and pulled out the bag. I jumped down and watched as he broke dried leaves off the twigs and sprinkled them in the crease of a rolling paper. Then, like a pro, he rolled it into a perfect cigarette.

We sat in a preschool version of a circle. Me and Khory, Diego and Rainn, and Jay close, but not too close.

"Okay, who's first?" Jay lit the joint, took a drag, and held it to Rainn.

She took a drag and passed it to Diego. He took one, then gave it to Khory. I studied how they did it. I didn't want to be like the kid in the movies who barfed on his girlfriend's shoes. Khory took a small inhale, held it for a couple seconds, then exhaled. Seemed easy enough. She held it out for me, and I did what she did. Smoke went down my throat. I coughed, then turned away and cleared my throat. No puke. Hooray! I passed it to Jay.

"You're going to like this," Khory said.

I pulled her close to me. The joint came back to us. I did better this time, no choking or coughing. When I leaned forward to pass it to Jay, my head felt fuzzy, lightheaded, and more so after each turn. The rocks appeared to be soft like pillows, and the trees swayed even though the air was still. I studied my friends and started to giggle.

"How you feeling, dude?" Jay asked.

I inspected myself, studied my fingers and hands, and stretched my neck. It didn't hurt. My shoulder blade, nothing. I lifted my arms. They were weightless. I was pain-free.

"Awesome," I said.

I tried to squeeze my hand into a fist, but it didn't want to. A tic didn't want to. My hand fell open on my leg. I leaned against a rock, and the rest of my body went limp. Having no control over my muscles was nothing new, but most of the time they were tense and in motion. Now all my body wanted to do was relax and be still. This was an entirely new sensation.

Khory snuggled next to me. I breathed in coconut mixed with the sweetness of pot. That made me giggle, too.

"What?" she asked.

"Nothing. Just smelling your hair," I admitted, then put my head down. "It's nice."

She tilted her head to me. Not caring who was watching, I bent toward her and kissed her.

"Get a room guys," Diego said.

"If your dad knew what you were doing Troy, he'd lock us all in jail," Jay said.

"Maybe just you guys. He'd kill me."

Khory's muscles tensed. I wrapped my arms around her and kissed the top of her head. "It's okay. We're here." And nothing could hurt us.

. . . .

On the way home, Jay and I drove with the windows open while I sprayed air freshener. It was eleven fifteen. Hopefully Dad and Terri were asleep, or at least in their room. Our efforts didn't completely mask the smell, and I was sure they'd recognize it immediately.

I opened the front door, ran to my room for my pajamas, then locked myself in the bathroom.

Knock, knock. "Troy?"

Phew! Just made it. "Yeah, Dad. I'm home, just getting ready for bed."

"Okay, see you in the morning."

I sighed and stared in the mirror. My neck twitched. My hands clenched together, fingernails dug into my palm. Repeat. I counted to ten, bent down, and touched the tile floor. Then I grabbed my hair and pulled as hard as I could. They were back in full force, and all at one time.

Trying to hurt yourself was like tickling yourself. It never worked. No matter how hard I dug my fingernails into my palms, they wouldn't bleed. But that didn't stop me from trying. I bent my finger back waiting for a crack. That didn't come either. The only thing that did was tears. A lot of them. And the realization that those wonderful pain-free hours were all I would get.

I went back to my room, crawled into bed, and pulled the blanket over my body. I inhaled, but I'd washed off Khory's sweet smell along with the pot. I grabbed my phone and opened my list. Tonight definitely qualified as pain-free. I checked off number three.

1. Meet someone with Tourette syndrome—COMPLETED
2. Get my first kiss—COMPLETED
3. Be pain-free—COMPLETED
4. Find a babysitter for my baby brother—IN PROGRESS
5. See the space shuttle—MARCH 20?
6. Talk about Tourette in public
7. Give away my Tim Howard autographed picture
8. Drive a car
9. Talk to Mom
10. Commit suicide

Then I closed my eyes and pictured Khory curled up on the couch watching the movie about kids with cancer. How would she feel when her boyfriend died?

MARCH 15

Monday mornings sucked more than the *Batman v Superman* movie, Mrs. Hill's geography tests, and Bradley's messy, crooked desk. I refused to open my eyes, even to pour milk in my cereal, and acknowledge whoever entered the kitchen and banged around the coffee machine.

Milk dripped down my chin, and I breathed in the aroma of coffee that was now across the table from me. I wished I liked the taste, because a shot of caffeine would have been extremely helpful.

"Good morning," Dad said.

"Morning," I mumbled.

My eyes were still closed, but my ears must have been wide-awake, because they caught three sighs and four throat clearings. Way more than just the normal getting your voice to work after being silent for eight hours.

I forced myself to open my eyes. Dad's hands were wrapped around his coffee cup, and he stared at the steam like he was waiting for it to reveal the location of the holy grail.

Did I want to know what was on his mind? If it was good, he'd just spit it out. Did he smell the pot? I knew the air freshener wouldn't work. My neck was fully awake now and twitched ten times in a row. My hand squeezed, and the cereal fell off the spoon.

"What?" I asked.

"I cleared my schedule for next weekend. I thought we could see the space shuttle and make a weekend out of it."

"Really? Awesome! Thanks."

"And what would you think about Khory and Mr. Price joining us?"

Spending a whole weekend with Khory? "Oh yeah!" I said. Pieces of shredded wheat and milk flew out of my mouth. "Sorry."

"And about Khory, there is something else I wanted to talk to you about."

My neck twitched. I knew seeing the space shuttle wasn't the thing freaking him out.

"Now that you have a girlfriend, we need to talk about sex."

Dad kept his eyes on me like he needed to stress how serious this was, but his hands fidgeted with his coffee cup, and he had the beginning of a sweat mustache. If I wasn't on the receiving end of this, it would have been comical.

"Dad, let me save you the trouble." And humiliation for both of us. "They taught us all about it in health." And you didn't have to actually be involved with someone to hear things. Didn't he ever ride the school bus?

"I know, but I want to make sure you have all the correct information."

"I'm in tenth grade. It's a little too late to be questioning the education system."

"Please Troy, this is hard enough, if you can't tell."

"Sorry, go ahead. But I have to be at the bus stop in twenty-five minutes, and I'm not ready yet."

Dad let out a big exhale. "The most important thing is that you treat Khory, and any future girlfriends, with respect. Sex is not a game or a tool. You don't use someone just for that."

I nodded and took another mouthful of cereal. I got it. Respect.

"Now I'm not recommending you go out and have sex, because you are still young and this is your first relationship, but if it does come to that, make sure it's what you both want."

"I will."

"So you know the basics right? Intercourse, penis, vagina?"

I practically choked on a wheat square. "Dad, really? We don't have to do this. I know what all the parts are and where they go."

He nodded and wiped his upper lip. "What about blow jobs? Of course that's the slang term."

I dropped my spoon in the bowl and balled up my napkin. My appetite had officially disappeared.

"We learned that, too." I would have proved it by saying the technical names, but I couldn't remember them.

"If you're sure."

"I'm positive. And if I have any questions, I'll ask."

"Then just one more thing." He put three square plastic wrappers on the table. I prayed they were the hand wipes that came with rib dinners, but we hadn't had ribs in weeks. Dad was sharing his condoms with me. This was something I'd never recover from.

"So to be clear—"

"Respect and condoms." I stood up and brought my bowl to the sink before he decided I didn't get it and needed more details. "Thanks for the talk Dad, but I have to finish getting ready."

He sighed and took his first sip of coffee.

"And thanks for making time for the trip. It means a lot to me."

That brought a smile to his face. At least someone would have happy thoughts this morning.

· · · · · · · · · ·

After Terri left for work, I sat by the living-room window and waited for Mrs. Price to drop Khory off. Her parents said she could come over for a few hours after school today. To work on homework only. If we didn't get all our homework done, they'd know we wasted our time doing who-knows-what, even though they knew exactly what that was, and Khory wouldn't be allowed to come over again.

My stomach was queasier than if I'd ridden a roller coaster. I wasn't sure if it was from her coming over or the visuals from Dad's sex talk that continuously invaded my brain.

The silver Mazda pulled into the driveway. Khory got out of

the front passenger seat, slung her backpack over her shoulder, and practically skipped to the front door. I let her in and made sure to lock it. As soon as her mom drove away, she let me know the rest of the rules.

"Make sure all the doors are locked, no going out, except to the backyard, and absolutely no going in your bedroom." Khory winked at me. "So that means I want to see it."

A girl in my room? I would have bet a million dollars against myself of that ever happening. My neck twitched ten times. Twenty times. One, two, three, four, five, six. Did I just say *sex*? Seven, eight, nine, ten.

"Let me check it first to make sure there's no dirty underwear on the floor." I was getting better at this conversation thing, and it helped hide the fact that I was freaking out. Except the tics didn't let me hide anything. And did I count out loud?

I ran to my room. Of course, it was clean. I had no idea what a cool room looked like, but I bet it didn't involve posters of the solar system and rockets put up by an eight-year-old.

"Knock knock." Khory walked in, stood in the center, and turned in a circle. "It's like outer space in here. This is great!"

"Well, I figured this was the next best thing to being there."

Khory moved to the bookcase. "I didn't realize you were such a big reader."

"I used to be. I didn't go out much, so I read a lot. I still don't go out much, but now I play video games." I took her hand and pulled her close to me. "Video games are very important for hand-eye coordination, problem-solving skills, and teamwork."

She laughed and stared in my eyes. I kissed her before my body melted into a pool of sludge, then rubbed my hands on her back. They squeezed her shirt. If she noticed, she didn't mind.

Her body fell into mine, and then . . .

Jude cried from across the hall.

"Damn," I said.

We moved away from each other, and Khory followed me to his room. He peered over my shoulder and smiled a big four-tooth grin.

"Khory's going to hang out with us today." I lifted him out of the crib and laid him on the changing table.

"Hi, Jude. Did you have a nice nap?" she asked.

I changed his diaper and grabbed the blanket. We went to the family room. Khory sat on the floor next to him and took trucks and blocks out of the toy box while I got our backpacks. We had to get our homework done. Our parents would never believe we spent the whole time playing with a baby. Their minds were really inappropriate. I sat with my math book open on my lap and watched them stack blocks.

"I wonder if my parents would let me babysit," she said. "Do you still want to find one?"

"Yes. I was thinking that same thing. About you babysitting." It wasn't just for me, but it seemed no shadow could dim the light that covered her face right now. One step on her list for survival and another step on my list for death.

"You never told me why you can't babysit anymore. Are you bored with this job, or is there some hidden terror you're not telling me?"

I rubbed Jude's hair. I'd never get tired of being with him. "Well, one time he had explosive diarrhea. But that's it. Really."

She crinkled her nose.

"I'm going to see my mom, but the plane tickets are serious money, so I'm going to work some odd jobs. Walk dogs, cut grass kind of thing."

"Too bad Dad won't let anyone touch the grass. Just think, if we both made money, one day we could go on a real date, you know, to the outside world. Somewhere nicer than Taco Bell." She sighed and brought her knees to her chest, but the light didn't fade. "Being allowed to go places without a chaperone feels really good. I love the freedom. I don't want to be all talk like, yeah, I'm going to travel the world but not actually do it."

"It's good to start small. Restaurants. Movies. Work up to the big things."

"You're right." She sat up straight. "I'll be brave. I'll be like the Katniss of babysitting."

Her attitude was addictive. "Yeah, and I'll be like the Peeta of . . . something."

Khory pulled Jude onto her lap. I leaned against the couch, pulled out my phone, and opened to my list.

"Don't take my picture. I look terrible!" Khory grabbed the phone from my hand.

I gasped. My list. I lunged at her and snatched it back.

She stared at me. Eyes wide. Her mouth open. She probably wanted to ask what the hell I'd just done. I prayed she didn't. How would I explain it? I dropped my arm by my side and clicked the button to close the notes.

"You have an actual list? I thought it was just ideas, like one day I want to see the space shuttle."

"Well, you know I like organization," I said and bowed my head. That was the first time I used my obsession as an excuse.

She reached her hand out. "Can I see it? The list?"

"No way, too embarrassing." I didn't care how many times she flipped her hair. "It's really no big deal. I already told you the stuff on there. See the space shuttle, find my mom, those kinds of things."

"Then show me."

I stuck the phone in my backpack. Her eyes followed it until it was out of sight. She frowned.

I put my head down. It wasn't a lie. I wasn't thrilled for her to know that in my entire life I never expected to get more than a kiss.

"Okay, fine, don't show me," she said. "But at least tell me what brave act you're going to do?"

Even I knew that "okay, fine" meant something different when said by a girl with her lips pressed together. Just like she knew I was hiding something. And for a girl to think her boyfriend had a secret was deadly.

I went through the list in my mind. Driving. Telling people

about the Tourette. I'd already missed a bunch of opportunities for that one. Really, how difficult could it be to talk to a bunch of smart-phone-addicted kids who didn't pay attention anyway?

And Khory. We sort of talked about it already when I mentioned Mom. So why was it so hard to say, "Hi, I'm Troy. I have Tourette syndrome."

"I'm going to drive," I said instead. Chicken. "And what makes that list-worthy is that my Dad won't let me."

I grabbed my math notebook and flipped to our assignment. "We have to get this done, remember? I want you to come back."

Somehow, between playing with Jude and distracting her from my list, we got our homework done. Okay, we squeaked it out at the very last minute, but everything was finished. At least for her. My dad didn't give me that ultimatum, so I saved my work for later.

That wasn't a good idea now that I was trying to read *A Fare-well to Arms*. I couldn't stop thinking I'd missed another opportunity to cross something off the list. And it should have been an easy one. If I couldn't actually say the name *Tourette* with Khory, what hope did I have with anyone else?

I sighed. Despite my fear, it had to be done. It was on the list for a reason, and I had to stick to the plan. There was no choice but to stop being a baby, suck it up, and do it. Who cared what the kids said or did? I wouldn't be around to hear it for much longer. And that concluded my pep talk for this evening. I shut off the light and lay in the dark. Rah, rah, cheer, cheer. I was getting closer.

MARCH 17

Khory was going to be the perfect babysitter. She knew it. It was obvious the night she met Jude. Unfortunately, it wasn't my choice.

Which brought up two problems. The first was money. Everything came back to that. Money to find Mom, money for Gravity Redefined, and I guess money for my funeral. Not that I needed one. I wouldn't be there.

To solve problem number one, Dad had to agree to pay someone to babysit. I didn't know the current rate, but it had to be more than an iTunes gift card and the occasional twenty-dollar bill he gave me. Which led to the second, and equally humongous, problem.

I had to take myself out of the equation. If it was just about money, why not just ask for more? That's what made this problem so huge. Obviously, I couldn't admit the real reason I needed to find a replacement babysitter, so there was only one choice: tell him the truth. Sort of.

The question was, which option to use?

Option one: guilt. In this one I would explain that after six years,

I finally had a social life. Of course, that meant money! And since I was more comfortable leaving the house these days (a small lie), I thought I'd do some odd jobs around the neighborhood.

I sighed. I wasn't sure that would work. It would mean convincing him I wanted to go outside and work until my muscles ached and my sweat stank so bad I offended myself. Any other kid would just ask for more money.

Yeah, it had to be option two: extreme guilt.

This had the same guilt-provoking reason as the first, with the addition of being an opportunity for Mr. Price to get used to Khory's independence.

Since I wasn't as experienced at the whole smothering-your-kid-with-guilt thing as adults were, I had to be sure I didn't overdo it. Too much and Dad would say no. Too little and he'd say no.

Jude's voice came through the monitor. Not a cry, but the ramblings of a baby deep in conversation with the stuffed turtle in his crib. I tossed my geography book on the table and went to his room. We went through the routine, then to the family room and plopped down in our usual spots. His smile warmed me. I slumped against the couch. I was going to miss knowing if he'd have lots of friends and what he would be when he grew up.

I grabbed my book and opened to page 285, but the words swam around the page and my eyes crossed. Homework wasn't going to happen right now. It could wait anyway. I needed to spend as much time with Jude as I could so that he'd remember me.

My hand squeezed together, released, then squeezed again. Jude held a bear out for me. I took it and squished. He frowned. His teeny hand and fingers morphed into a twisted, broken skeleton. I pushed a train toward him. I had to talk to Dad tonight.

"Jude, you want Khory to babysit you, right?"

He looked up from the train at the sound of her name. Yeah, who wouldn't.

· · · · · · · · · ·

Dad rolled up his uniform sleeves and started making dinner. A bag of green beans in the microwave, pork on a plate to go in next, and instant mashed potatoes in a pot on the stove. Besides the hum of the microwave and occasional bang of a spoon, the kitchen was silent.

Bad day? Was he tired? Maybe tonight wasn't the best night to talk about babysitting, but Khory and I had everything worked out. She'd ask her dad. I'd ask mine. Then we'd compare notes, we hoped while our dads talked and worked out the details. We didn't have an alternative plan if one of our parents was cranky.

I set the table, and Dad brought two plates over. His eyes drooped. He sighed and plopped into the chair.

"Bad day?" I separated my food.

"*Huh?* Yes, I went to a call of an overdose. A teenager. Beautiful girl, smart, but played around with heroin like it was candy. I was with her parents when they signed the paperwork to commit her to a rehab facility." He slumped in his seat and stared at his food.

Heroin's hardcore. I heard rumors about people doing it in my school. Even after teachers had shoved antidrug information down our throats every year since seventh grade. I know I smoked pot, but I wasn't being judgmental. Heroin and pot, there was no comparison. Right?

"How was your day?" he asked.

"Good. Same as usual," I said.

Dad sliced open his pork, and I caught a smile as the steam escaped from the middle. Microwaves can be temperamental. Most of the time our food required a second heating. He fed Jude a few tiny pieces of pork and a glob of mashed potatoes. Jude ate it like it was chocolate cake. Just wait, buddy, you'll get the good stuff soon. I counted and cut my food into ten pieces.

"So . . ." I started.

Then stopped. What was my problem?

Dad watched me. Waiting for another knife incident? It pissed me off, so I just spit it out.

"Can Khory babysit Jude a few days after school? I was thinking about doing some neighborhood jobs. Oh, and you'd have to pay her."

Dad stopped chewing and tilted his head. Wasn't that clear? Okay, now I understood why we had debate projects in school. I took a deep breath: time to present the arguments.

"See, now that I have a girlfriend, I'll have to get Khory a birthday present. And Jay always drives, so I want to pay him for gas. Sometimes we get food. So it would be good to pay my way."

See what a good friend I was? Dad nodded, but before he could speak, I went on. Option two: extreme guilt.

"It would be good for Khory, too. She's a really responsible person, and if you let her do this, it would show her parents she can be independent. She has dreams and goals. To go out places. To travel. After school's done, of course."

I let out a big exhale and squeezed the fork. "Wait! Please don't tell her parents about traveling. It's just an idea."

"Troy, it's okay." He put his hand on mine. I let go of the fork. "I won't say anything. Actually, I'm happy. I would hate for her, or you, to be afraid to explore the world."

Yeah, goals, I got you. I had them, too. I moved the food around on my plate. "So, she can babysit?"

"I figured the money issue would come up sooner or later. I should have offered to pay you more long before this."

"But I don't want you to," I said. "I kind of want to go out and do stuff." I didn't know what else to say. He'd never believe lines like "the hard work makes me feel good" or "I feel like I've accomplished something." Please, I only felt that when I'd beaten a video game. So I left it at stuff.

"I'm really happy you are getting out of the house, meeting friends, and that you have a girlfriend. I hated seeing you sit home every day. I wasn't sure what to do, but you've taken charge and done it yourself."

If his minispeech wasn't such a shock to me, I'd have made a joke about it being a therapy-type revelation Hardly Qualified would have been proud of. But that much emotion from him made my neck twitch faster. I didn't know he was capable of it.

"So, that's a yes to Khory babysitting?"

"Yes," Dad said.

"Can you talk to her Dad and let him know? It'll probably be better coming from you."

"Sure. I'll call him after dinner."

"Thanks!" My body tingled. My face scrunched up. Good stress.

"What about you? Have you thought about what you want to do when you graduate?"

I moved pieces of pork around my plate and regrouped them. We never talked about it because there wasn't anything to say. I couldn't tell him the truth.

"I like space," I said.

"Yeah, I kind of figured since you still have the posters in your room, and the only place you've ever asked to go was the Air and Space Museum."

Not true, Dad. I asked to see Mom.

"You are smart enough to do anything in that field you want. Maybe you'll get some ideas this weekend."

Smart enough maybe, but not controlled enough.

We finished eating and cleared the table. I offered to do all the dishes while Dad gave Jude a bath to speed things up. Khory texted and said she talked to her parents. Her dad was nervous but could be swayed if my dad sold it right. *Ugh.* Good luck with that. Dad was a facts-only kind of guy. There were 6,232 burglaries last year, and 2,177 robberies. Oh, and this year we'll have to add one more to the drug-overdose count.

I filled the sink and swirled the bubbles around like I was five and taking a bubble bath. I'd washed one pot by the time Dad came back in the kitchen with a wet shirt and Jude in Thomas the Train footie pajamas. My neck twitched double time.

I took a deep breath and let it out. I squeezed my hand, and water and soap squirted from the sponge across the counter. I tried something new to relax. With my eyes closed, I pictured an empty warehouse. Then the space shuttle behind the gray rope. Then me.

"Hank? Hi, it's Clark."

I spun around flinging soap on the floor. *Mr. Price, please don't let us down.* I dried my hands and grabbed my phone.

ME: They're talking.
KHORY: Are you listening? I will now
ME: Yes

I lingered by the sink pretending to wash dishes. I didn't want Dad to think I was eavesdropping, but if he wanted privacy, he could have gone in the other room.

"Troy wants to start doing odd jobs around the neighborhood," Dad said. He put Jude on the floor, then sat at the table and flipped through the mail. He nodded a few times and mumbled, "*um huh.*"

My phone beeped.

KHORY: They're talking about you.

ME: Good?

KHORY: Yes.

"It's been a big change, but I'm glad he's getting out there."

Ugh. I hated when people talked about me, and knowing Khory was listening made it ten times worse.

Dad listened, then frowned.

"I understand. Yes. I can't imagine. *Um huh.*"

KHORY: They're talking about me

ME: Good?

KHORY: No

My chest tightened. Not good about her, or she couldn't babysit? I squeezed the sponge over and over. Decision made after a two-minute conversation? I threw the sponge in the sink, went to the table, and stood next to Dad. He stared at the mail and shuffled through the envelopes again. He glanced at me, then put them in a neat stack and turned them face down.

"Jude is eleven months old," Dad said to Mr. Price.

I stared at him. Give me something. A hint. Good or bad. I brought my hands up, palms open. Dad shrugged. Mr. Price was still undecided. Well, that was encouraging. Anything's better than a flat-out no.

"Yes, we have an alarm," Dad said.

KHORY: No

What? I collapsed in the chair. How could Mr. Price say no? Khory and I needed this so much.

"I understand. Yes, absolutely. *Um huh.* See you then. Bye." Dad peeked at me, scooped up the mail, and stood up. "He said no. Well, not right now. He wants to give it some thought."

"Okay," I mumbled.

Dad hiked Jude up on his hip and sighed. He looked worn out, but his face softened. I appreciated him trying, and my heart ached knowing the secret I kept. These were little steps for him. I wished they'd come sooner. I turned away and put my head down.

"He did say he'd think about it," Dad said. "Are you sure you're okay?"

"Yeah." But it was a lie.

I went to my room and lay in bed. This would have been huge for Khory and her dad. By the time we graduated high school, they would have been ready for anything. Then it hit me. Actually, smacked me in the face. I said *we*. When *we* graduated. That was two and a half years away, and I'd be a memory by then.

My neck twitched ten times. Fast and hard. I rubbed it, then rolled over on my right side. It hurt that way, too. See, nothing had changed. I wasn't having second thoughts. Somehow Khory's life would be great, and just because mine seemed incredible right now, it didn't change anything. Especially when I knew Khory would be brave like Katniss and leave. I pulled my phone off my night table, went to my list.

1. Meet someone else with Tourette syndrome—COMPLETED
2. Give away my Tim Howard autographed pictured
3. Get my first kiss—COMPLETED
4. Be pain-free—COMPLETED
5. Find a babysitter for my baby brother—IN PROGRESS
6. See the space shuttle—MARCH 20?
7. Talk about Tourette in public
8. Drive a car
9. Talk to Mom
10. Commit suicide

MARCH 20

Imagine Dragons music played through my phone. I popped up and threw off the blanket. Saturday morning. Seven o'clock. I had to pack, then pump coffee into Dad so we could pick up Khory and Mr. Price. We had a space shuttle to see.

I grabbed my phone and ran to the kitchen. Jude's voice met me before I got there. He was in his high chair up to his elbows in a yellow mashed-up something that couldn't be identified without a forensics kit. But he obviously liked it, because he palmed the concoction into his mouth.

Terri sat across from him, her hand wrapped around a steaming coffee cup. Her body may have been in the upright position, but her brain wasn't. She lifted her head a millimeter. "You're up early."

"The Discovery! We're going to the Air and Space Museum today." I checked the time on my phone. "Where's Dad? Did he pack already?"

"Why don't you have breakfast? Your dad should be up soon."

I poured cereal and milk into a bowl and sat next to Jude. The cereal wasn't appetizing after seeing the mush stuck to his arm. Either that or my stomach wasn't calm enough to actually eat anything, and it wasn't ideal to mix food, a queasy stomach, and a long car ride with my girlfriend.

I poured breakfast down the sink and went to my room to pack. Dad and Mr. Price thought it would be fun to do the tourist thing in Washington, D.C., first. Whatever. As long as I got to see the space shuttle and spend all weekend with Khory. I dumped the books out of my backpack and stuffed in an extra pair of jeans, underwear, and a shirt. I got dressed, balled up my pajamas, and stuck them in, too. Then brushed my teeth and took my medicine. Ten minutes. Ready.

Dad, on the other hand, stood by my bedroom door in worn-out sweatpants and a T-shirt. I raised my eyebrows. I wasn't what anyone would call fashionable, but even I wouldn't go outside like that.

"Don't worry. I'll change."

Seven thirty. I texted Khory. Based on the number of bottles and brushes in her bathroom, packing could take a while.

ME: Are you awake?

KHORY: Yes.

ME: Ready?

KHORY: Yes. Waiting for you.

I went to Dad's room. His bathroom door was closed. What if there was traffic? I took a deep breath and leaned against his bedroom doorway. The invisible hand squeezed my chest. My neck twitched, and my hands squeezed together. What if the car broke down and we never made it? I hit my chest to jump-start my lungs and tried to take a breath. A tiny bit of air got in. Just enough to keep me from passing out.

Dad came out of the bathroom. "Relax. I'm going to fill a travel mug with coffee. Give me ten minutes. Why don't you put my bag in the trunk?"

"Okay." I picked up his duffel bag and went to the car. I must have gone through a thousand rounds of ten before he finally came out and said it was time to go.

. . . .

Khory waited for us on the driveway. Her hair was shiny and smooth, and the sun highlighted strands of red.

Dad pulled to the curb.

"Don't park on the grass," I said. "Mr. Price is very anal about his yard."

"I'm good. I'm on the street."

Khory ran to the car as I got out. She gave me a quick kiss and bounced up and down. I thought space was my interest, but I loved that she shared my excitement. She glanced at my dad, then at me and back to my dad. Wait. I knew that move. They had a secret.

"Go ahead and tell him," Dad said. "It was your idea."

"Do you remember when Jay told us about Gravity Redefined?" Khory asked.

The zero-gravity place where you could feel like an astronaut? The one that was thousands of dollars?

I nodded, but with all my twitching and scrunching, they probably didn't notice. "Yeah," I said.

Khory beamed. "Mrs. Frances knows one of the people who works there. He runs the academic program for high school students."

My body tingled. I wanted her to say we'd be going there, but it was thousands of dollars.

"Okay," I said.

"Not just okay. Mrs. Frances arranged for us to get a tour and for you and her to do the simulator." She grabbed my hand. "Aren't you excited?"

"I'm . . ." I looked at Dad. Not that I didn't believe her, but I must have heard her wrong. "Is this true?"

"Yes. Khory came up with the plan and worked out all the details."

"And Mrs. Frances is going, too?" I asked.

"Of course," Khory said. "She said it's part of the summer program she mentioned. Apparently, you're the guinea pig."

I figured eventually I'd be the test subject for something, but I assumed it would be a radical non-FDA-approved medication or electroshock therapy. Who knew it would be for something as awesome as zero gravity?

I pulled Khory to me and hugged her. "Thank you. Thank you," I whispered in her ear. I squeezed her tighter. With her close, the pain and embarrassment were tolerable. She was the drug I needed to survive.

Mr. Price walked up, and Khory and I separated. We stuffed their bags into the trunk and got on the road. Gravity Redefined was in New York, so we were skipping D.C. and driving straight there. I sank into the seat and watched her read *Lord of the Flies*. We promised to get our homework done in the car, so I turned back to my own book, read, and reread the first page of chapter three before finally giving up. It was nowhere near as interesting as she was.

I reached toward her hand and held it, which made the urge to touch it nonexistent. Khory glanced over and smiled, even when I squeezed too hard.

She put her book down. "So, have you gotten any calls about jobs?"

"Yeah, I've gotten two from women." *Ugh.* I sounded like a player. Heat rose in my cheeks. I needed note cards to talk to her, or an earpiece with someone cool feeding me lines. "I meant guys wouldn't call me to do stuff like rake leaves and clean cobwebs."

"I think with the money you make, you should take me to New Mexico to see the world's largest pistachio."

I laughed. "Really, the world's largest pistachio?"

"It's a real place, I swear," she said.

"Okay, I believe you. I guess," I said.

"Well then, how about Missouri to hike the nuclear waste adventure trail?"

Her eyes twinkled. Her pink lip gloss sparkled. I wanted to taste the strawberry, but it would've probably made Dad turn the car around.

We spent the next three hours doing math and Chemistry homework and staring out the window. I watched the trees and signs fly by, but my brain couldn't just take in the scenery. I counted to ten. Then again. And repeat. I figured I'd break a record in the number of rounds counted in one sitting. Unfortunately, it wasn't celebration-worthy.

"Tonight we'll do a little sightseeing. Go to Times Square if you kids are interested," Dad said as we crossed the state border into New York.

"Sure," Khory said

"Okay," I said.

My neck twitched. Faster and faster. My muscles burned. I squeezed Khory's hand. She squeezed back and grinned. She was excited, but I wondered how I'd walk out there with all those people. I doubted New York City had a slow lane like PH High. What would happen after I took ten steps? What would I bend down and touch? If I wasn't trying to suck in air, I would have had another perfectly still moment.

Before I knew it, the six-hour ride was over. Mr. Price was talking hotels, and the skyscrapers were getting closer. Soon we were in the city. Khory and I tried to catch glimpses of the Empire State Building and Times Square.

We parked at the DoubleTree Hotel near Times Square and

checked in. Dad and I had a room on the fifth floor, and Khory and her dad were on the sixth. My hands tightened around the backpack strap as Dad and I got out of the elevator and I read the room direction sign. The good news was we weren't the last room. The bad news was we were three rooms from the end. Dad walked ahead of me as I calculated it would be at least four rounds of ten-count-bend-downs to get to it. I pushed away images of grime-covered shoes shuffling their way down the hallway, along with suitcase wheels that had been dragged up from the subway, and tried to convince myself this floor was sterile compared to what I'd touched in the hospital's bathroom.

When we got inside our room, I washed my hands. I moved the soap over my palms, the backs, and in between my fingers, then focused on my fingertips. Twelve counts of ten. Two minutes, right? Or was that for brushing teeth?

I dried my hands, went to the room, and fell onto the bed.

"Hey, I thought we'd get something to eat and walk around a little. Do the tourist things," Dad said.

I sat up. I didn't want to walk around. I didn't want to touch the street. This wasn't my idea of fun. It was exhausting enough to go where I had to.

"What's wrong? Are you upset we're not going to the museum? We thought you'd like this better."

I nodded. I would've told him the simulator was a dream come true if I could've talked.

Dad grabbed my arm and pulled me off the bed. "Come on, we're supposed to meet them downstairs."

The invisible hand wrapped itself around my chest again. Its hold was much tighter than Dad's. I'd prepared myself for the museum. The ten-count-bend-downs, the stares, people crossing to the other side of the room. It was a sacrifice I would suffer through for my list. But New York City? Eight million people? I couldn't do it. Dad's face swam around in front of me. My stomach rolled along the waves. I fell back onto to the bed before I face-planted on the floor.

"What's wrong? Are you feeling okay?" Dad asked.

Definitely not. I gasped. Air couldn't get to my lungs. I was suffocating. I squeezed the comforter. No! I had to die on my own terms. On the date I picked. Not because of a detour to the most populated city in the country.

"Troy, talk to me," Dad demanded.

His voice was as forceful as a CPR chest compression. I sucked in a huge amount of air and held it until it reached every millimeter of my lungs.

"I don't go out," I whispered. Air conservation was a necessity. Just in case.

"What do you mean? You don't want to go out?"

I shook my head. "I don't go out."

"Of course you do. You go to school and out with Khory and your friends."

"I don't walk unless I have to."

Dad's eyebrows scrunched up. Did I really have to explain it? That was him in the hallway with me, right? My heart felt heavy. Mom would have understood. But then Dad nodded.

"I guess I never thought how disruptive tics, the bending, could be." He sat next to me. "Are they painful?"

Now he wanted to know how I felt? After almost ten years?

"Some are. The bending is exhausting. And annoying. And embarrassing." I stared at my hands balled into fists.

"I'm sorry, I didn't even think. You've been doing it for so long now, I just see it as a part of you. Like someone who limps," Dad said.

"It's okay." But it wasn't.

Dad sat still. What a concept. I was jealous.

"How about I tell Hank we'll meet up with them later? You and I can order room service or go downstairs to the restaurant, grab some food, and talk some more. We never get time just the two of us."

The invisible hand tickled my chest at the thought of talking. We didn't do that. I took a breath. But maybe we could. I nodded.

Dad took out his phone and called Mr. Price while I counted. I shook my head and it felt good. Not as an urge that was fulfilled, but because I remembered the counting didn't work before the frustration overwhelmed me. I replaced the numbers with the empty warehouse and felt my shoulders slip down my back. My breathing steadied, and I stood up. I wasn't sure I was ready for Dad's questions, but at least I could handle the walk down the hallway.

MARCH 20

Over burgers and fries in the hotel restaurant, Dad asked me what happened upstairs.

"An anxiety attack." I was well researched.

"Do you have them often?"

I knew where he was going with this. For a cop so against drugs, he was pretty quick with the prescription meds as a cure.

"Not enough for more medication," I answered.

He nodded. "How is everything else? The Tourette and OCD. I'm sorry I didn't realize how you felt." He dropped the burger on his plate. The top bun bounced off. "I should have known. Seen the signs. But you're . . . different."

Different from Mom? "What do you mean? What signs?"

"It's how your mother was. She wouldn't go out, said she was happy spending quiet time at home, especially after you were born. But she was sad at missing the events in your life, like preschool graduation and school performances. If I'd recognized the depression earlier . . ." He played with his burger.

Is that what he thought?

"I'm not depressed," I insisted. "I have a girlfriend, friends, we're on our way to a zero-gravity simulator this weekend. I'm just tired. Tired of people, tired of the pain."

Dad's eyes went wide. It wasn't the same as being depressed. I was well researched on that, too. My neck twitched, and I squeezed my burger. I dropped it on my plate, wiped my hands on a napkin, and hid them in my lap. They squeezed together. Damn it, why couldn't I make them bleed?

I sat up straight. "But it's fine. Really. I'm used to it. Of course, some days are worse than others, but it's good."

"That doctor you used to see, the psychiatrist. Do you want me to call him again?"

I laughed. "Dr. Hardly Qualified? No thanks, he wasn't any help. Really, everything's fine. I've found my own relaxation technique. Sometimes I just forget to use it. Like upstairs."

I dragged a fry through the ketchup and ate it. Then another. And another. See, everything was normal. We were eating and bonding. But his brow was furrowed, his lips were pressed together, and he wouldn't take his eyes off me. I forced myself to finish the food, because what depressed kid would eat a huge hamburger, twenty-two fries, and a pickle?

· · · · · · · · · ·

I had two choices: either suffer through the annoyance, humiliation, and terror of walking the streets of New York City or stay at the hotel and risk Dad seeing me as a depressed, anxiety-driven kid who needed help before he followed in his mother's footsteps and ran away.

I wanted to pick the second one. I didn't care about New York City, Times Square, or anything else the place had to offer, but the look on Dad's face was clear: choice two came with conditions. Back to HQ, or worse.

So off we went.

We met Khory and her dad in the lobby at six o'clock. Her eyes were bright and her body moved far more than mine.

"We went to the Empire State Building. There are so many people Dad wouldn't let go of my hand. And when people bumped into us, and it's hard not to, he held on even tighter. But I loved the excitement."

I watched her eyes twinkle and her hair bounce as she talked. I was addicted to her and her emotions. She was better than any drug, and if she could maneuver through millions of people bumping into her, maybe I could find something to enjoy.

We left our hotel, and I took Khory's hand, hoping her dad wouldn't mind since someone was holding on to her, especially now that it was night. We walked down the street and turned a corner to the left. Right there in front of us was the biggest Light Brite I've ever seen. Welcome to Times Square.

The lights, noise, and crowds made me feel like I was inside a video game. My body was electric. I stopped, turned in a circle, and tried to take in all the lights. Buildings towered over us. Lights blinked and flickered to the sounds on the street below. It seemed like a jumbled mass of noise, but the place had its own beat, and my body thumped in tune with it. Okay, I admit it was pretty cool.

We walked down the street and went in and out of stores like Godiva Chocolates, M&M's World, and Midtown Souvenirs, with our dads following close behind. I fought the urge to count as we walked, but my brain was sucked in. I counted, then fought the pull to touch the ground. A few times I got away with half a bend, like a bow. The heat in my body grew as I waited for someone to bow back, but the tourists with "I Love NY" shirts and phones out all stared toward the skyline. Everyone else pushed through the crowds without a word. It seemed this was the one place you could really be invisible.

So I didn't fight it. I let my neck twitch and hands squeeze together. My face scrunched up, and I bent halfway. I was like a Broadway dance routine repeating the sequence until the big finale: the full bend-down.

That's when I saw the third invisibility level in this city. A homeless man slumped against a wall. A scruffy brown beard that may have been another color when clean, a tattered winter jacket, and his life in a bundle beside him. He picked up a used cigarette from the ground and put it to his lips. His eyes were vacant like there was nothing worth seeing anymore. The only ones who saw people at this level were either the height of five-year-olds or someone like me, who touched discarded gum on the sidewalk.

Khory was used to the ten-count-bend-down, but after our big talk at lunch, I felt Dad studying my every move. I glanced back at him. He smiled, or attempted to, because it was the lamest thing I'd ever seen. His lips may have turned up, but his eyes were all sadness and pity. In the one place I could have been invisible, I'd created my own audience.

MARCH 21

Through the car window I watched the skyscrapers turn into neighborhoods. We passed signs for roads leading to Ossining, Peekskill, and the West Point Military Academy. The map on my phone said we were heading north. The towns turned into fields with cows and horses, until one of the fields sported a two-story gray building with ground-to-roof windows. My face was plastered against the car window. I couldn't read the name on the building yet, but I saw the shape of airplane wings hiding behind it.

I spun toward Khory. She stared at me with a humongous grin. Her eyes brighter than the north star.

Dad pulled the car into the parking lot, and there, in big black letters, were the words "Gravity Redefined" and a picture of an airplane angled toward space. He barely stopped the car before I burst out and ran toward the building.

They met me at the door, and we walked into the lobby. Dad pulled a letter from an envelope and handed it to the man in the glass ticket booth.

"Go on in Mr. Hayes. Mr. Armbretch will meet you in the lobby."

I grabbed Khory's hand as we went through glass doors. My heart thumped in time with my neck twitch. My hands squeezed tight, and Khory's fingers were caught in the middle.

I dropped her hand. "Sorry. Did I hurt you?"

She rubbed her fingers, then shook her head, but she put her hands in her jacket pockets.

The lobby was a big, bright, round room with a glass-dome ceiling and SUV-size models of Enterprise, Challenger, and Discovery. There was also a car-size model of a Boeing 727. Panels on the walls explained the history of space flight and the history of the company, and there were pictures of celebrities who apparently went through the program, including an actor from the *Star Trek* series and a real-life astronaut.

Mrs. Frances and a short, older man wearing a gray flight suit appeared from double doors in the back and came toward us.

"I'm glad Khory told me how much you love astronomy," Mrs. Frances said. "Who knows, we may be standing next to a future astronaut."

"That would be great," I said and pushed out thoughts of my future going in a different direction.

Mrs. Frances turned to the man waiting patiently next to her. "Troy, Khory, this is Mr. Armbretch. He heads up the Gravity Redefined Education Program."

"Nice to meet you." He shook our hands.

The round of handshaking continued with our dads as my neck twitched, my hands squeezed together, and my face scrunched up. Even though my eyes bounced around, I caught Mr. Armbretch's look. He glanced at Mrs. Frances, his lips pressed into a smile like a wax statue, but I knew what he was thinking: *Him, a potential student for the education program and a real astronomy career?*

"Remember, I told you Troy has Tourette syndrome," Mrs. Frances said.

My face burned, and my neck twitched too fast to count.

Mr. Armbretch nodded, then explained the program. "Our goal at Gravity Redefined is to introduce astronomy to high school students, specifically those who wish to make this field a lifelong commitment." He sounded like a brochure. "We hope to do that with a hands-on approach that includes real-time experiments, seminars from industry professionals, and our simulator."

He clapped his hands together. "Well, now that I've given you the official company spiel, let's have some fun. I am sorry to say I only have approval to take two people on the simulator, so Mrs. Frances and Troy will follow me while the three of you will attend our Gravity Workshop. You won't experience parabolic flight and the effects of space, but you will learn about it, as well as the sciences behind space flight, and enjoy a few hands-on experiments."

My heart sank. Khory should get to go since she was the one who planned all this. I turned to her but didn't know what to say.

"This is for you." She grabbed my arm. "I hope this comes close to making your dream come true."

I caught my breath. I felt like a traitor. She had no idea what she just said, what she just did for me. And she would hate me when she found my actual dream was to die.

Mrs. Frances and I left the others with a group of people who had gathered near the lobby doors and followed Mr. Armbretch down a hallway with more pictures of astronauts, airplanes, and shuttles.

"We're headed to a conference room where you will check in and watch a preflight orientation video. It will explain the procedure and what you will be experiencing when you're up in the air."

We turned a corner, and he showed us into a large room where eight other people were waiting. There was no question I was the youngest, but even though it felt like butterflies were slamming around in my stomach trying to break free, I definitely was not the most scared person. That award went to a tall blonde lady. Her eyes were wide, and her hands shook despite the guy next to her holding them.

The excitement and the shaking lady were making my neck twitch at rapid speed. One twitch hit a nerve, and a sharp pain stuck me in the shoulder blade like a dagger. A definite ninety on the rate-the-pain scale. I bit my lip, and now that hurt, too. *Relax. If you don't, you'll barf on the plane.* I hoped that pep talk would work, but my talks usually sucked, and the urges to twitch, squeeze, and scrunch were stubborn. I skipped past HQ's breathing advice and went right to the image of the space shuttle and empty warehouse.

I pictured the body, wings, and wheels, and the pain in my back lessened. I took a few deep breaths. Oxygen in. Carbon dioxide out. Repeat.

"How are you doing?" Mrs. Frances asked.

"Good." I said, telling the truth for a change. "I'm really excited. This is the best thing anyone has done for me. Thank you."

"It is my pleasure, truly," she said. "Just promise me if I get sick on there, it will be our secret."

"Deal." I twisted my shirt, then turned to her. "Mrs. Frances, why me? Why didn't you take Mr. Frances to try this, or another student? It can't be just because Khory asked. I don't think she has that kind of power over anyone but me."

Mrs. Frances smiled. "Well, let me tell you, Mr. Frances is extremely envious, but he'll get over it." she said. "And why you? Because you have the most potential out of anyone in the class. In all my classes, actually."

"Potential?"

"To do anything you want. To be anything you want. I hope you don't let anything hold you back."

"Okay, everyone, have a seat and we'll get started," Mr. Armbretch said. "Troy, can you please kill the lights on your left?"

I flicked the light switches off, then sank into a chair. Except for the screen with the company's logo, the room was black. My muscles relaxed even more. I loved the dark and its gift of invisibility.

The video began, and a woman's voice came on.

"Welcome to Gravity Redefined. Today you will board a modified Boeing 727 that will take you to twenty-six thousand feet, then climb at full speed before nosediving. This will cause weightlessness, or zero gravity. During your time on the airplane, you will engage in approximately fifteen parabolic maneuvers. As you experience weightlessness, you will be able to float, flip, and soar just as the astronauts do."

There were mumblings and cheers throughout the group.

"If anyone is pregnant, has a heart condition, or is sensitive to motion sickness, they should excuse themselves at this point."

I had no idea if I had motion sickness. I'd never been on a plane before, or a roller coaster, but I did love the feeling of jumping over speed bumps on my bike. Did that count? It didn't matter. I had to experience this.

When the lights came on, everyone scanned the room, probably wondering who would be the first to puke. My money was on the blonde woman. Her face already had a green tint.

Next we were directed to locker rooms where we changed into flight suits and were given bottles of water. Then it was through metal detectors and X-ray machines, like at the airport, to the tarmac outside and the plane. My heart pounded.

Everyone rushed toward it like it was the lunch line and today was pizza today. With each step my neck twitched faster, and the urge to scream my excitement built up in my throat. I clamped my lips together. Mrs. Frances turned to me before she boarded the plane.

"Are you okay?"

"Great." I said. "You?"

"I think so."

I followed her up the ramp and into the empty fuselage. The walls, windows, floor, and ceiling were covered in white padding. The plane could double as a kids' gym or a psychiatric facility.

"Everyone please strap yourselves to the rope running along the sides of the plane," Mr. Armbretch said as he strolled through the cabin to check that we did it right. "We'll fly for approximately thirty minutes to our desired altitude, then the plane will fly upwards. I recommend you sit as still as possible. That's when people usually get sick. If you do, each flight suit has a few barf bags."

Good to know. I stuck my hand in my right pocket. Yup, there they were. I pulled one out and showed Mrs. Frances. She nodded and patted her right pocket. I stuck mine back in but kept my hand around them. I squeezed, then opened. Repeat.

"Flight crew, strap yourselves in," a voice announced from speakers in the ceiling.

Mr. Armbretch, a tall man, and a taller woman strapped themselves to the rope near the back of the plane and sat down.

The engines roared to life. The plane rolled forward. Faster and faster. Then up. My ears clogged. I swallowed hard, and they cleared. I wasn't great at making small talk, especially with a teacher, but Mrs. Frances didn't seem like she wanted to talk anyway. Her eyebrows were furrowed, and she stared at her hands.

"It will be fine," I said.

She nodded.

We sat quietly. I focused on where we were going.

"We're going up," Mr. Armbretch said. "Remember, stay as still as possible."

Really? He had to say that? The nose of the plane turned up, and my neck twitched. A wave of nausea rolled through my body. My hand squeezed around the bags again. I closed my eyes, tensed my muscles, and begged them to stay as still as possible. It was easier than I thought because suddenly each muscle felt like a hundred pounds. My neck wanted to twitch, but it was too heavy and collapsed near my shoulder. My shoulder didn't have the strength to meet it. I sat there lopsided.

"Get ready, we'll unbuckle in . . .," Mr. Armbretch said.

The weight of my arm lessened. I lifted my head.

"Five, four, three, two, one. Now!"

We unhooked ourselves from the rope. I expected to float up, but I stayed on the floor. I pushed against the wall and zoomed to the ceiling. Ah, now I got the importance of padding.

Mrs. Frances unhooked herself as I pushed off the ceiling with my finger and floated toward her. She smiled, gave me a little push, and laughed as I bounced off the wall. This was the opposite of being stoned. Then I'd been too lazy to lift my hand, but now I felt like I was made of air. My neck twitched, but there were no muscles to hurt. My head just lobbed to my shoulder, then bounced back up.

I spun around and did a forward roll. Then did a backflip and saw the blonde lady. She was still green and curled into a ball clutching a barf bag. What would happen if something escaped it?

"Back to the straps everyone. Round one is just about up," Mr. Armbretch said.

My heart sank as I strapped myself in.

The plane climbed again. I forced myself to stay still, squeezed my eyes shut, and balled up the barf bag to distract my neck. I listened to the engines until the noise stopped and Mr. Armbretch announced it was time to unhook again.

Round two of 1.8 g's to weightlessness. Mrs. Frances and I grabbed hands and did rolls together. Round three, we opened our water bottles. Bubbles escaped and floated around the cabin. We chased after them and gobbled them up. By round four, we were all experts. Even the blonde lady uncurled herself and "swam" by me.

For the next twenty minutes, I floated up and crashed to the floor. The weightlessness was a high, better than any drug. I was a cloud, big and puffy. No bones or muscles to hold me down.

I turned to Mrs. Frances. I wanted to hug her. "You have no idea how much this means to me. Thank you again for arranging this."

"My pleasure. You are a very special person. Do you know?"

I didn't know. Not in the way she meant. Kids at school called me special, but it was their way of saying I was a freak without getting in trouble. Mrs. Frances was sincere. Something I'd always remember.

I sighed, sank into the padding, and tried to get the weight-lessness feeling back. The wheels touched the ground. My neck twitched, and the shooting pain came back. I closed my eyes and imagined a cloud. For a few seconds I was floating.

MARCH 22

I would have loved a day off to recover, since we got back late last night, but we were forced to go to school because of tests. And I would have given anything to be back on that plane instead of in math with Mr. Nagel. I tried to get the feeling back, being pulled by the g-forces, then floating through the cabin, but every time my fingers touched the grimy school floor, I crashed back to reality.

Of course, Jay, Diego, and Rainn knew about it even before we went, and it seemed the entire school knew by the end of block two. It was a schoolwide game of telephone. I hoped this turned out better than the one I played in kindergarten when I said, "The dog shit on the carpet." Wouldn't you know it, that time everyone heard it correctly.

As soon as I walked into science, Mrs. Frances popped up and stood in front of the class, although no one noticed but me. People were deep into conversations about boyfriends, girlfriends, and an Instagram picture of a girl named Trish.

"Phones away everyone," Mrs. Frances said. "Troy, Khory, come up, please."

Up where? To the front of the class?

Most of the class slipped their phones into backpacks. I wanted to personally thank those who kept theirs out and their eyes off me.

"Yesterday Khory, Troy, and I went to Gravity Redefined, the company sponsoring the summer science program. I would love to talk about the workshops and simulators, but today I will give you a break from me and let you hear it from them."

Mrs. Frances took a step toward her desk, leaving us on display like animals in the zoo, which actually wasn't a far-off description of high school. I wanted to disappear into the wall, but my face was so hot, it had to be bright red and sticking out like a beacon. Thanks for blindsiding me, Mrs. Frances.

"Khory, you did the vomit comet?" Abhy asked, getting to the good stuff. No one wanted to know about a workshop.

"No," she said. "But Troy did."

Suddenly all twenty-five pairs of eyes were on me. No phones out. No heads on the desk. They stared at me. I took a step back.

One, two, three, four, five, six, seven, eight, nine, ten.

The invisible hand squeezed my chest. No sliding in slowly. No nice to meet you. Just right in for the squeeze. I planted my feet and took as deep a breath as I could, but a two-year-old couldn't live on that amount of air. My neck twitched. My hands squeezed together. I pictured the empty warehouse. A little air got in. Then I thought about floating and being the big, puffy cloud. I closed my eyes and put myself back in the plane.

Khory squeezed my hand. That one touch seemed to transfer her bravery like she was a superhero and her power was mind control. I lifted my hand. It wasn't weightless, but it wasn't balling itself up.

"So it's like floating," I said. "Kind of like you're a cloud. Really light. And you don't have to do much to move, just a push off the wall or ceiling. But if you push too hard, you'll bounce around like a Ping-Pong ball. It's kind of hard to explain. You really had to be there."

I opened my eyes. Talk about looking like an idiot. Everyone stared at me, but this time their noses weren't crinkled, they weren't pointing or laughing. They were smiling.

"What else did you do? I've seen videos of astronauts doing flips and stuff," Eric said.

"I did that. Front flips, backflips. We opened water bottles and chased drops of water."

"Did anyone get sick?" Esther asked and glanced at the teacher.

"No, I did not," Mrs. Frances said.

"But there was this one lady." I turned to Mrs. Frances. "The blonde lady, remember? She was pretty green for a while."

"So, would you do it again?" Spencer asked. "What was the best part?"

"I would do it again in a second. I'd live on that airplane if I could." I stared at the sea of faces. Everyone focused and interested.

Not even Mrs. Frances commanded this kind of attention. They wanted to know what I had to say.

"The best part was that my body wasn't in pain. For the first time since I was six, my neck didn't hurt, my hands didn't hurt. It was like I didn't have Tourette at all." I gasped. I said the word. In front of all these people. I squeezed my eyes shut. Then my hands. No laughs from the class, no comments about disinfecting my seat. I opened my eyes. They were still interested.

So I went on.

"That's why I do these movements. The neck twitches. It's Tourette. And when your head bobs to your shoulder ten, twenty times a minute or more, your muscles burn. But in the zero-gravity plane, I was like a cloud. Or a jellyfish. No muscles, no bones, just air."

"Yeah, I never thought that you'd have pain like that. Sorry, dude. But it's so awesome that the experience took it away," Abhy said. "Mrs. Frances, will we do that in the summer program?"

"We are still working out the details, but that is what we have planned." She nodded toward Khory and me. "Okay, class, if there are no more questions. We have our new chapter to go over."

Khory and I went back to our seats. My legs were shaking, and my stomach did flips. I actually said the word out loud, and to people notorious for teasing me. I didn't mean to, it just slipped out. And I survived it. Khory smiled at me as she leaned over and grabbed her notebook. I grinned back like I'd just leapt a tall building in a single bound.

Mr. Price changed his mind about Khory babysitting. Sort of. She could take care of Jude only if her mom came over, too. Taking care of a baby was a huge responsibility, her dad said, and she had to be ready. But Khory and I knew the truth: he had to be ready. Hopefully he would be soon. I had a deadline.

After school, I rushed home and changed for my first job, cleaning rain gutters for a man who had broken his leg playing football. Mr. Cooper would never ask anyone to do household chores for him, but since he had broken his leg playing football (which he repeated several times), he couldn't get on a ladder. The cast would be on for six weeks since it was a bad break, as happens with tackle football (sigh), and his rain gutters couldn't wait that long. So basically, could I clean them? Yes, yes, I could.

But first I had an amazing idea to check out. I told Spencer I'd live on the airplane if I could, then I thought, why not? I grabbed a snack, sat down at my laptop, and googled International Space Station.

The idea of living in weightless conditions was intriguing, much better and more productive than living stoned. And no way I'd be able to get the smell of pot past Dad forever. NASA's website had a lot of information on the space station: bios on past and current crew members, experiments like engineering designs and biomedical research, and classroom Skype lessons. Some astronauts were lucky enough to have spent a year there. That's a good start, but I wanted to know if I could stay longer.

The doorbell rang. I closed my laptop and dashed to the front door.

"Hi," Khory said.

She practically glowed. There was no shadow today. I wanted to pull her toward me and kiss her soft, strawberry-flavored lips. Then let my hand slide down her hair and get lost in the curls at the end. Instead I moved to the side and let her and her mom in. We closed and locked the door.

"Are you ready to babysit?" I asked.

"Yes, I'm excited. What time do you have to leave?"

"Soon. I'm not sure how much work I'll be doing, and I didn't get much homework done when I came home."

I went over Jude's routine with them. He was a pretty easy baby, and I already knew he loved Khory. She walked to the garage, and I got on my bike.

"Tell Jude I said hi. Remember, he likes his blanket with him in the family room, and there are little containers of mashed fruit in the pantry."

"Are you sure you're okay with this? You sound like his mother." She kissed me. "If I have any questions, I'll call you."

"I love you," I said.

"I love you, too."

Mr. Cooper's house was two stories with a tall, peaked roof and a yard Mr. Price would be proud of. Clearly the owner hadn't let a broken leg keep him from chores on the ground. There wasn't a single layer of dust or speck of dirt anywhere. I wiped my hand on my jeans before knocking.

Mr. Cooper opened the door, and it was clear why he needed someone to clean his rain gutters on the second story. He may have played football, but he was no Peyton Manning. He had a large stomach that hung over his jeans and goggle-thick glasses. Even if he didn't have a cast up to his knee, I wouldn't have recommended he climb to the top of a ladder.

I smiled, then introduced myself. Mr. Cooper studied me and scrunched up his face. "You okay? Something wrong with your neck? You're not on drugs, are you?"

My face grew warm, and I wanted to shrink into a ball. Was I limited to one explanation in my lifetime?

"No, Sir." Not the kind he meant. "It's Tourette."

His face scrunched up a little more, then he shrugged his shoulders. "Whatever."

I said it again. Twice in one day. And he didn't care either. I practically floated behind him to the garage.

I climbed to the top of the ladder. He watched for a few minutes, maybe to make sure I wouldn't fall and break my leg, then went inside. When the door clicked, I pulled out my earbuds and turned on music. Today was a great day for Shinedown.

I thought about the space station. I had questions—well, one big one that Mr. Armbretch could probably answer, if he didn't laugh me out of the room first.

ME: Assuming I can get there, would it be possible for me to spend the rest of my life on the International Space Station?

Mr. A: Why would you even consider that? Didn't you see Matt Damon in The Martian? All he wanted to do was get back to his family.

ME: I don't care about a family or kids.

Mr. A: Well, did you ever think someone else might want a turn? Or funding could run out? And we have no idea what long-term zero gravity does to a person.

ME: Dude, does it look like I care?

I came back to reality and focused on my job before I fell off the ladder. I pulled out sticks and twigs, got the hose and washed away leaves and cobwebs, then made sure the water flowed freely. Sweat dripped into my eyes. A shower was mandatory as soon as I got home, but the physical activity felt good. It lessened my stress, which lessened my tics.

Tourette. I still couldn't believe I said it out loud in class. "Tourette." I said it again, although no one was on the roof to hear me. I still didn't like the sound of it and wouldn't be shouting it in the hallway, but I'd completed another item on my list. Another step toward number ten. But the more steps I took toward it, the less sure I was about my final destination.

MARCH 25

A little time with Khory, another job, and a TS meeting. I had actually looked forward to today. It could've been the day I shared my story. If I could talk about Tourette with my science class, why not with a bunch of ticcers who would definitely understand? And if I could share good news, maybe the Isenhours would take the Tim Howard picture for David.

I peeked in on Jude, who was still sleeping. He'd be asleep for the night by the time I got home. I sighed. We still had time. And with the way life was going, we might've had even more.

The silver Mazda pulled up, and Khory got out. I met her at the front door, and she waved to her mom.

"What's going on? She's not staying?"

"No. I'm on my own today. Surprise!" Her eyes twinkled, and she grinned. "But I'm a little freaked out, so don't make a big deal about it. Okay?"

"Okay. I promise."

Did this mean I found a babysitter for Jude and could check

it off my list? I wanted to pull out my list right there. But really, I wanted to celebrate for her. This was a huge step toward her freedom. I hated to leave.

I kissed her. "Sorry, but I have to go."

"Go. Do your sweaty work and leave me in this incredibly air-conditioned house."

I kissed her again, then rode to Mrs. Blackwood's house with a surge of extra energy. The house was similar to Mr. Cooper's but weathered and worn. Maybe she called me because her neighbors complained. People in my neighborhood were notoriously cranky about messy yards.

I knocked on Mrs. Blackwood's door. My neck twitched, and my hands squeezed together. I didn't want her to think I was a crazy drug addict. Be the cloud, I told myself, be the cloud. My shoulders relaxed a bit.

The curtains near the door moved; then the door opened. I stood as straight as possible, but there was no need. The woman who opened the door was old—original American settlers old. And her eyes were so cloudy, she wouldn't see me even on a sunny day.

"Are you Troy?" she asked and squinted at me.

"Yes, Ma'am."

"Would you mind cleaning the porch? I have been told I need to paint. And try not to hurt the little critters living in the corners."

I glanced around and wondered what her idea of "little" was.

"What a nice boy. My kids are grown and claim their lives are too busy to come help."

I hoped she would skip the whole I-raised-those-kids-and-wiped-their-dirty-noses part. And to give them the benefit of the doubt, based on her age, her kids were probably old themselves and hired teenagers to clean cobwebs, push lawn mowers, and paint. Hmm, I should've gotten their names. Jobs = money, and money = a plane ticket.

Mrs. Blackwood went inside. I turned on Shinedown and fought with a spider determined to keep his home, but I won in the end and relocated him to the grass. I finished the job in forty-five minutes, took the money, and graciously accepted the compliments on my work. Of course I'd help her again. Because I was such a nice boy. And I needed money.

· · · · · · · · · ·

I rode my bike to the city bus stop, locked it in the bike rack, and took my position away from the people on the bench. Most were regulars, and you'd think we'd nod to each other, or maybe say "hey." But no. They shifted their gaze away from me, just like the first time. Did I really have to explain it to everyone? Maybe I should just wear a sign on my back.

When the bus came, I counted my way to the back, slid into the seat, and leaned my head against the window. The door closed with a *whoosh*. So much for my big breakthrough.

The bus sped around a corner. The buildings grew larger and closer until the bus pulled to a stop. I shuffled out and made my way to the hospital, bending down and letting my right fingers drag across the rough sidewalk. Then ten steps, and my left fingers dragged on the ground. It felt good to be balanced.

At the front door, someone zipped around me and opened it. I didn't even know anyone was near me. That would have made a perfect anti-crime commercial: kid, totally oblivious to anything except the chewed gum on the sidewalk, robbed as he enters the hospital.

"Thanks," I mumbled.

"My pleasure, Troy," Mr. Isenhour said.

I glanced at him. He smiled, but something about him told a different story. His hair stuck out, and the muscles in his face were tense. Mrs. Isenhour didn't look much better. Her head turned back and forth, and she had dark lines under her eyes that weren't from makeup. I thought about handing them the folder and picture, but this wasn't the time for that discussion.

Mr. Isenhour took his wife's hand. "Do you want to go to the bathroom before we go in?"

She obviously didn't have the same issues with the bathroom floor that I did, or he never would have suggested it. Unless he didn't know. But they looked like they shared a lot. Especially the bad stuff.

She put her head down and shook it.

"David had a few rough days at school," he said.

"Sorry." I was. I knew it sucked.

242

I followed them into the meeting room but stayed in the back as they moved toward the front. Without the company of Khory, I felt like a beacon, bright and flashing, calling people to stare at me. Even in this group where people saw me, not the tics.

Susan started the meeting. For a second, I thought about sharing my zero-gravity experience to introduce myself, an icebreaker kind of thing, but then Mr. Isenhour started talking about David's week.

"As you know, David was allowed several exceptions because of the Americans with Disabilities requirements. Well, a few of his classmates didn't like the idea. I'm not sure if they were jealous, but they took it out on him." Mr. Isenhour took a deep breath. Mrs. Isenhour had her head down but kept turning it back and forth. "He's been bullied all week. Called names, pushed around on the bus, and one child ripped up his notebook."

"I'm so sorry to hear this," Susan said.

"I hope those kids were suspended," a man two rows in front of me said.

"They were suspended. The school did a good job of taking action, but the incidents set David back emotionally. We had just gotten him to a good place at school."

I sank in my chair. I hated to say that it would only get worse, but his mom would know all about that. No way she had a fantastically wonderful childhood. Which brought me back to the question of why they wanted kids in the first place.

The rest of the meeting was filled with ups and downs. People on meds and off, being a productive member of society and locking themselves in their houses. I wanted to share, tell them about my zero-gravity experience and feeling like a cloud. I even half raised my hand. But what was the point? Yeah, I'd had some good days, a few really excellent ones, but as I listened to the stories, I knew things would eventually go downhill. Even the part of me that hoped I could be positive, liked, and hopeful knew the truth and was done with the reminders.

So as soon as Susan made her closing statement, including "please take some coffee and cookies, or they will go to waste," I burst through the front doors and onto the sidewalk. What exactly was I hoping for? To find someone like me. That's what I'd put on the list. And I did it, but deep down I wanted something else. I didn't believe knowing other ticcers was the key to happiness, but maybe I'd hoped they'd have answers, ideas, something to take the pain, loneliness, and embarrassment away.

The only answer I got was that we were one big group of alone. No matter what we did, there would be us and then the rest of the world.

Shoes click-clacked on the sidewalk behind me. I turned and walked toward Mrs. Isenhour.

"Sorry to hear David is having a rough time," I said. "Please take the picture. Maybe it'll cheer him up."

Mrs. Isenhour nodded and took the picture. "Thank you. Will you let us give you a ride?"

I knew that look. Khory had it sometimes when she looked at me. She wanted to help, but on Mrs. Isenhour it was almost pleading.

My arms lifted. It was an urge, but not a tic. I wanted to hug her. Have her tell me everything would be okay even though we both knew it wouldn't be. But I couldn't do it. She wasn't my mom. Only David could feel that kind of comfort. I let my arms fall.

Mrs. Isenhour put her hand on me. "Please."

I couldn't trust what might come out of my mouth, again not a tic, but maybe a cry. I pressed my lips together and nodded. I slid into the back seat of a Toyota 4Runner and gave Mr. Isenhour my address to put into his phone's GPS.

"Did you meet him?" Mrs. Isenhour asked.

Him? Oh, Tim Howard. "No, my mom sent it to me."

That got a peek at me from the rearview mirror. Did my anger seep through?

"You live with your dad?" Mr. Isenhour asked.

Or maybe he realized my parents weren't together.

"And stepmom," I said.

"We would love to meet them," Mrs. Isenhour said.

Of course. No decent adult would drive a teenager home and not want to meet his parents.

"Um," I started. Apparently my lack of conversational abilities wasn't limited to pretty girls.

Mrs. Isenhour turned around.

"They don't know I'm here. That I go to the meetings. I tell them I'm at a friend's house or my girlfriend's," I confessed.

That brought a smile to her face. What? She encouraged lying? That wasn't going to go well for her when David was my age. I may not be popular, but I've seen and heard things worth lying about. Oh yeah, and I may have done some myself.

"You have a girlfriend," she said. "I look at you and see possibilities for David. High school. Friends, girlfriends."

I wasn't expecting that. Of course there were good days and bad days, but overall, high school was a nightmare. And my girlfriend? I've only had one.

"Who in your family has Tourette?" Mr. Isenhour asked.

"My mom."

"So, your dad is like me. A non-ticcer. He may still find the meetings interesting. I've learned a lot myself. Being on the other side has its own set of problems and responsibilities."

I had never thought of it like that, but maybe that's what Dad meant during our talk in New York.

"I can talk to him if you want. Father to father."

Really? What would he say? Your son has been sneaking off to meetings because he doesn't want you there? "Thanks. I'll think about it, if that's okay."

"Of course. You just let me know."

"I'm sorry about the problems your son is having," I said.

Mrs. Isenhour gave me that look again. Wanting to help but mixed in with helplessness.

Mr. Isenhour pulled the car into my driveway. The drive was much quicker than the bus that made several stops before mine. Most of the inside lights were off, which meant Jude was asleep and Dad was relaxing. No need to disrupt a quiet night.

"Thank you for the ride," I said.

I got out of the car. Mrs. Isenhour lowered her window and held a piece of paper out to me.

"I hate to go behind another parent's back, but I'm also not comfortable with you riding the bus at night. Here are our phone numbers. Call us if you want a ride."

"Thanks." I spun around so she wouldn't see my quivering lip.

I went inside, closed the door quietly, and crept to my room. I wasn't in the mood for small talk, and even though it was still early by my standards, I got ready for bed and crawled under the covers.

I went over the conversation again. My life made Mrs. Isenhour happy? Obviously she didn't know the details. I picked up my phone, texted good night to Khory, and shut the light off. Okay, some of the details were pretty awesome.

MARCH 27

"Turn those screens off and get some fresh air," Mrs. Levine yelled from the top of the basement stairs.

We sighed and moaned. Leave our haven to search for fresh air in this polluted world?

"Fine," Rainn mumbled and shut off the TV.

We grabbed our phones and jackets and headed outside to the backyard. Khory and I lay on the grass and held hands. It was actually nice outside. A movie scene type of night with soft grass and a cloudless sky where you could connect the dots with stars. Which I did in groups of ten.

Jay sat across from us texting a girl he liked who obviously didn't like him or she'd be here. Rainn and Diego were to his left, for once not making us all gag. Diego was reading.

"It's Friday night. Put the book away." Rainn tried to swat it out of his hand.

Diego moved it out of her reach. "I need to study for my driver's test. Did you know that it's illegal to play in traffic?"

"I'll make a note," she said.

"It is also illegal to tie your dog to the roof of your car."

"If you don't put that book away, I'll tie you to the car," she said.

"You won't be whining when I get a car and we can drive to the lake or the park at night. Hint, hint."

I glanced at Rainn. She lifted his book back up.

"I cannot wait till I don't have to drive with my parents," he said. "My mom never stops yelling at me: 'Both hands on the wheel. Don't you dare touch that radio. And if I ever catch you texting and driving . . .'" He dropped his head in his hands. "Her nagging is more distracting than texting."

"Yeah, right? As if adults are better," Rainn said. "My mom talks on the phone while driving, and not hands free, by the way. It's just so important that she plan her gym and strawberry frappuccino dates. My dad speeds and drinks coffee. He has a stick shift, so I'm not really sure how he gets all that to work."

"Well, after tomorrow, I won't have to deal with it," Diego said. "Troy, do you have your license?"

"No," I said. My eyes back to the stars.

"Why not? You're sixteen, right?"

"My dad won't let me." I said.

Jay glanced up from his phone. "What? No way."

Being a teenager and not being able to drive was horrible enough to pull Jay away from his crush. Yeah, it was up there for me too on the list of very bad. I sat up. "You know he's a cop. Well, he's seen tons of kids die in car crashes. He doesn't want me to be like that."

"Oh, man, that's sad. I swear I'm not going to text and drive," Diego said. "Rainn's going to be my DT."

Knowing them, a DT was something perverted. I wasn't going to ask.

"What's a DT?" Of course Jay was willing to go there.

"Designated texter," Rainn and Diego said at the same time. Then they turned to each other and kissed. *Barf.*

"My dad told me one story. A guy was driving. And his girlfriend leaned over." I paused and scanned the crowd. They stared at me. My neck twitched, and my face scrunched up. Just like talking about zero gravity in science, my friends were interested in the story, not my freakish moves.

"Dude, come on," Jay said.

I shifted toward him, well, really away from Khory. We didn't talk about things like this.

"Okay, she leaned over to him. Put her head in his lap and—" I couldn't say the rest. My face was hot.

"Dude, she gave him a blow job while he was driving?" Jay said. "Damn."

I nodded. "The guy must have closed his eyes or went crazy." Which was just a guess since I had no actual knowledge, but I would have gone insane if Khory did that to me. "Then he drove into the oncoming lane."

Khory gasped and grabbed my arm.

I continued. "They ran into a semi. His girlfriend sat up at the wrong time and—" I slid my hand across my neck.

We were all silent. What could you say to that?

"So, your dad won't let you drive because he thinks you'll let Khory give you a blow job and you'll get yourself killed?" Jay asked.

My cheeks were on fire. *Khory* and *blow job* in the same sentence was enough to blow my mind.

"Ha, ha, ha," Khory said.

I left it that way. No one had to know my dying wish had been to kiss a girl for the first time. But they were friends, right? And interested in my story. If I could speak in front of a room full of judgmental, self-centered kids and still have the guts to go to school the next day, why not them? My tongue moved behind my teeth trying to form the words.

"No. He thinks I'm unreliable," I said. "He thinks I'll swerve into traffic and kill myself. And someone else. Because of the Tourette."

"*Duh.* I hate to tell you, dude, but it's not a secret," Jay said.

I fell back on the grass and closed my eyes. Of course I knew it wasn't a secret, but I still hated how the word sounded and what it stood for.

"So you'll never get to drive?" Diego asked.

"Well, I wouldn't say that. I'm going to borrow his car. Just for a few minutes. A quick trip around the neighborhood," I said.

"You're going to steal your dad's car?" Jay asked.

"I think of stealing as not giving back. This is borrowing. It's the only way I'll get to drive."

I did believe that, but knowing Dad would ground me for life if he found out started a massive wave of tics. Rapid-fire neck twitches that scraped the back of my head across the grass and dirt. I counted to ten. Over and over. My hands squeezed together. The darkness was a lifesaver.

Jay leaped up. "Hey, I have a great idea. I'm going to teach you to drive."

I sat up. "You're kidding, right?"

"Wait, maybe his dad has a point," Diego said. "No offense or anything, but maybe you're better off riding a bike the rest of your life."

"Would you be okay with riding your bike after you pass the test?" I asked.

"Good point," Diego admitted.

I turned to Khory. "If I don't drive, you'll either have to ride on the handlebars or chauffeur me around for the rest of our lives."

"Not going to happen," she said.

I grabbed her hand and squeezed it, then put my arm around her.

That's the second time I let myself dream about a different number ten.

. . . .

"Hands at ten and two. You don't get to drive with one hand until you're more experienced like me," Jay said. "Okay, start your engine."

A race-car analogy probably wasn't the smartest thing to say right now, especially since we were in his Mustang. Jay and I were in the front, and Khory, Rainn, and Diego were in the back. We buckled our seat belts. I turned the car on, then gripped the steering wheel until my knuckles turned white.

My neck twitched. I counted to ten.

"Move the wheel slowly. Not too much unless you're turning."

I had the general concept, gas on the right, brake on the left. *D* meant drive. *R*, reverse. But I listened to Jay's step-by-step directions because it was his car, which he so stupidly put in my hands. And I wanted this so bad I would have kissed his shoes if he asked. It also gave me time to finish my round of ten.

I inched to the left, away from the curb in front of Rainn's house, and pulled into the center of the road.

"Stay on the right," Jay said. "But careful not to hit the curb or take out any mailboxes."

Gotcha. Sounded easy enough. And it was, until we passed a few. Then they taunted me like a new person's lunch tray. I wanted to touch them. More than that. I wanted to plow them down.

My right arm jerked to the right and my left arm pulled to the left. Breathe. One, two, three, four, five, six, seven, eight, nine, ten. Repeat. I pressed the gas, and the car lurched forward. I took that as a beginner's mistake and pressed the gas again. The car jerked down the street. My foot felt heavy, and the bottom of it tingled. It was an itch that could only be scratched by slamming down hard.

I gripped the wheel tight. My right and left arms pulled in opposite directions. If I'd had any strength, I would've yanked the wheel in two. New-driver syndrome and Tourette wasn't a good combination. I didn't want to believe that Dad had a point.

"You're doing great," Jay lied. "Make a right at the stop sign. And don't be afraid to go faster."

I nodded, pressed the gas pedal harder, and went faster, to twelve miles per hour. I backed off and got it to ten.

"This is like a baby train at the mall. Go faster," Diego said.

Rainn giggled. "I rode my tricycle faster than this."

"Guys, be nice and let him focus. Remember, this is his first time driving," Khory said.

Jay's leg bounced. He was getting impatient, too. I didn't want to stop, so I pressed the gas a little harder. Twenty should be okay. Even. Divisible by ten. I made a right again, a little too quickly. Khory grabbed the back of my seat.

"Sorry," I called out.

"It's good," she said.

I made another right and got in the groove. My shoulders relaxed, the tics slowed down, and my body sank into the seat. I picked up the speed and was cruising at thirty now. This was exactly what I thought driving would be. Freedom. Power. I could go anywhere. Do anything. Music would have been great right now, maybe Shinedown humming in the background, drums pounding, guitars screeching.

"Now you got it," Jay said. "Don't know what your dad was worried about." He leaned back in his seat.

The darkness disappeared, and the streetlights lit up the road like a concert. Then the one-lane residential road magically turned into a three-lane highway. Shit!

My hands tightened around the steering wheel. Cars beeped and whizzed past me. Horns blared.

Jay sat up and grabbed his hair. "Dude, you were supposed to turn right. You're heading toward the bridge. You gotta turn some-where."

One, two, three, four, five, six, seven, eight, nine, ten. Repeat. Out loud this time. "One, two, three, four, five, six, seven, eight, nine, ten."

Jay was back to his role as a driving instructor. "Get off the road! Turn. Make a right. Now!"

I swung the steering wheel to the right. Khory, Rainn, and Diego tipped like dominoes. The car bumped as I ran over a curb. I pulled into a parking lot, turned the car off, then leaned back and exhaled.

Diego laughed and punched my arm. "Started slow but ended like a roller coaster. So, what did you think?"

"When I get over the fact that we may have died, I'm sure I'll have loved it." I opened the window for some air.

"Good evening," a man's voice said next to my ear.

I jumped and smacked my knee on the steering wheel. Leaning inside the window was a man. But not just any man, like say an ax murderer, which I would have preferred. The light from his flashlight reflected off his badge. He was a cop.

He cleared his throat. "Hello, kids."

"Hello," I choked out.

"License and registration please."

I turned to Jay who rummaged in the glovebox for his wallet. Earbuds, papers, and a Twix fell out.

"Put your hands on the dash," the cop told him.

"Sir, it's my car." Jay reached across me and handed the cop his info.

"And your license?" The cop asked me.

"*Uh,* I don't have one," I said.

"Please step out of the car."

Khory gasped as I fumbled with my seatbelt and finally unbuckled it. I got out of the car. My neck twitched. My hands clenched together. Opened and closed. Tighter. The cop scrutinized me. From head to toe. He watched me tic. His hand moved to his gun. I didn't want to look at it. I tried to focus on his scrunched bushy, blond eyebrows. But I had to. My eyes darted from his face to his gun. Face. Gun. Repeat.

One, two, three, four, five, six, seven, eight, nine, ten.

"What are you doing? Are you on drugs?" He grabbed my arm,

pulled me to the front of the car, and pushed me forward. "Hands on the hood. Everyone else, hands out the window." Then he called for backup.

I knew what he thought. I was dangerous. Some crazy druggie or psycho, and we all knew what happened to them. I couldn't see inside the car, but my friends could see me. I was in the spotlight. My humiliation lit up like the star of a viral video, but the life and times of Troy Hayes wasn't a show anyone would want to see.

"Officer?" Jay called from the passenger seat. "Can I tell you something, please?"

The cop leaned toward Jay. "What?"

"He's not on drugs. He has Tourette syndrome. He's completely harmless."

During a neck-twitch explosion, no doubt brought on by hearing that word, I caught the cop studying me. His eyebrows were still scrunched. Maybe that was his normal face. Or maybe he was trigger happy.

"I don't know what that is," the cop said. "Sit still. We'll be going to the station soon to call your parents."

"What?" Khory screeched.

My heart ached. But that was nothing compared to what the Prices would feel when the police called their house. I wanted to tell her I'd take care of everything, but Officer Blond still had his hand on his gun. For all he knew, Tourette syndrome was code for attack the police.

Headlights pulled up behind Jay's car. A door slammed and another cop sauntered up.

"What's up?" he asked.

The first cop filled him in. Erratic driving. Bizarre, possibly drug-related behavior from the driver, who doesn't have a license.

The new cop leaned toward me and studied my face way too long. "What's your name?"

"Troy," I answered.

"You look familiar. What's your last name?"

"Hayes." Why couldn't it have been something more common, like Jones or Gomez? There were at least five Joneses in tenth grade alone. He had to know other people named Hayes. Besides his boss.

I counted to ten. Airplane. Floating. Repeat. Count. Airplane. Floating.

"I know, you're Captain Hayes's son. He has your picture on his desk."

Now wasn't the time to be sentimental, or wonder which picture he decided to display to the entire station, because I was busted.

"Does he know you're here?"

"No, Sir."

And I would have liked to keep it that way. But any chance of that died when Officer Blond asked everyone to step out of the car and Jay's rolling papers fell to the ground.

MARCH 27

The last time I was in a police car I was ten. It was just after Mom left, and the kids on the bus had really ramped up their teasing. I'd asked Dad to drive me to school because at that age everyone wanted to be a cop and I hoped it would make me look cool. I'd imagined they'd ask me questions like: have you seen a bad guy, or did you arrest anyone with your dad? I even had a few stories made up about psycho-killer shoot-outs just in case anyone asked.

No one ever did. And riding in the police car didn't make anything better. Instead, it gave the mean kids something else to tease me about. They called me crazy and said I needed an armed escort to take me to school.

This ride in the police car wasn't any better. I would have chosen school over the place we were going. I glanced at Jay. He stared at his lap and twisted the end of his shirt. I didn't want to think what Khory was doing right now. Probably terrified at what this would do to her parents and grasping at any coping techniques Rainn gave her.

We drove to the back of the police station, got out of the cars, and followed Officer Blond to the door. I tried to hold Khory's hand, but the officer behind us yelled no touching. I guess in case we decided to pass a weapon to each other or escape. We weren't criminals, not really, but I wasn't going to tell them that. I kept my mouth shut, focused on relaxing my muscles, which wasn't working at all, and did what I was told.

On TV, prisoners were handcuffed, fingerprinted, then thrown into a jail cell with a passing "you have the right to remain silent." Tonight there was none of that. We went inside and straight upstairs. I guess that was a perk of being the captain's son.

I'd never been to Dad's work, but there was no mistaking this was the detective bureau. It looked just like the ones on TV. Desks in groups with computers, papers, and pens scattered around. Coffee cups everywhere, and the big whiteboard with burglary, robbery, and auto theft totals on it. Besides us and the two cops, the room was empty.

I turned my back to the desks even though the pull of crooked pens and messy papers reached out like an octopus's tentacles. It was torture how people left their things carelessly lying around. I faced my friends. Khory's eyes glistened with tears. Rainn and Diego stared at the floor, and Jay was still twisting his shirt.

He leaned toward me. "I'm so sorry. I didn't know they fell out of the glovebox."

"Have a seat, guys," Officer Blond said. He handed us each a piece of paper and pen. "Write your parents' names and phone numbers. Except yours. I know your Dad's number by heart."

My shoulders slumped.

Khory practically fell into the chair behind her. I walked over, but Rainn zoomed in front of me and sat next to her. She held her hand and whispered in her ear. Khory nodded and wiped her eyes.

I sat in the chair across from them. Yes, it was my fault we were here, and I would take the blame for everything, but I was her boyfriend and should have been the one holding her hand and comforting her. I took a chance and stretched my foot toward her. She glanced at me, gave me a small smile, then her foot met mine.

Rainn scooted closer to Diego. I rolled my chair next to Khory. We held hands, despite what the officers said, and she rested her head on my shoulder. I took a deep breath, smelled her coconut shampoo, and sighed.

"I'm sorry," I said. "I should have told Jay no."

"It's not your fault. We all thought it was a great idea. But your dad may have a point. Your driving is a little scary."

I chuckled and leaned into her.

"Dude, is that your dad?" Jay asked.

My body froze. Like I said, it never happened for a good reason.

I turned toward the open elevator door. It was him. Feet planted on the floor and arms crossed over his chest, which left a perfect view of the gold badge clipped to the front of his jeans. His lips were pressed tight, but when I met his eyes they screamed disappointment. I looked away.

Dad talked to the cops for a few minutes. His hands moved to his hips, and he nodded. Was it a good nod like "they're just stupid kids"? Or was it a they-need-to-be-taught-a-lesson kind of nod?

Dad shook the cops' hands and came over to us. "I'm Captain Hayes, Troy's father. Officer Parker told me what happened tonight—"

Mrs. Price burst into the room and ran straight toward us. Mr. Price was right behind her. My guess was they had broken a few traffic laws themselves to get here. "Khory? Are you okay?" Mrs. Price asked. "We got the call. The police. I'm so glad you're safe."

Khory stood up and her mom hugged her. "I'm fine," she said, then tried to push herself away, but her mom held on tight.

"What happened?" Mr. Price asked.

Dad stepped forward as everyone else's parents stepped off the elevator. They spied their kids, ran to them, and gave them the head-to-toe visual inspection for scrapes or broken bones.

"I'm Captain Clark Hayes, Troy's father. My officers called and informed me they had our kids at the station. Apparently Troy was driving erratically and without a license. He's sixteen but strictly forbidden to drive."

I stared at my shoes and bounced my leg up and down to the count of ten. My neck was out of control, and every time my head twisted up, I saw everyone staring at me. I begged them to look away, but it was all in my mind. Any progress I'd made in the last week was gone. I fought the urge to run away and lock myself in a room with no windows, or hide under the blanket like I did when I was a kid.

From the corner of my eye, I saw Khory's purple shoes take a step toward me, but then a man's blue-and-black Adidas sneaker blocked it.

"Several laws were broken tonight," Dad continued, "including driving without a license, reckless driving, and possession of drug paraphernalia. A pack of marijuana rolling papers was found inside the car."

"Drugs?" someone's father asked. "Were you kids doing drugs?"

"They were mine," Jay said.

I was sure Dad would assume we were all involved. A drug-taking, driving, TS kid would send him over the edge. I met his eyes. *What are you going to do to me that will top what I planned do to myself? Try me.* I dared him.

The room was silent. The tension was thick like syrup but smelled like sweat. Dad shifted his feet and ran his hands through his hair. I let out a big exhale.

"Because our kids didn't harm anyone and have no criminal records, the officers agreed not to file charges against them. But they need to understand just how serious this was. They could have been hurt or hurt someone else. A car is a four-thousand-pound weapon." He looked at each one of us. "Do you understand?"

"Yes, Sir," we answered in unison.

Dad turned to the parents. "They are free to go under your supervision."

We leaped out of our chairs. A few rolled back and banged against the desks. The parents thanked Dad, I'm sure realizing it was really him who'd saved us from a night in jail or a permanent juvenile record. Then the relief on their faces quickly changed to anger, and they pulled their kids to the elevator. It would be a long night for all of us.

"How could you be so careless and deceitful?" Mr. Price yelled in Khory's face. "We give you freedom, and this is what you do? Endanger yourself? Do you want us to lose you, too?"

I totally expected Khory to crumble. Fall into a little ball right there on the tile floor that was probably as dirty as the hospital bathroom floor. That's what I would have done if I was her. But she wasn't me. She was brave. She stood up straight and looked her dad in the eyes.

"Freedom? You let me go to Rainn's house. That's it. No school dances, no dates." She glanced at me. "You just started letting me go to Troy's house. I'm a prisoner. Why don't you just wrap me in bubble wrap so I don't even get a paper cut?"

I shifted my feet and focused on Dad. He turned around and sorted through some files.

"Khory Lynn Price. You think you're a prisoner? Well, you got it. You are forbidden to go anywhere except school. Not Rainn's house. Not Troy's house. And no boyfriend."

Khory ran out of the room. Her mother followed, tears running down her face. Mr. Price shot me a look that made me long for a jail cell with steel bars between us. Just as I was about to beg for police protection, he went after his family.

The room was silent. I stood in the middle of the discarded chairs, and the urges grew. Tingled at first, then invaded every muscle in my body. I started to straighten the chairs, close to the desk but not touching. One. Two. The third one had loose wheels. It rolled to the desk and banged into it with a thud. I pulled it out and tried again.

"Let's go," Dad said. His sneakers stomped on the concrete floor.

"I'll be right there." I backed away from the chair. It stayed. I sighed and moved to the fourth one.

"Now. We have a lot to discuss, and we're not doing it here." He grabbed my arm and pulled me to the elevator.

Two chairs were crooked in the center of their row. I turned back to them. "Let me just—"

"I said 'now.'"

I stopped, yanked my arm, and faced him. He'd never been like this. But I'd never been like this either. What kind of trouble could I get into when all I did was homework, video games, and babysit my brother?

The heat rose in my body. No matter how many times I counted to ten or imagined myself floating, I couldn't cool down. Didn't he remember anything we talked about in New York? Didn't he pay attention to Mom at all when they were married?

I spun around and stomped to the chairs. Giant leaps got me there in six steps. Seven, eight, nine, ten.

Two chairs were still out of place. I pushed the first one in and caught Dad watching me. His mouth and eyebrows softened. I hated pity more than I hated people thinking I was a freak.

I fixed the chairs, put three pencils in a jar on the desk, and straightened a stapler. Then I stalked past Dad and into the elevator.

. . . .

We walked through the station's parking lot to his car. When the doors were closed, that was Dad's signal to go. At me.

"How dare you put your life and your friends' lives in danger."

He leaned close to me, grabbed my shirt, and smelled it. Then grabbed my hand and did the same. I yanked it back.

"What are you doing? Leave me alone." I scooted closer to the passenger door.

"I'm checking for a pot smell to see if you're high and stupid," Dad said. "Officer Parker told me how you were driving. Jerking back and forth on a busy street. Did you not understand why I forbade you to drive?"

"Yes, but you don't understand."

"Understand what? That you want to kill yourself?"

My chest tightened. I spun to him. My mouth opened, but I was speechless. Did he know?

"Because that's what could happen if you drive," he finished.

He turned the ignition key, and the car came to life. He pulled out of the parking lot and headed in the direction of home. I put my back to him and stared out the window at the lights and neighborhoods where families were actually enjoying each other's company. I should have been relieved he didn't know my plan, but for some reason I wasn't.

"Listen, I know you have friends now, and a girlfriend, and I'm thrilled for you. You are a great kid and really deserve to go out and have some fun. Just let me drive you there. Anywhere you want to go, I'll drive you."

I appreciated his offer. Really. Not that I was going to tell him right now, especially because he missed the whole point. It wasn't about going somewhere. It was about being able to do things without the fucking tics and obsessions getting in the way. Just once.

I didn't answer him. Instead I counted to ten. My neck twitched. Faster. My hands squeezed together. I wanted to scream, so I bit my lip as it tried to burst through.

We rode the rest of the way home in silence and parked in the garage. I was done, but Dad wasn't.

"You're grounded. No more going out with your friends. No more jobs. Your friends cannot come here, and no more rides from this kid Jay. If you need to go somewhere, Terri or I will take you. Otherwise you go to school and come home."

It wasn't a surprise, but my heart ached at the thought of not being able to see Khory after school. And everyone else.

"How long?" I asked.

"Until I can trust you to follow the rules," Dad said.

Well, you know what, Dad? You should have told me that a long time ago. And acted like it. I got out of the car, stomped ten steps, then bent down and pounded the floor. And repeat until I got to my room and slammed the door.

I texted Khory.

ME: I'm sorry. I love you.

I stared at the phone for a while waiting for her to text cute little hearts.

Nothing.

I got into bed and turned off my light. I was ready for the day to be done. And the next eleven days to be done. I didn't need this shit anymore. Before I put the phone down, I opened the list and checked off "Drive a car." I sank into the pillow. Only two more left.

MARCH 28

The first thing I thought of when I woke up was Khory. I grabbed my phone. Nothing. No texts or phone calls from her or from anyone else. But it was only nine in the morning. Everyone was probably up late getting screamed at, so naturally they'd sleep in late. That's the lie I told myself, anyway.

I texted Khory again.

ME: Hi. Sorry again about last night. I hope things were better when you got home.

Was she curled up under her purple comforter deciding if she wanted to talk to me? I wouldn't blame her if she didn't. Khory was brutal to her parents in front of us. I can't imagine what happened when they were alone. No doubt having the police call brought back memories and nightmares they wished would never come back.

Did that make Khory realize having a boyfriend like me was more trouble than it was worth? Because now she'd never get to go anywhere.

Despite the fire in her eyes when she talked about traveling, she'd never be free. Neither of us would. We were both strapped to something. Me, the physical pain and the emotional pain when I faced people outside the security of my room. For her, the dangers that lurked around every corner. She'd never be free if she kept looking over her shoulder.

I opened my bedroom door a crack and peered down the hall. Empty. I crept to the bathroom, took one clonidine pill and one Lexapro, and counted what was left. Twelve in each. I added two pills from each bottle, including the melatonin, to the stash in the back of my drawer. Monday I would ask Dad for refills.

My neck twitched. I squeezed my hands together. Dad's voice seized control of my brain. The conversation from last night played on repeat. My neck twitched faster. The picture of me plastered on the hood of Jay's car took over. It wasn't Dad, but it wasn't better. I squeezed my hands even tighter.

A burning sensation grew in my stomach. It traveled down my arms and into my hands. I whirled around the bathroom and gnashed my teeth together. My eyes landed on the towel rack. I grabbed it with both hands and wrenched it from the wall. Two holes stared at me like eyes. Judging. I held the rack like a bat and swung.

Smack!

Dad's voice drifted down the hall followed by Terri's. I stared at the big hole in the center, then dropped the rack, raced to my room, and slammed the door. I locked it and jumped in bed.

There was a bang on my door.

"Troy?"

My doorknob turned.

"Troy, I know you're awake. I know you were just in the bathroom," Dad said. "What the hell happened?"

I flipped over and faced the wall. I begged myself not to grunt or moan or yell.

"Open the door."

I bit my lip.

"I'll give you some time to calm down, but we're going to discuss this," Dad said.

I waited a few minutes to be sure he'd left, then grabbed my phone, fingers crossed for a text. From anyone.

Nothing.

One more try to Khory. I didn't want to seem desperate, and three texts really wasn't, but I didn't care because I *was* desperate.

ME: Hi. I don't know what to say. Just let me know you're okay.

The phone beeped before I put it down.

My heart stopped for a second. Would it be good news or bad? I hoped to see a heart emoji or smiley face as a clue. Nothing. Just words.

KHORY: No more boyfriend and Khory isn't allowed to use her
        phone anymore.

A sharp pain stabbed my heart. Then my chest burned. It was exactly what I thought a broken heart would feel like. I grabbed my hair and pulled as hard as I could. I begged for pain, but my body wouldn't listen. It wasn't on my side. My neck twitched fast. I whipped my head up and down praying for a snap or crack.

I dug my nails into my wrists. It wasn't enough. The scissors were sharper. I could feel them through the mattress. The pain could be intense. I leaped out of bed and lifted the mattress. Ran my finger along the green handle and then squeezed the blades in my hand. But if I went too far . . .

April 6 was coming. Ten years. I had to wait. I dropped the scissors and mattress, then let my body go. I twitched and squeezed until my muscles were on fire and definitely over one hundred on the pain scale. When I was too weak to move, my body sank into the bed and slept.

The knock on my door woke me. I rolled over and opened my eyes.

"Troy? You've been sleeping most of the day. Are you hungry?" Dad asked.

I rubbed my eyes and stretched. My legs were sore, and a sharp pain ran down my left shoulder blade.

"No," I said.

"You want to come out and play with Jude?"

"I have homework. Maybe later." Lie.

"Listen, I'm not upset about the bathroom. We'll fix it, okay?"

"Okay."

"Are you going to come out?"

"I have homework."

"Well, let me know if I can help."

"Sure." I should have called his bluff. What did he know about Pre-Calculus?

But it wasn't all a lie. I had work to do, just not for school. Nothing had changed. Last night had made me realize how stupid my dream of living happily ever after with Khory and without the tics and obsessions was. It wasn't possible. Which meant I still needed money, and if I couldn't work, I had to find a cheaper way to get to Schenectady.

MARCH 29

I faced my locker and counted my money. Ninety dollars. I needed at least fifty more. The bus was the cheapest way to New York, but still more than I had.

I wasn't against begging and trying out the guilt-trip approach again. I knew what Dad had said, but keeping me inside would set me back at least ten steps in my progress to be the well-rounded kid he wanted. Grounding me just wasn't productive. Really, how harmful could pressure-washing an old woman's deck be?

I played the script over in my mind when a pair of arms wrapped around me. They were smooth with light-pink nail polish. I turned around. Khory gave me a big kiss and leaned against me. I put my arms around her and breathed in the sweet smell of strawberry.

"I wanted to call you, but my dad grounded me and took my phone. I only get it at school in case there's an emergency." She stood up straight, scrunched her eyebrows together like her dad, and pointed her finger at me. "No need to have your phone when you're safe at home."

She went for the deep, throaty voice most grown men have, but it sounded more like a thirteen-year-old boy. I held in my laughter.

"He actually said 'safe at home.' So I said he couldn't guarantee that. I could fall down the stairs or the house could explode."

"You didn't say that, did you?" I asked.

She nodded.

Didn't she realize her dad would freak and was probably calling around for a full-time babysitter or a realtor to find a one-story house? Did she realize she just upped the security on her prison?

"I know, I shouldn't have, but I was so upset." She ran her hand through her hair. "I thought about running away and actually pulled out a bag. Then I thought that maybe I could go to Schenectady with you." She smiled and winked.

We walked down the hall to the cafeteria. Was she joking? Of course she couldn't go. My list had a different ending than hers. We couldn't run away together. Even if she went to Schenectady with me, there was no happily ever after.

"If he thinks he's going to stop me from having a life and freedom, he's crazy."

I loved that she was a fighter and added to her list. But I was stuck with mine. She kissed me, and I followed her to the middle table. Jay, Rainn, and Diego were already there.

"My mom wasn't really upset about the driving," Jay was telling Rainn and Diego. "She was pissed about the rolling papers. She spent the entire weekend tearing my room apart looking for drugs.

And I mean the entire room. Drawers, closet, the box of stupid pictures I made as a kid."

I tried to imagine Jay as a first grader. That box was probably full of pictures of crayon-colored cars.

"She was convinced I had heroin or cocaine or some other hardcore freaky drug hidden. She didn't believe me until there was nothing left to go through. Good thing we smoked it all. Still, she grounded me and threatened weekly drug tests. Which I'm not sure was just a threat."

He sighed and dropped his wrap. Nothing killed an appetite like the thought of peeing into a cup for your mom. All I needed was for Mrs. Davidson to give my dad that idea.

Rainn and Diego weren't grounded. I didn't know his parents, but hers were pretty chill. It was her house that we'd walked away from to smoke pot and to drive. Maybe because marijuana was technically an herb.

"I did get a long lecture, though," Diego said. "Excruciatingly long."

"My mom was shocked your dad never taught you to drive. Mom claimed it disempowered you," Rainn said. "So I thought she was cool with the whole thing, but then the lecture came."

She glanced at Diego, then focused on straightening her lunch bag.

"What's going on?" I asked. I knew the signs. They were hiding something. Yeah, they said *lectures*, but there was more to the story.

Rainn looked at Diego. He shrugged.

"So they said they couldn't believe we got in the car with someone who has no control over anything and we couldn't hang out with you anymore. Or Jay, because they think he's on drugs," Rainn said. "We're really sorry. Don't take it personally. They don't know you, Troy."

Except hers did. I'd been to her house often enough for her mom to check out my lack of control. She noticed because she'd offered to help me one day with some oil or witchcraft remedy. But I wasn't supposed to take it personally. I straightened my lunch bag, sandwich, and drink, because that's what I did. But I really wanted to squeeze the crap out of my sandwich.

"Hey, Troy, our parents are jerks. Okay, maybe you're not the best driver, but you're cool. They can't tell us who to hang out with," Diego said.

"Yeah, don't worry about it. You probably had enough grief with your dad," Jay said. "He was so businesslike, which is a hundred times worse than ours since his business is being a cop."

I looked up from my lunch. The four of them were waiting for my story, so I told them about the sniff test in the car, the "I told you so" about driving, and that I was grounded, too. There wasn't much to say after that, so we ate in silence. To some degree, today life sucked for all of us.

I went with that feeling when I walked Khory to class after

lunch. Who cared if I was late to math again? Who cared if Mr. Nagel gave me a detention? I really didn't give a shit, and for a few seconds I thought about telling him that.

"Even though my parents are being jerks, I don't regret anything," Khory said. "I still love you, and somehow we'll make it work."

Khory to the rescue again. If I told off a teacher, her dad would never let me see her.

"Thanks." I kissed her. "I have to get to class."

"Oh, no! We have midterms next week. You were supposed to help me tomorrow when I babysat Jude." Her eyes were wide. Failing wasn't an option for her. "I still have questions. What am I going to do?"

I couldn't stand to see the panic on her face. But there was no way her dad would let her come over.

"Maybe you should find someone else to help you," I said.

"There's no one else. You are the only one who explains it clearly." She put her hands on her hips. "I want you. That's it. No discussion. That's what I'll tell my dad."

Yeah, like he'd care. "Listen, you can't bring up my name. No more boyfriend, remember?"

"I don't care what he said, or about math. I can't live without you." She had tears in her eyes.

I should have been a man and told her I wouldn't be around forever. She'd have to learn to let me go. If I broke up with her now, she'd be over me before April 6. But when I looked at her, my legs weakened. My heart ached. I wanted to hold onto her until the very last second. Even though I knew it was inevitable, I couldn't bring myself to. I wanted to spend as much time with her as possible.

"You can't come to my house because my dad will definitely call yours." I shifted my feet. "Can you sneak out? I'll ride my bike to your house. We can take a walk or something."

"Yes! There's a park near my house. It's on the main road at the top of the hill. I'll meet you there." She wiped her eyes, and her smile lit up the dreary hallway.

"Ten o'clock." I leaned over and brushed my lips on hers. "I love you."

"I love you, too." She turned and skipped into her class.

MARCH 29

For once giving Dad the silent treatment had an advantage. Usually it meant missing out on great takeout food or choosing a movie to rent. Tonight it allowed me to hide in my room right after dinner. I left just to take a shower.

My towel hung over the shower-curtain bar since the towel rack I'd snatched off the wall yesterday was propped up behind the door. We'd have to talk about that at some point. I hoped not tonight.

At nine fifty, I stuffed pillows and balled up a blanket under my comforter to mirror a person sleeping. It looked as fake as it did in movies. But what the hell, if he realized I was gone, I'd be busted whether a lumpy imposter was there or not.

I turned off my lights, opened the window, and climbed out. Good thing we had a one-story house. I had no experience sneaking out, but it was obvious being quiet was key. Our garage door made a lot of noise when it opened, so after school I hid my bike in the bushes. I hopped on and rode to the park near Khory's house as fast as my legs would allow.

The park was easy to find. At the top of the hill, just like she said. The lamppost helped. I coasted to the mini-playground, leaned my bike against the metal fence, and sat at the picnic table. Jude would love to crawl around the fort and one day climb up the rocket ship.

In the beam of a streetlight, I saw her running toward me, backpack bouncing on her back. I met her halfway, then hugged and kissed her. Electric currents flew through me. It was the contact our bodies made, and the thrill of our secret meeting in the dark.

We walked to the table and straddled the bench.

"I brought my math books just in case we actually decided to study." But the smirk on her face told me she didn't care about the midterm. She took the backpack off and dropped it on the ground.

"So, what did you tell your parents?" I asked.

"We haven't really talked much since Saturday night, except for Dad lecturing me, so it wasn't strange that I locked myself in my room. What about you?"

"Same, but I did make one of those body pillows in case he decided to check on me."

She laughed. The lamppost highlighted the red shine in her hair.

"I thought this might be a fun place for you to take Jude."

"You think my Dad will ever let me babysit again? Doubtful."

I gasped. She had to babysit. I already checked that off my list. It was getting too close to find a new babysitter.

"Maybe if my dad talks to yours again, he'll agree," I said. "Or maybe at your house."

She shrugged, then her shoulders drooped. I took her hands, pulled her to me, and ran my hand through her hair. Soft and silky. I forced the list from my mind, leaned closer, and kissed her. She opened her mouth, and my tongue found hers. My other hand reached for her breast as her hand slid across my thigh. I was calm and energized at the same time. I moved my hand under her shirt. Jolts of electricity shot through me.

She let out a little squeak. I moaned. A car engine rumbled.

Khory pushed me away. Headlights passed the park's entrance and continued down the road.

"Cars can't see us this far from the road," I said.

"I know. I thought it might be my parents." She sighed. "So, when are you going to Schenectady?"

The magic was gone. Thanks, Mr. Price.

"I don't know yet. Why?"

"Maybe I wasn't kidding earlier. Maybe I'll go with you."

As exhilarating as these few minutes were, I couldn't let myself dream about that kind of happily ever after again. I wasn't Prince Charming. I wasn't capable of rescuing anyone. Let's be honest, I wasn't nearly as lucky as Shrek.

"How much is a plane ticket?" she asked.

"You can't go," I said.

"What?"

"It's not that I don't want you to. Really. I've got this fantasy thing going on in my head about us being together forever," I said.

"But it would make things so much worse for you. He'd never let you out of his sight."

She scowled. "How much?"

"It's really expensive. Like five hundred dollars."

"Well, what else? A train? A bus? I know you have the prices. Probably in a nice little spreadsheet on your phone."

I cringed. It was true, but I didn't expect her of all people to throw it in my face.

"I'm sorry. I didn't mean it like that," she said.

Like what? You didn't mean to make fun of my OCD?

"Don't you want me to go?" she asked.

Her hair fell over the side of her face. Did I ever tell her what that did to me? I picked up my phone and opened it to the notes section. I had info on every possible route to Schenectady. I read them to her with the prices.

"You're not kidding! Do you have enough for a bus ticket?"

"Almost. But since my dad won't let me work right now, it's going to take a little longer."

I had to get away and think before she announced she had hundreds of dollars stashed in her bedroom and would be ready to go at midnight. I scanned the park. "*Um*, I have to go to the bathroom."

I needed to give her a reason why she couldn't go with me, besides her dad, because she was so mad at him she wouldn't care. I stepped away from the playground, down a tree-lined path, and headed toward the bushes. I collapsed on the ground and dropped my head in my hands. Wasn't this what I wanted? A girlfriend who loved me so much she'd follow me anywhere? Okay, it wasn't what I had originally asked for, but who knew this would be so much better than one kiss? Who would have even thought it was possible? Or that I'd be the one to leave?

My hands squeezed tight and pulled my hair. It felt good. I did it again. Harder. Repeat. Harder. I hoped it would stimulate my brain. It didn't. I stood up as clueless as before, but now with a few strands of hair wrapped in my fingers, and walked back to the table.

Khory stared at my phone. In the glow of the lamppost, I saw her eyebrows scrunched together. Didn't she understand the prices? How could she not? With my OCD, if I wrote something, everyone understood it.

She glanced up at me, and I realized she wasn't confused. She wasn't reading the travel list.

We stared at each other for a very long second. I would have sworn that time froze, but it didn't because I was counting. As soon as I reached ten, I lunged toward the phone, but she pulled it out of my reach. I fell against the table.

"What's your List of Ten?" she asked barely above a whisper.

"It's not what you think," I said. "Can I please have my phone?"

I leaned toward her and reached out. She got up and paced the picnic area. For a second I considered grabbing her, but the phone didn't matter anymore. She knew what the list said and what it meant.

"I can't believe I helped you do these things and all this time you were planning this. The whole zero-gravity thing. And I kissed you. I was your first, right?"

I nodded. Tears ran down her face. She tried to swipe them away with her fingers, but there were too many.

"Can I explain?"

She shook her head. "So now that I was dumb enough to help you with your plan, you're almost there. Were you even going to come back and say goodbye, or just kill yourself there?"

My stomach tumbled. "I'm not going to do it. Things are different now." I would've said anything to get her to stop crying, even a lie. I took a step toward her. She tensed and pressed herself against the fence.

"How could you even consider it? We have things to do."

"Listen, I still wanted to kiss you and talk about Tourette in front of people. And there are things I need to work out with my mom. But you're right, life is a gift, so my list turned into one like yours."

"You lied to me. We shared our secrets. I told you my biggest fears, and you just lied to me."

"Okay, I didn't share everything, but you can see why, right?"

She shook her head.

"Fine. You have this big dream about the future. I'm happy for you. But don't stand there and judge me when you have no idea what my life was like."

My neck twitched. I counted to ten. I wanted to scream. Throw something.

"I'm in pain every day," I said. "The only time it goes away is when I'm so drugged up I can't function. Or stoned, which isn't much better because I can't live my life like that. I'm tired of the fear and ridicule in people's eyes when they see me. Am I a freak or a psycho that needs to be wrestled to the ground?"

Khory stared at the ground. Reality is hard to look in the eyes.

I squeezed my hands and dug my nails into my palms. "I hurt Jude. Did I tell you? I squeezed his hand so hard he cried. I could have broken his fingers because I couldn't control the tics. I cut myself with a knife. And scissors. Not because I wanted to die, but because it was more painful to fight the urge."

She looked up, her eyes wide.

"I thought life would be so much easier for everyone," I said.

I collapsed on the bench. Even as I tried to make her understand and convince her I changed my mind, I still felt the same. Yeah, I'd met the most amazing girl in the world and had real friends who overlooked everything, even if their parents didn't, but the reality was, they wouldn't be around forever. They'd go to different colleges or move to different cities. Find different friends. The only things that would stay were the pain, loneliness, and embarrassment.

"I'm not going to tell you I understand what you feel, but everyone has pain. Some that will never go away," she said.

Her eyes were dark except for the sparkle of tears.

"I want to be brave like you. And I'm working on it," I said. "Maybe someone knows about a new medication I haven't tried. Maybe I'll ask Rainn's mom about some herbal or mystical concoction. If she'll talk to me."

That brought a tiny hint of a smile to her face. I'd take any little bit I could get.

"So what happens when you see your mom? When number nine is done?"

"I get answers to questions that have haunted me for six years. And then I come home to you."

"And what about number ten?"

"I told you, things changed." I got up and moved to her. I wrapped my arms around her. She hugged me back.

"Please believe me. What can I do to prove it?" I glanced away. I couldn't look her in the eyes. "Please don't tell anyone. Not our friends, my dad, or your parents. It's done. No one needs to know but us."

She dropped her arms and pushed me away. She studied me. "You promise things have changed?"

"Yes, I promise." I was surprised at how smoothly the words rolled out of my mouth. But that was the definition of desperation. It made a person lie to anyone, even to the one they loved the most.

• • • • • • • • • •

My neck twitched in triple time during the twelve-minute bike ride home. I didn't realize it could go that fast. A stabbing pain made itself at home in my left shoulder blade. Then something popped.

I dumped my bike in the bushes, crawled back through my window, and went straight to the bathroom. I accidentally caught sight of myself in the mirror. My head was bent toward my left shoulder. I tried to straighten it, but the pain went from seventy to one hundred.

I got in the shower and let the water pound it.

The hot water usually loosened my muscles, but tonight it had a lot to work through. I was almost at scalding before the pain went from one hundred to ninety-five. Then ninety. And all the way down to fifty, where it hung out for a while. I washed myself and let the rhythmic sound of pounding water calm my brain.

When the pain was down to twenty, my head was now sort of in the upright position. I got dressed, took my medicine, and went to my room.

Dad sat on my bed, hands in his lap.

"Shit!" I screamed.

"Sorry, I didn't mean to scare you," Dad said.

"Why are you in my room?"

Was he going to subject me to weekly drug tests? Did he search my room when I was in the shower? I glanced around for anything that could be used against me. I tried not to focus on my mattress and the scissors waiting for me.

"The Prices called," he said.

I leaned against the wall and crossed my arms.

"I know you and Khory snuck out, and we will deal with that later, but first tell me about the note. The one that said you were going to kill yourself."

So much for true love. My neck twitched. The pain rate of twenty was going back up.

"Is it true?" Dad asked.

I wasn't in the mood for this conversation again tonight. The talk with Khory left me emotionally and physically exhausted.

"It was," I said.

"Was? Not anymore?"

I shook my head. I had the right to remain silent.

He stared at me. Studied me. Like he was trying to read my mind.

"What changed your mind?"

If this was an interrogation technique, it was pretty damn effective. My tics ramped up. I tried hard to calm myself, but I couldn't clear my mind enough to picture anything.

"My life got better. I have a girlfriend and friends. At least I did until recently." Having one friend was good, but add a girlfriend, more friends, and BAM! Instant social life. I could play the psychology-interrogation game, too.

"Let me ask you something: does any of this have to do with the driving stunt?"

I wish I knew what Khory told her parents. A note was one thing. A list with details was another. But I'd been lying for so long, what was one more?

"No," I said. "That driving stunt was the only way I'd ever get to drive."

"We could have talked about it. Found some way that was safe."

"So all those times I asked, and brought home papers from school, you never thought those were good times to talk?"

Dad sighed and frowned. "I was worried. Not about you, you're responsible. It's the Tourette."

"I am the Tourette!" I put my hand over my face. "Never mind."

"No, let's talk. Like we did in New York. I'd hoped after that you would have come to me with these feelings."

"After one talk we're supposed to be best friends? If I didn't tell Khory, did you really think I'd tell you?"

Dad put his head in his hand. "I'm changing my schedule so I'll be home before Terri leaves. That way you won't have to worry about watching Jude."

What? Suddenly I'd gone from being the babysitter to having one. I pressed my lips together and put my hands behind my back. They squeezed and opened. Squeezed and opened. Repeat. Of course I couldn't hide the neck twitch, and now the pain was down the right side of my neck, too.

"I want you to focus on yourself right now. Being a teenager is hard enough without the added pressure you have," Dad said. "I also think talking to someone again might help."

Did he have a suicide checklist or something?

1. Don't leave the kid alone

2. See a psychiatrist

I refused to go back to Hardly Qualified. I scrunched my nose and sighed.

"If you don't want to see the same person, we can find you someone else. We can talk about that later."

I slumped against the wall. Dad got off the bed, came over to me, and put his hands on my shoulders. There were tears in his eyes.

I twisted away from him.

His hands dropped, and he stood there for a minute. My neck twitched. My face scrunched.

"Don't stare at me!" I yelled.

"I—" he started. Then he turned and shuffled out.

All I wanted was to be free, but now I was more trapped than before.

My phone vibrated. There were seven texts and three voice-mails from Khory. At least she had the decency to make it an even ten. Did she do that because she understood me, or was it just a coincidence and she really had no idea how my brain worked? But how could she when I didn't get it myself?

I scanned the texts. They were all pretty much the same. "I'm sorry, I feel guilty, I love you." Her first voicemail gave the details.

"I know you said you weren't going to do it anymore, and it's not that I don't believe you, but I couldn't stop thinking about it. And if something changed your mind and you did it and I didn't say anything . . ." By that point she was crying.

Maybe she really did get me, because a part of her knew I was lying. And maybe I would have done the same thing. Especially if I already knew what losing someone felt like. But I wasn't her. I was the one who had to live with myself, and I couldn't do that anymore.

MARCH 29

I yanked the schoolbooks out of my backpack and shoved in clothes, medicine, a toothbrush, and deodorant. Then I pulled my blanket to the pillow and turned off my light. Dad said a lot tonight; I'd hoped he was as emotionally done as I was and wouldn't want to talk anymore. I needed at least an eight-hour head start.

I opened my window, climbed out, and got my bike from the bushes. I needed help. Actually, I needed money. The problem was, you couldn't just ask anyone. Money was so damn hard to come by, especially for teenagers, and everyone wanted to keep it for themselves for crap like ten-dollar coffees. I had to find someone close to me, like a family member or a really good friend.

Family was clearly out, and since Khory would never give it to me because she knew I was full of shit, Jay now had the distinction of being my closest friend. Lucky him.

I'd never been to his house, but I knew where it was. He lived three houses down from Khory. I slowed down as I got near her house. Her bedroom light was on. Was she lying on her bed or taking the pictures of us off her bulletin board? I knew she loved me, but I wouldn't blame her if she wanted to break up. This was a problem as far from simple as Pluto was from Earth. Simple would have been you kissed my best friend. This one was way too complex for me to understand.

I sped up and stopped at Jay's. Even in the dark it was clear his parents weren't as obsessed about gardening as Mr. Price. Other than that, the house was the same, two stories, brick, with two trees in the front yard.

I leaned my bike against one, ran to the door, and dried my hands on my jeans. His parents' first impression of me sucked since I almost got their son arrested, but I was desperate. I took a deep breath, knocked on the door, then paced the porch.

My neck twitched. One, two, three, four, five, six, seven—

The door opened. "Can I help you?"

I spun around and faced Jay's mom. She glared at me and put her hands on her hips. Eight, nine, ten.

"Mrs. Davidson, I'm really sorry to bother you, but it's an emergency." I went for a manners-and-desperation combo. The best tactic for a sweaty kid full of adrenaline and twitching up a storm.

"It's late and he's grounded," she said.

Good thing it wasn't a life-or-death kind of emergency. But then I probably wouldn't be knocking on his door.

"I know. And I'm sorry, but it will only take a second. It's very important."

She inspected me. One, two, three, four, five, six, seven, eight, nine, ten. My neck twitched, and my hands squeezed together. Sweat dripped down my chest. Her eyes wouldn't leave me. I stood there and took it. I had no choice.

"Wait here. I'll get him." She closed the door and left me there.

I waited, counted to ten four times, and prayed she wasn't calling the police.

The door opened again. "Sorry, my mom's a little cranky. Come in," Jay said.

"It's okay, she's allowed to be. Look, I need a favor. I need to borrow some money. I'll pay you back. I promise." I shifted my feet.

Jay inspected me the same way she did. Genetics always amazed me.

"You okay?" he asked.

"Yeah. I'm going to see my mom in New York. That's why I've been working. I almost have enough for the bus ticket, but I just need a little more."

He leaned against the wall. "You didn't ask your dad?"

"I can't," I said. "We got in a fight. Plus, their divorce was really bad. They haven't spoken in six years." I looked him in the eyes, pleading. "And before you ask, Khory and I had a fight too, so I can't ask her."

I stuffed my hands in my pockets and turned toward the door. "Never mind. I understand. I don't want to get you into more trouble."

Jay stood straight. "No, it's okay. I've got money in my room. Come on."

I let out a big sigh. "Thanks. I really appreciate it. You have no idea."

I followed him to his room. It was exactly what I expected. Clothes on the floor, an unmade bed, and shelves of model cars. He was the opposite of me in every way.

Jay opened his desk drawer and pulled out sixty dollars. All he had.

"Is this good?" he asked.

"Yeah, perfect. Thanks again. I'll be back in a couple days, and I'll pay you back."

"No problem."

We walked back down the hallway to the front door.

"What's the rush?" Jay asked. "Why don't you wait until you have money for a plane ticket? It's got to be better than taking a bus."

"I know. But plane tickets are majorly expensive, and since I'm grounded, my dad won't let me work."

"Ha, you'd think work would be a punishment." He nodded toward my bike. "You riding to the station?"

"Yeah. I have a few things I need to get first, though. Eight hours is a long ride. I need something to keep me busy."

"Next time you should suck it up and fly."

"No kidding."

"I hope things work out with your mom." Jay patted me on the back. "And Khory."

"Thanks. Me too."

I put the money in my pocket, then rode to the bus station. It was farther than I'd ever ridden, but I had to save every penny for the trip. What if Mom wouldn't see me? I had to stay somewhere. Or go back home.

I pedaled and coasted for twenty minutes. I didn't count the miles. I pushed out images of Dad going back to my room for another talk. As long as my phone didn't ring, I was good. And once I was on the bus and out of Richmond, there was nothing he could do. I pedaled faster.

• • • • • • • • • •

It took me thirty minutes, not twenty, to get to the bus station. I stored my bike in the rack, raced to the ticket booth on wobbly legs, and bought a one-way ticket to Schenectady since that's all I had the money for. Then I sat down to wait.

The place was a ticcer's nightmare. Even in the dim light, I saw chewed gum smushed on the floor like polka dots and a greenish-brownish-blackish grime smeared on the walls. I crossed my arms and tried to ignore the tingling in my fingertips. I would have traded the touching tic for anything right now. The arm flap, the curse words, even screaming *bomb* in a theater.

Based on the red-versus-blue graffiti, it seemed like gangs actually fought over this place. I knew it was a territory and pride thing, but I would've gladly handed over the nauseating aroma of urine and puke-crusted walls for a nice, open place under a bridge.

I chose a bench far from other people as a favor to them since I was dripping sweat from the bike ride and probably had the stench to go with it, but close enough to the ticket booth so that I wouldn't be mistaken for a runaway-in-hiding or a victim-to-be.

The clock ticked slowly. If I ticced that slowly, I wouldn't have been sitting here right now. You know you've lost it when you wished you were a clock.

I tapped my feet, counted rounds of ten, and fought the urge to play on my phone. Eight hours was a long time to have a dead phone battery. Ten minutes was a challenge. To pass the time, I went over my plan, which was extremely disorganized for me. Basically, I would arrive in Schenectady, take a cab to Mom's house, and knock on the door.

After then it was up to her. She'd either let me in or slam the door in my face. She wasn't crazy about seeing me when we lived together since I constantly mirrored her tics and touched her plate, so why did I think this would be different? Maybe the fact that I spent eight hours on a bus to see her would give me an edge and guilt her into letting me in. Maybe if I said I had to pee really bad. The alternative was to stand outside, yell everything, and possibly pee on her grass. Of course, that meant attention on me, so no thanks.

I dropped my head in my hands. Music, pieces of conversations, and the clang of the metal gate separating those with tickets and those without rang in my ears. My hands squeezed together and hit the side of my head ten times. With my right hand. Then with my left.

I glanced up. A black guy on the bench across from me had his eyes closed and earbuds in. He didn't notice me. The gray-haired couple on the opposite side of the bench looked away. Did it ever occur to them to help me? What if this was a medical emergency? I didn't see them reaching for their phones or yelling to the ticket lady for help. But if I walked over and touched them, all of a sudden it would be the emergency of the century. They'd call the police and yell that some crazy kid infected them. Why wasn't there any in-between? I was either completely ignored or a complete lunatic.

The speaker squawked and spit out a stream of static before the announcer got out the word *Schenectady*. The freaked-out couple eyed me, then stood up and sprinted to the bus line. I grabbed my backpack and followed them. One part of me thought about brushing my arm against theirs or literally breathing down their necks. Maybe it was the fed-up side. Or the dark side.

I sighed. My neck twitched. People took their time finding seats and stowing their luggage. One, two, three, four, five, six, seven, eight, nine, ten. Repeat. Finally it was my turn to get on.

This bus was longer than the city bus but had the same issues of aisle seats and seatmates. That wasn't going to work. I'd reach over and touch someone and be thrown off before we made it out of Virginia.

Back to a police department, charged with inappropriate touching, drugged-out behavior, and being a runaway. And they'd call Dad.

I made it up the steps and did a quick scan. The back seats were taken, but there were enough open ones on each side, so I could get a window. And the line behind me wasn't too long, so I could get a seat to myself.

I started down the aisle. One, two, three, four, five, six—the first open seat was at least six more steps. I stretched my steps as wide as I could—seven, eight, nine, ten. The people behind me sighed as I bent down and touched the floor. I stood up, took three more steps, and slid into a seat on the left counting the rest of the way to ten.

Not surprisingly, everyone else behind me scooted past my seat and found others farther back. I was alone when the doors finally closed. I put my back against the window, my legs across the seat, and closed my eyes. Soon my body moved in time with the bus's rhythm and not its own.

MARCH 30

A big, old-fashioned wall clock greeted the bus as it pulled into the Schenectady station. Eight thirty in the morning. I rubbed my eyes and stretched. It wasn't the best sleep I'd ever had, but it had to be enough. My brain couldn't be foggy today.

I glanced out the window at the people leaning against the walls and hanging out in groups. They stood with their arms crossed, smoking and frowning. The bus doors opened; I started my ten-count-bend-down. My back screamed from the stiffness. A thirty on the rate-the-pain scale. No big deal. I'd been worse.

This station was similar to the one at home. The smell of bodily functions gone wrong indicated no one bothered to clean it. Not to mention the overflowing garbage cans and paint-chipped walls. Outside the sun was shining and the temperature was crisp, reminding me I was in the north. How could anything bad happen on a day like this? It was so damn bright and cheery.

I turned on my phone, and it beeped immediately. Messages from Khory. None from Dad, which meant he went to work before

I supposedly left for school. Part of his new adjusted schedule so he could be home to babysit both his boys.

Of course, Khory wouldn't miss the fact that I wasn't in school. I scanned her texts. More of the same from last night but with a touch of added panic. She pleaded for an answer so she would know I was okay. In other words, tell me you're alive and didn't kill yourself.

School just started, so she'd be in Language Arts, but I knew her phone would be close. I sent her a text.

ME: I'm fine. Just sick.

And in case she felt the need to call her parents, or mine, to check on me, I added a little bonus for her.

ME: I stayed up late talking to my dad, so I'm tired too.

I barely had my finger off the Send button before it beeped.

KHORY: Sorry you're sick. Glad you talked to your dad. I love you.

No smiley faces with heart eyes, but she seemed to believe me, if you could believe a text message. But I didn't have time to worry about that, I had to get to Mom's house. I used the map app to track the route and distance. Only fifteen minutes from here by car. Walking would add another hour and a half, especially the way I walked.

And I had a time limit. I had to be at Mom's before Jay and Khory met in the lunch room and he innocently mentioned that he had loaned me money for a bus ticket. I debated texting him and asking him to keep it quiet, but I had already taken money from him that I wouldn't be able to pay back. So that gave me three hours before phone calls were made and Dad sent the Schenectady Police Department to find me and haul me home. I put on my jacket, calculated the money I had left, and walked to the cab waiting on the curb.

· · · · · · · · · ·

The fifteen-minute cab ride wasn't long enough for me to get it together. I stared out the window trying to come up with a better plan. Something besides, "Hi, remember me?" I kicked myself. Me, Mr. OCD, should have written note cards, or at least key phrases on my hand, but I had nothing. The most important conversation of my life, and I was stumped.

Office buildings, houses, and churches zipped by. My neck twitched. My hand squeezed together. I counted to ten. My face scrunched up. Repeat.

"Kid, we're here. 5220 Hawkwood."

Already? I was sure I hadn't made it nine rounds of ten yet, but the driver, half turned in his seat, had his hand out. I paid the bill, plus a tip, then grabbed my backpack and scooted out. I stood on the sidewalk and watched him leave. Then I turned to the house.

It was smaller than mine, light gray with white shutters and columns on the porch. A tan Ford Focus sat in the driveway. It was the kind of car I'd pick. Not sporty or flashy like Jay's, but something that blended in with everything else.

I started toward the house, taking small steps for a change. It took thirty-five steps and three bend-downs to get up the driveway. My neck twitched. I took four more steps and did another bend-down. Up close the columns were dirty and had cobwebs. She needed a teenager to clean them.

I started another round, walking up the brick pathway.

One, two, three . . .

I was on the porch.

Four, five, six . . .

I peeked in the front window. A couch and lamp. No people.

Seven . . . eight . . . nine . . . ten.

My neck twitched four times. My hands squeezed together.

I raised my hand to knock, but it just grazed the wood. Not even loud enough for a dog to hear. I pressed my hand against the wood. My stomach flip-flopped.

Just do it.

Rat tat tat.

I waited. My hands in my pockets, then out. My neck bobbing to my left shoulder, then to my right. My stomach rumbled, but the thought of food made it nosedive, even though I hadn't eaten since yesterday afternoon.

The door opened.

Mom.

She wore jeans and a T-shirt and had the same long, brown hair, but curlier I think. And gray at the temples. She looked older and had wrinkles by her eyes. And the scar on her chin. It was her. The left side of her face scrunched. Then the right. I grabbed the wall and squeezed tight.

Her mouth dropped open. "Troy," she said.

I nodded.

She peered around me. "Are you here with your dad?"

I shook my head. "I took a bus."

"I can't believe you're here." She smiled, studied me from head to toe, then took my hand. "Come inside."

I followed her inside to the living room. It was as plain as the outside, but homey. A white couch and chair faced a fireplace, and a shaggy blue rug partly covered hardwood floors.

She turned toward me and gave me another once-over. Her chin trembled, and she pressed her lips together. I wanted to hug her and cry with her, but I wasn't ready for that. My hands squeezed, voluntarily this time. She left me. This wasn't a happy reunion. It was a question-and-answer session. Of course, if she hugged me, there wouldn't be anything I could do. I bit my lip. My neck was out of control. I lost count after four sets of ten, and I was usually a much better counter than that.

She pulled me close. I wanted to be strong, but who was I kidding? I had no control over anything. I put my arms around her and let the tears flow.

She hugged me, then stepped back and held my hands. "Your voice is so deep. You're so grown up."

The last time she saw me I was short and thin, but that was before years of meds. I was also pretty stupid then and believed life would get better.

"I didn't know you were coming. You should have called. I would have picked you up," she said.

She made it sound like I was welcome here and this was a normal visit. I guess my invitation got lost in the mail.

"How is everything? At home? Your Dad?"

"Fine," I said.

"I don't know why he didn't call to tell me you were coming."

I knew he had her phone number. I gritted my teeth and was just about to say I hated liars when remembered I was one.

"Dad doesn't know I'm here."

"What? We have to call him. He'll be so worried and send the entire department out to look for you."

"It's okay. He thinks I'm at school. I'll call him later. I just want to talk to you."

She was silent. Trying to think of the right thing to do? She was worried about that now?

"Okay," she said.

She led me through the kitchen to a sunroom where half the walls were windows. I sat on the edge a wood chair with puffy blue-and-white striped pillows, and she sat on a matching couch across from me.

Mom had the neck twitch that seemed to define Tourette more

than cussing. She tapped the arm of the couch in no specific pattern, and I had to look away so I wouldn't even her taps out. How could she be so careless?

I thought back to our shoes at the bottom of the stairs. I bet her house was filled with shelves of accessories, all of them touching. My hands clenched and went to my head. I grabbed my hair. They pulled and squeezed, but as usual, it wasn't hard enough. My neck twitched again. And again.

"I can't believe you're in tenth grade now. Are you still crazy about science and space?"

"Yes," I said. She remembered.

I wanted to tell her about the zero-gravity experience, and Khory, but I had to focus. This wasn't the time to play catch-up. I had a purpose. I just had to find the guts to bring it up.

"How long have you been here?" I asked.

"About two years. Since my mom, your grandmother, died. I was an only child, and even though we weren't close, the house became mine."

I stayed quiet and counted while I figured out where to go next. Small talk wasn't my thing, but I didn't want to piss her off with accusations, or she would never give me answers. I opened and closed my hands and tried to put some order to her tapping. This wasn't going according to plan. Oh, yeah, I didn't have one.

"I'm very happy to see you," she said. "You have no idea how much I missed you."

I watched her neck twitch and the left side of her face scrunch, then the right.

"Why?" I spit out.

Mom sighed and leaned forward. "I knew this was coming. I didn't realize it would be today, but I should have been prepared. It's not like me to be unprepared."

She tapped. "Why did I leave? I know this will sound corny, or like a cop-out, but I did it for you."

"You're right. It is a cop-out." It was the line everyone gave in every TV show and every movie: "I did it to protect you from the once-dead-but-now-back-to-life leader of the league of assassins." That's how lame her excuse was.

"I didn't have many friends growing up," she said. "Just a few who could look past the tics."

"So, did you think it would be different for me?" My neck twitched, and my hands squeezed together.

"I did because your dad was one of those. He treated me like the tics and obsessions didn't exist. I thought he could give you a normal life." She took a deep breath and let it out.

"Normal? For me normal is people asking for a new desk so they don't get what I have. Or people spitting on the floor because they know I'll bend down and touch it."

Mom's face scrunched up, and when it relaxed, there were tears in her eyes. Her tears should have put out the fire building inside me, but it was too hot to be smothered.

"If you knew it was hereditary, and your life sucked, why did you have me?" I demanded.

She shifted in her seat, wiped her eyes, then stared toward her hands. "I don't know. Maybe I thought it would be different for you. That I could help you more than my parents helped me. Of course, that was crazy, because I couldn't help myself."

"So, you went ahead and had a kid, then realized it was too much and just left?"

"I knew the risks, but I wanted a child so bad. And we were happy."

"But then I started showing the signs. And you couldn't love me like that." I gritted my teeth and squeezed my hands together.

"That's not true. I loved you. I do love you. But I couldn't see you like that. Knowing the pain I went through and that most likely you would, too. And that was my fault. The guilt was too much. I was afraid. Terrified I'd do something drastic."

I stared at her. Did she hurt me like I hurt Jude? Did she think about suicide? I ran my hand over my phone, knowing the list was safely inside. We could have shared our pain and feelings, maybe found a way to survive. But now it was too late.

"So you left with no one to help me."

"If I stayed, I wouldn't have been able to help. Do you remember what it was like living together?" she asked. "Our tics feeding off each other?"

"The shoes," I said. "It drove me insane when they touched.

Still does." I stiffened my neck and face muscles so I wouldn't look around and see things that had to be moved apart.

"I wanted you to have the easiest life possible."

I spread my arms wide. "You can see how well that turned out. I needed you. You understood. Instead I was stuck with someone who had no clue what to do. Except send me to a psychiatrist who made things worse. Dad doesn't understand what it feels like or what I need. He thinks everything is great, like I'm still in second grade."

Mom's shoulders dropped. She shook her head. "Your dad was so outgoing. I prayed you would get that from him. I just wanted to stay at home. I forced myself to go out after you were born. Took you to play dates, the park. I went to your school events. But it was too much."

"He did try to get me to be more social, but I fought him until he gave up," I said. "I'm the same as you. I don't go out if I can help it. Just school and the jobs I did to get the money for the bus ticket."

I forced myself to face forward, and the muscles in my body began to ache. Tourette wasn't the only thing that was hereditary. It was all the fear and anxiety that went with it. So despite her so-called best effort, I still ended up just like her.

"I'm so sorry," she cried.

I watched her body shake and listened to her sobs. My lips quivered and tears formed.

"It's okay," I choked out. I wasn't an asshole. I just wanted answers.

She nodded but continued to shake. I stood up, moved to her chair, and knelt down. She put my hand on her arm, then rubbed my hair. Soon her body was still, and my tears dried.

Mom popped her head up, her eyes wide as if she suddenly remembered I wasn't supposed to be here.

"We have to call your dad. He'll be so worried. Do you want me to call?" Mom asked.

"And say what: 'Surprise, it's your long-lost ex-wife'?"

She put her head back down.

"Sorry," I said.

He would find out in an hour when Khory and Jay compared notes at lunch. She'd call her parents for sure. Then they'd call Dad. It was probably better he heard it from me. Or from Mom. I took out my phone, brought up his number, and handed it to her. She stared at it for a minute, six ten-counts.

"It'll be okay," she said.

Was she telling me or trying to convince herself? She pressed the Call button. Her neck twitched faster. She tapped her fingers on the chair. The left side of her face scrunched, then the right. I should have been the one calling, but I couldn't handle the cop side of him right now.

The tapping stopped.

"It's not Troy. It's Jennifer," she said. "He's with me."

She stared at the table in front of the couch. I was relieved I couldn't hear Dad through the phone, but the fact that he was quiet didn't mean he wasn't mad.

"In Schenectady. He took a bus . . ."

Mom described my big surprise while I sat there. I'd done it. Number nine. I found her and told her how I felt. The fire was gone. I was cried out. There was nothing left.

"We can get a flight in the morning if you don't mind him staying overnight." Mom glanced at me. "Is that okay, Troy?"

I nodded. I could handle one night. This wasn't a big "let's be a happy family again" reunion. I wasn't nine anymore, and I definitely wasn't clueless.

While Mom and Dad worked out the details, I got up and stretched. I had no clue about decorating besides space posters, but this wasn't the flower-patterned-plastic-covered furniture I expected from grandparent-aged people. I guess Mom redecorated. Besides the furniture, there was a vase with flowers, a few candles, and a book. The only personal thing was a black-and-white photo of a woman dressed like she lived centuries ago.

I wandered toward the kitchen and the living room. She wasn't big on decorations there either, maybe because she had more important things to do than spend her day making sure everything touched. There were a few wire animal statues that I assumed were someone's idea of art, and they did pull me toward them, but not because I wanted to study the creativeness. I had the urge to bend them. The one with the cat's tail reaching up to the sky made my fingers tingle. I squeezed my hands together and moved toward the fireplace.

My fourth-grade picture stared at me from the mantel. I looked like the photographer just told me that Darth Vader was real. I had an eye tic that year. I would open my eyes as wide as I could, then I'd squeeze them so tight I was afraid they'd pop. I'd spent weeks wondering what gelatinous material would squirt all over Justin, who sat across from me and already hated me. I touched my eyes.

There was a baby picture of me, one of Mom and me when I was about three and could still take a decent picture, and another of an older couple. Probably my grandparents.

There wasn't anything else of interest in here. I wandered back to the kitchen. There were no pictures on the refrigerator, just a few magnets, including one of the Empire State Building, and a calendar on the side. I resisted the urge to flip to July to see if my birthday was circled.

What stood out the most was there weren't pictures of anyone but family, and no papers or mail with anyone's name but hers. No husband, wife, or roommate.

I went back to the sunroom. Mom held the phone to me. I took it and held it to my ear expecting this lecture to top the one after I got caught driving.

"Hi," I said.

"I'm glad you're safe," Dad said. His voice was quiet, but there was nothing calm about it. "We have a lot to talk about when you get home, but for now, just spend time with your mom. I'll see you tomorrow, okay?"

"Okay."

I put the phone down. Mom wrapped her arm around my back and turned me toward the kitchen.

"Are you hungry? I can make you a sandwich."

She talked at superspeed with the ticcing to go along with it. What did they talk about?

Mom motioned to a chair. I sat while she zipped around the kitchen making sandwiches with a side of fruit.

"You live alone?" I asked.

"Yes. Just me and Hitchcock, my cat." Mom sat across from me and pushed the plate across the table.

"Isn't it lonely?"

Her body stiffened, but her neck kept twitching and she tapped the table. Dad told her something. Was it the driving? The smoking? The note?

"No, it's not," she said, but she wouldn't look at me. "I talk to people on the phone all day for work, I'm a project manager, and I have a few friends I go to dinner with."

She smiled, but it wasn't the kind that made you welcome or

warm. It was fake. Yes, I'm lonely, but that's how I want it. Bullshit.

"Your dad says you have a girlfriend."

I smiled at the thought of Khory, but it faded pretty quickly. I was too unstable for her. Still, I told Mom about her past and her future. Everything except the way her eyes were like stars and her hair smelled like coconut. I had to keep some things to myself.

We talked about our lives, and underneath it all was loneliness. Staying inside, working from home, and living alone. Unless you counted a cat, but they're so damn independent, even they don't care about you.

I lay in the guest-room bed that night and opened my phone to the list. I checked off number nine.

1. Meet someone with Tourette syndrome—COMPLETED
2. Get my first kiss—COMPLETED
3. Be pain-free—COMPLETED
4. See the space shuttle—COMPLETED
5. Talk about Tourette in public—COMPLETED
6. Find a babysitter for my baby brother—COMPLETED
7. Give away my Tim Howard autographed picture—COMPLETED
8. Drive a car—COMPLETED
9. Talk to Mom—COMPLETED
10. Commit suicide

I pulled the white blanket over me. The weight of it held me down and comforted me at the same time. I opened my Methods to Die list. Gun, pills, scissors. Seven days left. That thought held me down and comforted me as well. Soon I would be free.

MARCH 31

Our flight was early, earlier than school. Not because she wanted to get rid of me, but because there weren't a whole lot of options between Schenectady and Richmond. I knew; I'd helped her search last night.

I repacked my backpack and brought it into the living room. Mom stood next to an end table with a suitcase.

"Where are you going?" I asked.

"To Richmond with you. I thought we could spend more time together."

Her neck twitched, and her fingers tapped the table. I tilted my head.

"Dad told you. About the note."

"Yes."

"Why didn't you say anything?"

"I was afraid you'd leave. That you would run away from here."

I squeezed my hands, then grabbed my hair. "So you're going

to move in and help babysit me? Won't that be uncomfortable with his wife and baby?"

She frowned. "No, I'll be at a hotel and come by after school."

"I don't need a babysitter. And you're a little late, don't you think?"

I stared at her until she turned away. I should have told her it was a waste of time and she should save her money. I'd already checked her off. She had no place in number ten.

Mom drove us to the airport, and we trudged on the plane with the rest of the sleepy passengers. I settled into the seat by the window and leaned against the side, hoping to fall asleep before I caught glimpses of the strange looks from other passengers. Their lack of coffee might have disguised our neck twitches as a bizarre synchronized dance team, but when the rest of the tics started, fear would set in.

The invisible hand tickled my chest. I took a deep breath to get as much air as I could before my chest tightened. Would someone slip a note to the flight attendant saying they thought we were terrorists? Or would they just jump us? Come on people, terrorists would never draw so much attention to themselves. Really, would anyone if they could help it?

Mom mumbled under her breath. Would her vocal tic make her scream *bomb?* I squeezed my eyes shut and rubbed my temples. I took another deep breath, but hardly any air got to my lungs.

Mom rubbed my arm. "It will be okay."

Did she think I was afraid of the plane ride? Please, I did zero gravity. After that, a regular plane was like riding a bike. But maybe she didn't mean the flight. Was it the passengers? Or Dad? That thought didn't help me breathe easier.

A flight attendant came over the speaker. I focused on her words. Seat belts. Exit rows. Flotation device. Dying in a burning plane wasn't a method I'd thought of.

The engines rumbled, and the plane moved forward. We made it this far. The throbbing in my head slowed. Air reached my lungs. Soon we were soaring through the sky. Some of the people in my area were asleep, and others had settled into their electronics. I pulled out my headphones. My plan was to zone out to music. I didn't want to think about the lecture I knew was coming from Dad, or how I'd escape twenty-hour supervision on April 6.

"I'm so happy you came," Mom said. "I should have gone back to see you a long time ago."

Of course she should have, and she knew she'd messed up. I stared at the way her neck twitched and face scrunched. What would our lives have been like if she had stayed? Us against the world, or us happily hanging out at home? More likely we'd be miserable. Despite what I'd always believed, I wasn't sure being together would have been better.

I sank into my seat and drank water while she had coffee. I listened to her mumble and tried not to do the same.

"I'm going to stay for a few days. Just to make sure you're settled," she said clearly.

I stared at her. Settled? It was my house. I settled in sixteen years ago.

. . . .

Dad didn't just pull the car to the curb to pick us up, he met us in the visitor's area as close to the gate as he could get. The next step would have been to show up in uniform and officially escort me off the plane. The glare he gave me made me think handcuffs weren't out of the question.

After an incredibly awkward greeting that was half handshaking, half hugging, and a lot of stumbling around polite words, my parents and I walked to the car.

I'm good by the way, Dad. Thanks for asking. He was strangely quiet, and a nagging feeling tickled my mind. It creeped me out. I studied him and Mom, waiting for a sign. A clue. Was he sending me to live with her in New York? That wouldn't fix anything. Of course it might have if he'd done it when I asked six years ago.

They stared straight ahead. No secret winks or hand signals. We got on the highway toward Richmond. I fell back against the seat, crossed my arms, and scowled. Dad eyed me from the rearview mirror. Finally, he remembered I was here. I kept the scowl.

"I know it wasn't just a note. It was a whole list," he said. "I also know what's supposed to happen after you talked to your mother."

I gasped and squeezed my hands. In anger. Well, it's official, I wasn't as good a liar as I thought. But I guess you believed people until they gave you a reason not to, and I gave Khory and Dad plenty. Just like I believed Mom would come back. Until she didn't.

"Now I understand about pushing to have Khory babysit. Does she realize you used her?"

"I didn't use her. I helped her. And you, too. Or would you have left Jude with some psycho nanny who locks him in his room or lets him sit in dirty diapers?"

Mom spun to me. "Troy, do not talk to your father like that. He's trying to help."

"You have no idea about helping or even Dad's version of it."

She faced front. Silent. That's right. You may say you love me, but you're too late.

"We are going home, so you can pack some clothes," Dad said. I leaned forward to hear as he continued. "Then I am taking you to a psychiatric hospital. They have people you can talk to. They will also evaluate you and see about changing your medication."

"What?" Mom and I practically screamed in sync.

"It's for your safety. And others," he said.

That's his way of helping? Locking me up until strangers declare I'm safe to be out in the world?

"What do you think I'm going to do? Take everyone out?"

"I don't want you to take yourself out either," he said.

My insides were burning. My chest was on fire. Soon any air in there would be snuffed out.

"Did you know about this, Mom?" I cringed when I called her

that. She wasn't anything like what a mom should be. She didn't deserve that name.

"I had no idea. We agreed I would stay with you while your Dad's at work. Clark, we need to discuss this. I'll make sure he's never alone."

Dad slapped the steering wheel and turned to her. "I'm doing what I think is best. It's not your choice. You gave up your right for input when you walked out the door."

"I did that for his own good."

"And look how well he's doing."

"You can't blame all this on me. You're the one who raised him."

It was a Ping-Pong game, and I was the ball. My head throbbed like I was really being smacked around. I rubbed my temples. One, two, three, four, five, six, seven, eight, nine, ten. Repeat. The neck twitches, hand squeezes, and face scrunches were at superspeed. I closed my eyes and pictured the airplane, but Hardly Qualified walked in. I tried to float, but I was shoved into a police car. I couldn't even remember the feeling of floating.

The car slowed, and Dad parked in the driveway. I kicked open the door and ran inside. The house was still. Quiet. Like it was holding its breath. Terri and Jude weren't here. She'd taken him away so I couldn't see him before they locked me up. Not even to say goodbye.

My hand squeezed as though Jude's hair was wrapped around my fingers. Dad was right, I was a danger to others, and no one could counsel or medicate me out of it. No amount of time in any hospital could change that.

I stood in the hallway and debated which way to go. It was too early. I still had seven days. My hands squeezed together. I pulled my hair and searched for something to break.

A door slammed behind me. "Troy, let's talk about this," Mom said.

Sorry, I'm all talked out. I couldn't wait anymore. I ran to Dad's bedroom, closed the door and locked it, then pushed his night table in front it. I held my breath as I stepped into the closet.

The metal box was in the same place on the upper shelf. I ran my finger along the opposite shelf and found the key.

"Troy. Where are you?" Dad's voice boomed from the other side of the door.

I grabbed the box and key, went into the bathroom, and locked the door. Dad would figure it out soon. Locked doors were an easy clue, especially for a cop.

My fingers trembled and my neck twitched as I put the key in the box's lock.

Click.

I lifted the lid and stared at the gray metal. I ran my finger along the barrel. My neck twitches slowed down.

They pounded on the bedroom door. "Troy, open the door," Dad yelled. "Do you hear me?"

Of course I heard. He was kind of hard to miss. I lifted the gun out and checked for bullets. Loaded. Of course. It was for protection, and what kind of help was an unloaded gun?

The pounding continued. Mom begged me to open the door. I held the gun in my hand and slid down the wall.

A loud bang shook the bathroom door. He tried to kick open the bedroom door. "Damn. Troy, open this door or else," Dad demanded.

Or else what? It was almost comical at this point. His threats, his plan. They were nothing compared to mine.

Another bang turned into a crash. Their voices were louder. Right outside the bathroom door. My neck twitched, and pain shot down my back. I gasped and for once didn't bother to count to ten.

"The gun's gone," Dad said.

The grip of the gun fit perfectly in my hand. I put the barrel to my head.

"Jennifer, move away from the door," Dad said.

"Stay out. I have the gun to my head."

"Okay. We won't come in. Please just don't do anything," Mom said.

Her voice was soft. Was she really there, or was this all a dream?

"Clark, leave us. Let me talk to him," Mom said.

The bathroom door moved.

"Don't come in!" I scooted to the corner, faced the door, and brought my knees up.

"I'm not. I'm not coming in." She let out a big breath. "I'm just sitting against the door. I told your dad to leave so we can talk. Ticcer to ticcer."

We already talked, and it was pretty damn revealing. Jude would grow up and leave. Khory would experience life no matter what her dad said. And my future was pain, loneliness, and heartless people. I rested my arm on my knee. The gun was heavy.

"It sucks," Mom said. "It sucks, and no one can understand us without walking in our shoes. Not your dad, not your girlfriend."

Khory's face floated in front of me, her hair falling over one eye. She was so strong. After everything that happened, still fighting to survive. I tried it her way, but I wasn't that strong. Living was for the ones who wanted to go out and make a difference. What good was a person who sat home all day? I was just wasted air.

I pressed the metal to my temple. It wasn't as cold as I thought it'd be. Maybe because it had been resting in its cloth-covered box. Like a coffin.

"I remember when Khory's sister was killed," Mom said. "The story made the national news. It was our city, and someone your age. I couldn't imagine what it would have been like to lose a child. I don't ever want to know."

My hand squeezed around the gun. I didn't want her to feel like the Prices, but honestly, she'd lost me a long time ago.

"I was as miserable as you are and thought about killing myself, too. One day when you were at school, just before I left, I sat at home with a bottle of sleeping pills. All I saw was pain and loneliness in our futures. Then I pictured you coming home and finding me there. You alone with your dead mother."

She was silent, then let out a big exhale.

"I worked hard to get my life back. And yes, sometimes I'm lonely, but I go to meetings and I've met other people with Tourette. Some really special people."

I had special people, too, like Khory who made me forget to count and Jay who stood up for me to the cops. The police! Mrs. Frances picked me out of everyone for Gravity Redefined. Even Rainn and Diego were cool, even though their parents were stupid. Maybe there was hope. Mr. and Mrs. Isenhour found each other. The lady found her dog, and didn't she say that she'd be able to drive now?

I wanted to drive. I wanted to be free to feel weightless. To kiss girls. Mrs. Isenhour said I was a role model for her son. Me? I focused on the gun and rubbed my finger over the barrel. Then the trigger. The urge to squeeze it built up in my fingers. I gasped and dropped my hand.

My heart pounded. My finger tingled. I wanted to feel the trigger again. Harder. Was that my Tourette brain talking, or was I ready to give in to the exhaustion? I breathed in and out fast. One, two, three, four, five, six, seven, eight, nine, ten. Repeat. My chest tightened. My breathing sped up. Too fast to get air back in. The Tourette and OCD, they were responsible one way or another.

"I just want it all to stop. To go away. The pain, the anxiety, the fucking number ten." I brought the gun back to my head.

MARCH 31

CRASH!

The bathroom door slammed open and bounced off my leg. I winced. White splinters flew across the room, hit the wall, and fell into the sink. I moved the gun from my head. Mom and Dad stood in the doorway. Mom's eyes were red, and her cheeks splotchy. Probably what I looked like if I dared to peek in the mirror.

Dad's eyes went from mine, to the gun, then back to me. Sweat poured down his face. My hand squeezed the grip tighter, not ready to let go. My parents didn't move. I'd been so sure. I had my list. I'd completed just about everything. But now there was something else. A twinge of doubt? Actually, it was more like the spark I felt when I saw Khory and experienced weightlessness. I wouldn't call it hope, but it was far from despair. Could I make it last?

Mom found hope and so did Mrs. Isenhour. Enough to stay alive at least. Is that the kind of role model the Isenhours were looking to show David? A kid who survived. I had nothing else to offer, besides the picture. Nothing right now. But what if, in the future, I actually accomplished something great? Was I so sure about number ten that I wanted to erase that chance?

I stood up and turned the gun grip side-up toward Dad like he taught me. He took it, emptied the bullets, locked it, and put it in the box. The click of the lock made me flinch.

Mom took my arm and led me out of Dad's room. My tears flowed. I didn't bother to wipe them away. They calmed me and washed away every fear and every pain. At least for now.

"Oh, baby, I wish I could make it better. But I promise you there's hope. New medications, injections to dull the nerves. We can work on it."

We went to my room, and she looked around. "Just like I remembered."

Another reminder I probably should have updated my decorations sometime in the last decade.

Mom sat on my bed. I wondered if she felt the scissors under the mattress like I did.

"We can change your medication, but it would be more effective if we got you in the right frame of mind first," she said.

"Which means going to the hospital," I said. "How long will I have to be there?"

"I'm not sure. A few days maybe. A week?"

There were still seven days until the tenth anniversary. Still time to give life one more try. It wouldn't hurt to try things Khory's way. I doubted she'd be willing to teach me, but maybe I could watch from afar. I was good at sitting in the back. Mom opened my closet, pulled out a duffel bag, then went to my dresser and pulled out jeans, T-shirts, underwear, and socks. I looked around my room and frowned. I hated to leave it.

"Don't worry, you're coming back," Mom said.

I nodded and watched her stuff the clothes in a duffel bag. Dad stood in the doorway.

I followed him out.

· · · · · · · · · ·

Dad pulled the car to the front of a building that, ironically, was attached to the building the TS meetings were in. If I was still here when the next one came around, maybe they'd let me go. That had to look like progress, which I guessed I had to show to get out of here.

We parked, Dad grabbed my duffel bag from the trunk, and Mom and I followed him inside. The walls were a light green, like mint-chip ice cream. They were either going for cheery or calming. Rainn would have loved it. It made me hungry.

A few kids strolled by me on their way somewhere, but no one seemed in a hurry to get there. Thankfully, none bothered to glance my way.

My parents signed papers, then came over to me followed by a woman in green scrubs and shoes that clomped when she stepped.

"I'm Ms. Fenske, the day nurse assigned to your section.

Parents, this is where you leave him in my hands. I will take very good care of him, I promise."

Already? We had more time to say goodbye the first day of kindergarten. I stood up and Mom hugged me. She held on until Dad put his hand on her shoulder.

He took my hand and pulled me close to him. "Troy, it's just a few days. Everything is going to be fine."

"Okay," I said before my voice cracked. Tears already blurred my vision.

They turned toward the door. I shuffled behind Ms. Fenske. It was five counts of ten from the check-in desk to my room. I looked back at them just as they peeked at me. It felt like my heart ripped in two. I counted to ten. And again. I could have stayed in the hallway and done this forever, but they turned and walked away. I took a deep breath, went in, and leaned against the wall while Ms. Fenske rummaged through my duffel bag and pulled out my phone.

"Electronics are forbidden here. As are tennis shoes with laces." She held out her hand.

I kicked my shoes off, put them on the bed, and reminded myself I had agreed to this. Even though it wasn't really an option.

"A nurse will bring you your medication. Dr. Gannon was able to fit you in today, so your first therapy session will be in twenty minutes. After that I will show you around. The lunchroom and the common area where we have group therapy. A few kids do their school worksheets in there, too. Keeping up with school is very important; you don't want to fall behind. What grade are you in?"

"Tenth."

"I'll make sure you get the right ones."

How long did she think I'd be in here?

"Even missing a few days can be a big deal in terms of work." She scanned the room, maybe to see if all the sharp objects were confiscated. Hard to have weapons when the only things in here were a bed, a night table with no drawer, and one of those clothes cabinet things, open and empty.

She scooped up my shoes and phone. "Do you have any questions?"

Questions. I had a few. Would this doctor get me fixated on something as equally disturbing as the number ten? If I stayed in my room, was that a sign of depression? And I guessed asking if I could go home was out of the question. I shook my head.

I followed Ms. Fenske back down the hall and around the corner. Twelve sets of ten. She was careful not to get too far ahead, probably in case I decided to run away. I went into a small, plain room big enough for a coffee table and three black leather chairs, one already filled. Ms. Fenske hovered in the doorway until the doctor motioned for me to sit; then she backed away and closed the door.

"Troy, hi. I'm Dr. Gannon."

He was the complete opposite of HQ. Younger, muscular, and

obviously not as stuffy, because he wore khaki pants and a light-blue button-down shirt.

"Have you had a chance to look around the place? Meet anyone?"

"No. I just got here."

"Okay. Well, there will be plenty of time for that. Just to warn you, you'll probably be disappointed. It's not like home or hanging at your friend's house; the only fun and games we can offer are puzzles. You're here to get your life under control, we don't want you to stay."

I nodded. I wasn't sure I'd ever hang at a friend's house again, but I knew this would never be better than home. Not for me, anyway.

"Well, let's get right down to it. I know you tried to kill yourself, and that's why you're here. Okay, you tried suicide as an option; that didn't work. Thankfully. I'd like to discuss other options with you."

I raised my eyebrows.

He smiled. "Ah, you thought this would be a lecture. I try not to do that since I can't begin to understand what it's like to be you. So why don't you tell me?"

My neck twitched. I squeezed my hands together. Repeat.

"How about school? Family. Your Tourette. I bet your muscles are constantly in pain."

My neck twitched faster. My hands squeezed tighter. Then my face scrunched up.

"Do you play video games?" Dr. Gannon chuckled. "I know,

dumb question. What do you play? I'm into quest-type games. I love collecting tools that lead to a treasure."

My hands unclenched.

"I'm currently playing *The Quest for Alien Artifacts,*" he said.

"I've done that one."

"It's great, but I'm stuck on level seven. Any hints?" He winked.

We spent the next twenty or thirty minutes talking about video games. I gave him clues, and he named games I hadn't played. Yet. He seemed cool. Hardly Qualified, coming from the age of stone tablets and chisels, never would have mentioned electronics. But that didn't mean the doctors were completely different. Dr. Gannon could still implant some phrase or number or letter into my subconscious that even Khory wouldn't have been able to get me to forget about. So when he decided to switch from games to life and living, I tried to tune him out and made a list in my mind of everything I wanted to ask but couldn't bring myself to.

1. Did Khory think I was dead?

2. Did Dad find all the weapons I hid?

3. Did Jude wonder where I was?

4. Would I ever be able to see him again?

And then Dr. Gannon said a word that caught my attention. *List.* He spoke my nongaming language. It was like he read my mind.

"By the time you leave here," he said, "you'll have a new list of tasks to accomplish. Ones that will help you feel better."

I thought about talking, asking him a few questions, but Ms.

Fenske opened the door and said our time was up. I sighed. The questions could wait. It's not like I'd be sprung tonight if I talked. She gave me a tour of the floor, including the nurses' desk and the common area where I'd go for group therapy, then led me back to my room.

She held out a mini–paper cup. "Here are your meds for today."

I stared at the pills. Clonidine, melatonin, no Lexapro, but a new one. "What's this one?"

She peeked in the cup. "It's a higher dose of Lexapro. For depression."

I nodded, swallowed the pills, and washed them down with the cup of water she handed me.

"Open your mouth, please, so I can make sure you swallowed them."

I did as I was told. Was all this worth it? I agreed to give the whole living thing one more try, but if I had to spend it being treated like a baby, then maybe I had chosen poorly.

"I left a few worksheets on your night table. You can do them in here or in the common room," she said.

A common room with other people? The past few months I hung out with people, but Khory was there to literally hold my hand. I wasn't sure I could do it without her. No big deal; I was used to being by myself.

"Dinner is at five o'clock, and you will have relaxing time before lights out at eight," Ms. Fenske said.

She seemed to have misunderstood her clients. Apparently, she thought this was an old-age home. Should I have expected a bingo tournament later?

"Thanks." I collapsed on the bed.

She took both cups and clomped her way to the door. It *whooshed* as it closed behind her.

I rolled toward the window and stared at my view, a mammoth air conditioner. It appeared wavy, like it was behind a force field, but I was the one enclosed. And it wasn't with high-tech lasers, just an extra-thick pane of glass. I guess bars on the windows seemed too much like a prison.

I slipped under the covers. The blanket was thin and offered no protection or comfort. My scissors weren't under this mattress. I was exposed and vulnerable, and for the first time, I didn't want to be alone.

APRIL 1

I was already awake when my door opened and a man announced it was breakfast time. I rolled away from the window as he put a tray of food on a rolling table and pushed it toward me.

"Meds first," he said and held out a cup like Ms. Fenske had yesterday. I swallowed the pills, he checked my mouth, then left me alone. I picked at the food that looked like pancakes but smelled like the school cafeteria. The silence surrounded me. I peeked out the door he'd propped open: the hallway was empty.

I took a bite of food. They weren't Terri's pancakes, but they weren't terrible. By the time I finished, the floor was a little more active. Figures shuffled past my room. One or two peeked in, but no one stopped to talk. Just like school, except we weren't free to leave. I kept myself busy by showering, getting dressed, and trying not to think that today was April 1. The anniversary was five days away.

Since my phone was confiscated, I couldn't check my list. Not that I had a lot left to finish. Just number ten. And if I completed that, I wouldn't be around to mark it off anyway. I sat straighter. That wasn't going to happen. I chose life. I jumped off the bed, snatched the worksheets off the night table, and went to the common room.

The room wasn't what I expected. It was empty except for a brown couch against one wall that clashed with the mint-green paint, two round tables, and eight chairs. My neck twitched, and I counted to ten. So much for company.

I crossed the room to the closest table, sat, and scanned the worksheets. *Lord of the Flies* passages and Geometry. Seriously? But I grabbed a pen from the center of the table and began reading. My eyes closed, and I rested my head in my hand.

Thud. I opened my eyes and popped my head up. A girl wearing black leggings and an AC/DC T-shirt was slumped in the corner of the couch. My neck twitched and my hands scrunched, but I managed to smile. She smiled, then stared across the room. I looked too, but there was nothing to see. I knew that look. I've had that look. Too much medication.

I focused on my papers again, and more people came in. Another girl and three boys. They moved the chairs from the tables, then pushed the tables out of the way. I watched as they put the chairs in a circle.

"Dude, you gonna help?" a tall blonde kid yanked my chair. I hopped up before he dumped me on the ground.

"Troy, you're here. Good." Dr. Gannon walked in the room and put a hand on the blonde kid's shoulder. "Ryan, this is Troy's first group session."

"Hey," Ryan mumbled.

"Hey." I got out of his way. He was the kind of guy girls at my school followed down the hallways. And the kind of guy who used his audience to humiliate me.

Ryan took a chair near the door, crossed his arms, and stretched his legs out. I sat across the room near zombie rock-and-roll girl.

Group therapy. Would this be like the Tourette support group, all accepting and forgiving? I scanned the crowd. No one looked excited to be here.

"Good morning everyone. We have a new member of group." Dr. Gannon nodded toward me. "This is Troy."

Everyone stared at me. My neck twitched ten times. I focused on my shoe and the circles where my laces used to be. One, two, three, four, five, six, seven, eight, nine, ten.

Dr. Gannon cleared his throat. "Lauren, you said you wanted to share."

He'd moved on. My shoulders relaxed. I glanced up. A girl with long, wavy red hair, Lauren, I guessed, let out a big exhale.

"It's the pressure," she whispered. "School, sports, clubs. I can't do it all."

"I think a lot of us here understand that kind of pressure. Please, continue," Dr. Gannon said.

And she did. Half speaking, half crying, she told us about having to get into a good college, the constant questions by her parents, and the comparisons with her friends. No matter what SAT score she got, someone bragged about a better one. Then Lauren told us how she dealt with it. She took a handful of pills.

But, like me, she changed her mind. And now we had to figure out what that meant.

· · · · · · · · · ·

A couple more people shared during group, talking about anxiety and anorexia. Ryan stayed quiet on his side of the room, and I counted rounds of ten on mine. When Dr. Gannon let us go, I went back to my room. I got the concept of sharing our problems; we all dealt with bad stuff. That's why I went to the Tourette group in the first place, to compare the bad stuff. And get answers. I still hadn't gotten any, and time was running out. I wanted this to work; I just didn't know how to do it. The thought made my brain hurt.

During the next three days, I spent less time by myself and more time around other people. And not because I had to. I did the lame worksheets in the common room, walked the halls, and sat in group. Okay, the last one wasn't a choice.

I met with Dr. Gannon every other day and actually talked about something besides video games. I told him about the embarrassment of this stupid disorder, my pain scale, and zero gravity. But I kept the number ten to myself.

He took me off melatonin, and my naps were replaced with putting together puzzles of cities I'd assumed I'd never see in person but still found myself interested in. If this whole future thing worked out.

When I told that to Dr. Gannon, he smiled. I doubt that's what influenced him, but on April 4, he told me this would be our last session here. I was going home.

My neck twitched. It was out of control. My face scrunched up. Good stress or bad stress? I wasn't sure.

"I'm happy with your current doses of clonidine and Lexapro," he said. "And, except for this brief tic explosion, I feel you are too."

"Yeah, it's fine." I said between face scrunches. "I'm not as tired as I was."

"Good. We'll keep monitoring it and change it if we have to. So, how do you feel about going home and back to school?"

School? And face Khory?

I shrugged, then stared at my lap. "I didn't tell my girl— ex-girlfriend I was coming here. She probably thinks I'm dead."

"Well, I'm not going to tell her. You need to start speaking up for yourself. If something hurts, say so. If there's something you love, say that, too." He reached down beside him, picked up a piece of paper and a pen, and handed them to me. "Let's make a list. Things you're going to do to help with the Tourette, OCD, and anxiety. What do you think you should call it?"

I tapped the pen against my leg and thought about my other list.

The one where I chose death over life because I had no choice. Now I had options.

I wrote the word OPTIONS in capital letters on the top.

"Good title," Dr. Gannon said.

And together we came up with four:

1. Adjusted medication
2. Chiropractor for pain
3. Therapy with Dr. Gannon
4. Visualization techniques

I chose two. The empty warehouse and the feeling of weightlessness. I already felt ahead in this game.

APRIL 6

My decision to live came with requirements. I thought my parents would be happy I chose life and give me a little breathing room, but that's exactly what they did not do. Mom decided to stay in Richmond a little while to help babysit me. I was cranky about it, but the alternative was more time at the hospital for mentally unstable and at-risk kids. I wasn't sure which category I fell into.

That was the first requirement: twenty-four-hour supervision. I wondered who had the overnight shift and would watch me sleep.

When I got home from the hospital Saturday morning, I noticed the knives were gone, the box of cold medicines and aspirins wasn't in the hall closet, and if I had to guess, the gun had disappeared, too.

To show good faith, I dug out the pills I'd hidden in the bathroom drawer and took the scissors from under my mattress. I handed them to Dad.

"Thank you," he whispered, then walked away with his head down.

It wasn't a surprise the second requirement was that he would dispense my medicine.

And onto the third: Dad would drive me to school every day, and Mom would pick me up. They weren't kidding about the babysitter thing, but honestly, I was happy to be off the bus. Or more accurately, not to have to walk down the aisle.

Monday morning, Dad pulled into the carpool line, I got out and turned toward the school. Apparently I left one prison for another. I glanced around for staring kids who might make a smart-ass comment about me getting out of a police car, like the ones in elementary school, but no one seemed to care. Probably because it was the butt crack of dawn and no one was awake yet.

"Your mom will pick you up after school," Dad said.

Like I forgot. "Okay," I answered. Like I had any other choice.

"Hopefully you and your mom will get to know each other better."

That would be one positive outcome of all this. I nodded, closed the car door, and began the ten-count-bend-down to my locker. Another positive fact was that it only took me eight ten-counts to get there from the carpool lane. It was ten rounds from the bus lot. I made a mental note to write these down. Apparently my OCD didn't just involve the number ten, but lists as well.

I scanned the hallways for Khory. I didn't call her when I got out of the hospital but probably should have sent her a text: "Hey, it's me, I'm alive." After that big reveal, though, I was stumped. I'd done so many things to her; a simple sorry wouldn't cut it. How does someone apologize for lying to their girlfriend's face about suicide and then expect forgiveness?

I opened my locker and dug out my books for B day. My neck twitched faster, and my hands squeezed tighter. I had until the afternoon to figure out what to say. I closed my locker, and the smell of coconut surrounded me. I turned around.

Khory stood in front of me with tears in her eyes. She wrapped her arms around me and buried her face in my chest. The smell of her hair made me weak. Funny, but I considered that a positive thing. Man, I was on a roll this morning. I hugged her. She pushed me back and crossed her arms.

"I know you went to your mom's."

I nodded.

She studied my face. Was she looking for the rest of the story? Or forgiveness? Happiness? A renewed sense of loving life, not that I'd ever had one? I still wasn't one hundred percent sure what I felt or what my face would show.

"I'm sorry I told my parents and your dad about the list. I was so worried." Tears trickled down her cheeks.

"It's okay. Really."

It wasn't a lie. I wasn't mad at her for trying to avoid having another dead person haunting her life. I told myself I wouldn't lie about this anymore, but I prayed she wouldn't ask if I'd given up the whole suicide idea.

I was only sixteen, and with medical advancements these days, I could easily have lived to be ninety—older if I had genes like Mrs. Blackwood. So at least seventy-four years of neck twitches, hand squeezes, and strange looks, which was the reason for the fourth requirement: I had to see a psychiatrist.

I took a chance, leaned in, and kissed her. Partly to taste the strawberry lip gloss, but mostly so that she couldn't read something I wasn't sure I could explain.

"I'm happy to see you," I said.

The bell rang. We broke apart to head to our first class. Khory dug in her backpack and handed me an envelope.

"Here. Let me know what you think." Then she walked into Language Arts.

I made my way to Visual Tech, leaned against the hallway wall, and stared at the envelope. I thought it might be a breakup letter, but she kissed me earlier, so maybe it was a love note. Plus, breakup would be by text. I opened the envelope and took out the letter.

Dear Judge,

Steven Wesley killed my sister, Krista Lauren Price. I know. I was there. People say I was lucky to survive, but since that day my life, and my parents', have been filled with fear and heartbreak. I'll never get my sister back, and I miss her every day.

I can't begin to imagine why someone would do what this man did to her, and for a long time I was so angry, the only thing I thought could make it right was for him to die. But now I truly believe that everyone on this planet has something to give. Something positive. At one point in his life, Mr. Wesley was a teacher. He could use the time in prison to teach others to read, or write, or do math. If there isn't anything productive he can share with others, he can do his part by being on trash or bathroom-cleaning duty so others can be free to develop skills and become functioning members of society.

With this letter, I am asking you to spare his life and not give him the death penalty. Everyone has a purpose. They just have to find out what it is.

Sincerely,

Khory Lynn Price

I took a deep breath and let it out slowly. Once again Khory proved how brave she was. If she thought *the guy* had a purpose, imagine how far she thought I would go. Did I have the right to waste it?

I folded the letter and put it back in the envelope when Jay caught up to me.

"Hey, dude, my bus was late. Sucks not to have a car." He smiled and threw up his hands. "Did you see your mom? How did it go?"

"It went okay. She came back with me. Make up for lost time kind of thing." I shrugged. He didn't need to know her real purpose.

"Cool. Gotta go. See you at lunch."

Then he was off at a pace I'd never be able to keep up with.

Friends. I had to add that to my new list. I took out my phone and opened to the note section. My original List of Ten pulled me down like gravity. Today was April 6, the tenth anniversary of my diagnosis. And like I planned, it was the death of something: my old life. Just not as final as I originally envisioned. I took a deep breath and clicked on the trash can. Already I felt lighter.

Then I started a new list.

1. Get to know Mom better
2. Only eight rounds of ten from the carpool lane to my locker
3. Friends (Khory, Jay, Diego, Rainn)

I didn't expect to have a lot, but really, how many people could you hang out with at one time? The more friends, the more drama. Then you had to add things like birthdays, and if you stayed in touch, you'd have to know their wives', husbands', and kids' birthdays, too. I smiled. There I was, thinking about the future again.

AUTHOR'S NOTE

When I was eight-years-old, I told my mom I wanted to die.

That was the year my life changed. Diagnoses, doctors, and medications became a regular part of life. We learned what Tourette syndrome was, experimented with medications, and participated in a study.

But having a name for what was happening to me didn't make things better. If anything, they got worse. I learned this disorder would never go away. No one else I knew had it, or at that time, in the 1970's, had ever heard of it. In fact, people didn't care what it was called, only that you acted strange and scary, and they were afraid of you invading their personal space. I spent a lot of time hiding in my room back then, getting lost in other people's stories.

I'm not going to lie and say I learned to adjust quickly. I thought about ending my life many times throughout my childhood. It took me a long time to get to the place where I am at today. Maybe because I didn't have the resources we do now, or books written about people like me.

I don't want anyone to think growing up was entirely miserable. I had friends, we roller skated, made up dances, and swam. Many people stood next to me, encouraged me, and counseled me throughout the years. And still do. I've come a long way. Do I still hate having Tourette syndrome? Absolutely. Do I let it hold me back? Absolutely not.

I'm happily married (28 years when you're reading this.) We have two children and two dogs. My life has been filled with careers that I love. I have no top-secret explanation as to how this happened, except possibly hope and love. From others and myself.

What compelled me to write this book? I get asked this question often, and there are several answers. To let those who have neurological disorders, or are contemplating suicide, know they are not alone. I am here. I understand. I'm living it. No one can really understand unless they are members of this group.

It is also to help others see us. The words in this book are bold and blatant. I don't sugarcoat anything for a reason. If we act like we're happy when we're not, or if we allow people to treat us poorly, we are not doing our part to make our lives, and those of others, better.

I'm writing this in 2020, and if this year has proven anything, it's that we must look beyond the mirror.

ACKNOWLEDGMENTS

Like Troy, I am obsessed with lists. So naturally I have one for the people who helped make this possible.

1. Deborah Warren you are an extraordinary agent and an extraordinary person. The day we met at the SCBWI Carolinas conference changed my life and not because you loved this story. Your kind and encouraging words made me believe this dream could come true.

2. Suzy Capozzi, my editor and story champion. My last big outing before the world changed was to New York where we met face-to-face. You shared your visions for Troy's story and I knew it had found the perfect home. I am truly grateful for the way you took care of us both.

3. Thank you to the entire team at Sterling—editorial, marketing, library marketing, sales, and designers—who got behind this novel made it the best it could be. Kalista Johnson, you identified my comma problems (too many and too few) thank you for helping me clean it up. Elizabeth Mihaltse Lindy, you clearly understood this story and it shows in your design of this stunning cover. Blanca Oliviery, thank you for answering all my questions, and letting me know if I was going in the right direction. Go Team Khory!

4. Rebecca J. Allen, Richelle Morgan, Michelle Leonard, Julie Arts, Jessica Vitalis, and Kate Manning. The most talented group of writers. I gave you a manuscript that was extremely personal and asked for your honest opinions. It is because of your honesty and encouragement that we are here today.

5. Helen Segel. My first reader. Number one fan. Mom. So here we are, career number three. I had my doubts, but you knew I could do it. Knowing you had such confidence in me made me want to give it all I had. And guess what? I have a book!

6. Barry, Danny, Debbie, Joanne, Julianne, Karen, Kelly, Mike, Neal, Phil, Rita, and Suzie. Writing a book isn't just about having an idea and learning the craft. A book is like a child and we know it takes a community to raise one. And wow, what an incredible community we have.

7. Julia and Joe Granieri. My martial arts instructors and friends. No words can describe how I felt when you gave me the opportunity to stand at the front of the class and represent your business. Thank you.

8. Debbie, Jimmy, Carly, Steve. We may be a small family, but the love and support we have for each other is bigger than the universe.

9. Society of Children's Book Writers and Illustrators (SCBWI), I wouldn't be here today if it wasn't for this organization and its amazing members. The conferences and events taught me how to write, allowed me the opportunity to find critique partners, and a venue to meet my agent.

10. Tourette syndrome support groups. I belong to several online, and although I don't contribute much, just knowing there are other people like me in the world makes the hard days easier and the pain bearable.

11. The21ders. The process of getting a book published doesn't stop when you have a contract and publishing date. In fact, that's when the hard work begins. Thank you all for your insight, knowledge, and most of all, friendship.

12. Last, but definitely not least, David, Aidan, and Riley. I love our creative household, and I love you all for cheering me on as I pursue this dream. You were the ones who said "sure, what the heck, do that manuscript critique." And the rest, as they say, is history.

RESOURCES

The visual aspects of neurological disorders can be compared to the top of an iceberg, while numerous other disorders and concerns hide below the surface. Anxiety, depression, and thoughts of suicide are a few that may be found there.

It is important to know that while many things in life can remain private between friends, suicide cannot be one of those. It is not something a person or friend can handle alone. If you or anyone you know has thoughts of suicide, please reach out. There are many avenues for help.

Tourette Association of America
Tourette.org

National Suicide Prevention Lifeline
1-800-273-TALK (8255)

Crisis Text Line
(Text HOME to 741-741)

American Foundation for Suicide Prevention
Afsp.org

Risk Factors and Warning Signs
afsp.org/risk-factors-and-warning-signs

National Alliance on Mental Health (NAMI)
Nami.org
1-800-950-NAMI